On the Eighth Day

Books by Antonine Maillet
available in translation

Christopher Cartier as Hazelnut, Also Known as Bear

The Devil is Loose

Evangeline the Second

Gapi and Sullivan

Mariaagélas: Maria, Daughter of Gélas

Pélagie: The Return to Acadie

La Sagouine

The Tale of Don L'Orignal

On the Eighth Day

ANTONINE MAILLET

Translated by Wayne Grady

This edition published in 2006 by Goose Lane Editions.
First published in French as *Le Huitième Jour* by Leméac Éditeur Inc., Montreal.
First published in English as *On the Eighth Day* by Lester & Orpen Dennys Limited, Toronto, 1989.

Cover illustration, *Musique sur mon village* by Nérée DeGrâce, 1984, oil on canvas, 35 x 30 cm. Artwork reproduced with the permission of the DeGrâce family.
Cover and interior design by Julie Scriver.
Printed in Canada.
10 9 8 7 6 5 4 3 2 1

Library and Archives Canada Cataloguing in Publication

Maillet, Antonine, 1929-
[Huitième jour. English]
On the eighth day / Antonine Maillet; translated by Wayne Grady.

Translation of: Le huitième jour.
ISBN 0-86492-454-2

I. Grady, Wayne II. Title. III. Title: Huitième jour. English.

PS8526.A4H8413 2006 C843'.54 C2006-900271-1

Goose Lane Editions acknowledges the financial support of the Canada Council for the Arts, the Government of Canada through the Book Publishing Industry Development Program (BPIDP), and the New Brunswick Department of Wellness, Culture and Sport for its publishing activities.

Goose Lane Editions
469 King Street
Fredericton, New Brunswick
CANADA E3B 1E5
www.gooselane.com

Translator's Note

"The primary decision any translator of Antonine Maillet must reach," wrote Philip Stratford shortly after finishing his translation of *Pélagie-la-Charrette*, "is what English idiom to imitate or invent to try to capture that droll, earthy, salty, poetic, archaic, innovative language that is the essence of her work." My solution, like Stratford's, has been to render Maillet's rich, rolling Acadian, blended with her own idioms and expressions as well as borrowings from Rabelais, Perrault, Molière, *Le Roman de Renart*, and Pascal, into the kind of English that a reasonably educated and moderately travelled Canadian might speak — not write, mind you, but speak — while yarning in a local tavern with a few close friends.

There were problems with that: no English-speaking Canadian need be as passionately concerned with the preservation of his or her language as Maillet is with the future of Acadian; nor has any other French-speaking writer since Rabelais been so adroitly placed between a fading oral culture and a burgeoning written literature. In the preface to her book-length study of the remnants of sixteenth-century French in the folk tales of Acadia — *Rabelais et les Traditions Orales en Acadie* — Maillet noted that it was her "taste for literary masterpieces combined with a passion for living, oral literature" that led her to "search for a link between the two art forms," and that link has in turn formed the basis of all her own writings, including *Le Huitième Jour*. But by and large, translating Maillet's Acadian idioms into figures of speech I have been using all my life — laced with a few gleanings from Shakespeare, Jonson, *The Dictionary of Newfoundland English*, and *The South Shore Phrase Book* — seemed the most natural course to take. For the overall tone of the work, however, the mock-heroic style of *Gulliver's Travels* probably presents the best model.

One of the most striking characters in *Le Huitième Jour* — the sower of chaos, Dulle Griet, also called Margot l'Enragée — may require some explanation. Dulle Griet appears in a 1564 painting by that name by the Flemish master Pieter Bruegel the Elder, who depicted her as a fiercely demented character brandishing a sword and carrying an armful of pots and pans as she strides through a nightmarish landscape crammed with clashing peasant armies, two-legged fish, collapsed buildings, ships' rigging filled with eggs and insects and sprouting teeth, and flying devils; in the background is the ominous red glow of a medieval town being blown to bits. Historically, Dulle Griet was the name given to the huge cannon of Brussels, the largest and most powerful in Europe, and Bruegel's tableau is his vision of the waste and insanity of war. Since "Dulle" is Flemish for "mad" and "Griet" is the diminutive of Margriet (Margot in French, Margaret in English) — and since the great fifteenth-century piece of ordnance in Edinburgh Castle, cast in Mons, Flanders, was called Mons Meg — I have called her Mad Meg. And as Maillet refers to Dulle Griet as "la Faucheuse" as well, I have sometimes called her the Grim Reaper.

— *Wayne Grady*

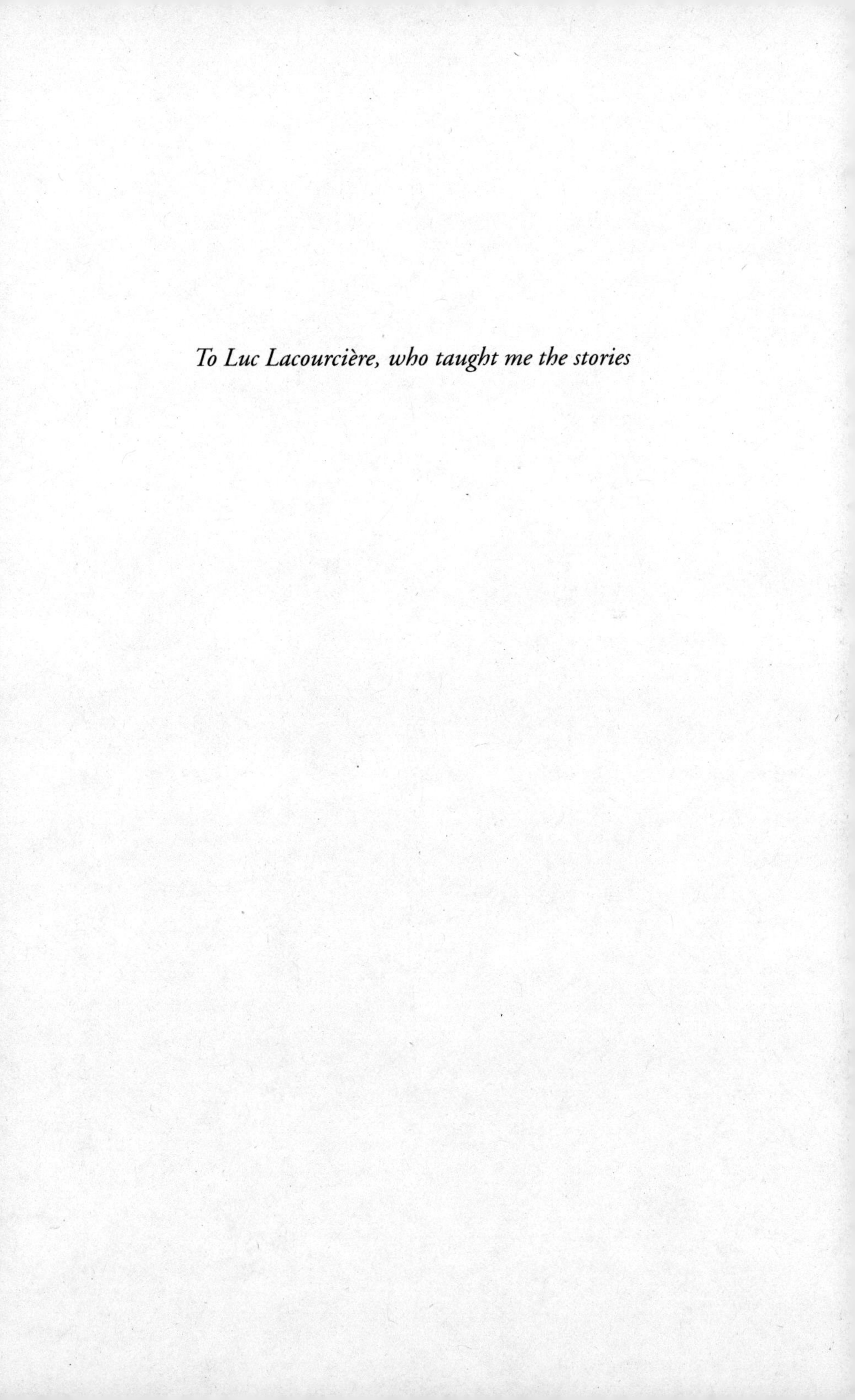

To Luc Lacourcière, who taught me the stories

Contents

Prologue

I came into the world with a birthmark on my left thigh, in spring, at noon, just as the angelus was announcing that the Word had been made Flesh. That was my sole legacy. Later, when my older brothers and sisters sat around the family desk in the evenings, inventing a country for themselves, and a language and an identity, I'd watch them, proud and imperturbable: I am Tonine, I have inherited the gift of speech, and my Original Sin is in plain view above my knee. No one else in the world — which is to say, no one within a dozen miles of Bouctouche — bore that name or those attributes. I was distinct, unique, and entirely myself, and that was that. I have never had anyone else's toothache; never uttered a cry that didn't come from my own throat; and it's my very own backside that's been whacked more often than it deserved because this me that I am has always demanded more than was her due.

It was about this time that I learned, curled up in a ball under the family desk, that I was directly descended from Adam and Eve, an odd couple who lived back at the beginning of the world and fell out with their relatives because of something to do with an apple. Just think: an apple! I could see them squabbling over a pear or a coconut. But an apple? Our yard was full of apples in the summer, and our cellar in winter. Couldn't someone have just let them into the orchard, this Adam and Eve, and told them not to make so much trouble for the rest of us?

And when I say trouble, I mean nothing less than the worst mess that any scatterbrain ever got himself into. Next to Adam and Eve, that little brat Norman who used to break my things and push me off the porch so my nose ended up in the daisies was an angel. And even Albertine, who used to tell lies — oh, such lies, telling us Shirley Temple was her cousin! — was like Saint Albertine compared to Adam and Eve. They may have stolen my slingshot, which was made out of real rubber, and my marbles, one after another, and my pencil crayons and my licorice sticks and my hazelnuts. But Adam and Eve, those sneak-thieves, they stole Paradise from me!

And all the time I was growing up, that stuck in my craw. I had a score to settle with those first parents of mine. No wonder I ended up writing books. You never start out writing books. You start out looking carefully at pebbles or shells; working out the age of a tree by counting the growth rings in its trunk; playing the monkey and climbing, climbing up to the highest branch, your eye riveted to the horizon as it flies by, drowning your cries in the wind. The highest branch is always the thinnest and driest, and crack! . . . you've gone too far. Scraped knees heal over, though. But the sign of Original Sin on my thigh, the gaping hole in my heart left by Adam and Eve, who bit into the apple . . . you drag a wound like that around with you everywhere, all your life, from age to age, from country to country, from book to book.

And yet, like all poets, inventors, explorers, storytellers, I still believe that one day I'll find . . . I haven't given up on Paradise. Not finally and forever given up on it. There is still a thread of hope. Maybe if we went back to the beginning of history. Everything began with the creation of the world. It took six days, they tell us, six short days, with a Creator who even took time to rest on the seventh day! Surely they can't be serious. No wonder we've been saddled with a hurried-up, makeshift world. An unfinished world.

Unfinished . . .

Doesn't the very word make you want to get out your pencil crayons, or your compass, scissors, protractors, T-squares, paint brushes . . . your pen? But what would that get me, except another book? No, the only hope lies hidden just over the horizon, in the folds of time, in the well of the imperceptible. The only hope lies in the eighth day.

I went home again this summer, one more summer, talking loudly, laughing hard, pretending to believe, as usual, that this year would be the one. The year of Halley's Comet. A comet brings luck, like the number seven or thirteen. Surely those are omens it drags around in its tail. The earth can only benefit from omens. Or at least it has nothing to lose, with sands invading its jungle, volcanoes erupting all over the place, and the poles shifting a few more cubits each year. Omens can only rejuvenate us, return to our planet a sense of that primordial time when it first emerged from the mud and began to harden and form a crust.

So though my head was empty, my heart and guts were full of thrilling dreams as I walked away from the ocean, with its dunes and marshes, and crossed the village, passing beneath the old clock tower that, half a century before, had spit its twelve noon-time gongs into my cradle, warning my parents — who didn't seem to be paying much attention — that this was a very irregular and defective word that had just been made flesh.

I didn't stop under the clock tower, waiting to count its strokes; the angelus doesn't ring at noon any more; it doesn't ring at all. Robichaud Brothers' general store no longer opens its doors at dawn, either, because it was torn down to make room for a parking lot on the square in front of the church. And the house I was born in has lost its porch, its poplars, and its backyard, where one day Old Man Ferdinand's pony tried to send a young trespasser to an early grave. The intruder who got the better of that barebacked pony also thought she had taught fate a thing or two at the same time, and played it one of those dirty tricks that's haunted her ever since . . . As if fate needs to be taught anything! But anyway, there's no need to waste time setting your course for destiny when it's lying there right under your nose. Because on the other side of the garden, just beyond the orchard and the top of the field and the fox cages, runs Doctor Landry's creek, which winds its way through the most beautiful woodland the earth has produced since the dawn of time.

Except that the foxes have lost their cages, which have lost their foxes, who must have drowned in the creek that now sneaks so shamefacedly through the roots and moss and isn't even deep enough to drown a dragonfly. I wanted to shout at it: What about the sea, how do you expect to reach it at this rate? And your source. You do have one, don't you? No, a thin trickle of water like you, who hasn't even the strength to flow downhill, you couldn't have a source. You must be running on memory, out of habit. Have you forgotten your halcyon days, when forest creatures for miles around came down to drink and admire themselves in you? Those glorious days when I, too, would bathe in you, secretly, splashing about in your forbidden waters, letting myself float right up to the gates of Paradise Lost . . . The door is open, my dear, just lift the latch and come in!

And in I went, left foot forward for luck, to have a man-to-man talk with none other than God the Father himself, who would please take the trouble to remake the world especially for me on this gorgeous afternoon in July, and according to my instructions. A bit bigger, please, higher and wider, with its right more left and its left more right, and with no nights, except for stars and fireflies. A world in which girls are also boys; where children are both children and grown-ups at the same time; where everything is both itself and something else — everything else — and is always able to start life anew. A world without limits, without worry, without end. The door is open . . .

This creek has to have a source. Without one, it would starve to death. And the poplars and birches that line it would dry up and turn back into bark dust. This creek of Doctor Landry's has its source somewhere higher up, beyond the edge of the undergrowth . . . perhaps deep in the heart of the forest?

This forest was off limits when I was a child, and yet was so near my creek that I don't know how I could have resisted its pull for so long. You can get lost in a forest, that's true, but . . . so what? You can get lost anywhere, in town, in a crowd, where people are like so many trees with intertwined branches. One forest is much like any other . . .

So I went in.

Go on, go ahead, challenge the limits of your village, push back the horizon that bars you from the north road. The forest, too, was created in those six days. It's real, it can be touched, smelled, it's alive, it feeds on ferns and moss, it nourishes all the creeks and streams that fling themselves into the ocean. You're only a few steps from home, so don't be afraid.

I'm not afraid, though I am trembling a bit. This tugging on my left thigh, where is it coming from? And these blue jays who won't stop hurling their warnings in twelve articulated cries. The forest is part of a conspiracy, but who's the other part? . . . A spring amuses itself by distracting me, roots by tripping me up, tufts of grass, leaves, and moss by breaking my fall. I'm not afraid, I'm not afraid. I follow my creek upstream to its birthplace in a cleft in the rocks, beneath the earth's crust, deep, deep . . . down to where the earth turns on its axis like a fruit on its stone, like me on my birthmark. Who called it a birthmark, anyway, instead of a beauty mark?

Suddenly, there's the cabin, at the foot of a giant beechnut tree. A shack. Boards wrenched from their wall studs, banging in the breeze. Yet the frame sits on a perfectly squared foundation. A dwelling much larger than it seems at first glance. I count the rooms, climb the stairs to the attic, a full storey complete with rooms, alcoves, closets, a hallway with creaking boards and a window in the gable wall. So those *aren't* bear traps I see from up here; those huge holes that surround this cabin are the cellars of other cabins, some bigger, some smaller, but all the same depth. They built well in those days.

In those days? What days?

"Anyone home?"

Silence.

Then, all at once, the squirrels start quivering again from tail-tip to snout; the rabbits leap up and disappear into a hole; the moss emits a soft, white mist; the fiddleheads play a jig; the crows complain that there's nothing to do; the birchbark rustles over its sap; tufts of marsh grass scrape their leaves, which rasp and bleed; blue jays sing out their twelve tones: Don't be afraid, Tonine! Don't be afraid, Tonine! I nearly laugh, I am upside down and wrong side up . . . What are you up to, you ominous birds? Never have I felt so amazed, so awed, so . . . alarmed.

Alarmed. I heard the word often enough in my childhood; in our part of the country it has a richer, deeper significance. It keeps its original sense of fright, but it also contains the idea of being alert, "all-armed." And the two meanings came sharply together here at the gate of my lost paradise, where I ventured every day after discovering that birthmark on my thigh. You have to be a little frightened and more than a little armed — with impudence, at least — to confront God and the Devil with the eighth day!

"Are you coming in or aren't you?" croaks a flayed voice that reminds me of that of an old servant of ours, whose stories always began with the words: *Once upon a time . . .*

1

How two heroes emerged from the woods
and a batch of bread dough

Ever since the Fall of Man, Master Goodman, like everyone else, has dragged his Original Sin around with him everywhere — bad-mouthing Eve, feeling sorry for Adam, and looking for ways to get around the law, that cursed apple, and the flaming sword that guards the gate to Eden. It was a Tuesday or a Thursday — one of those happy days when the girls wiggle their hips, the boys wiggle their moustaches, and old couples like Goodman and his wife wiggle each other just to see if they're still good for something.

"Good for nothing!"

Such was Goodwife's conclusion after years of fruitless contortions on the part of this son of Adam, who was barely able to get a rise out of his Adam's apple. Good for nothing. The words stuck there in Goodman's throat, choked, strangled, letting out only a single, jumbled complaint: What did I do to God to deserve this! And the quarrel would begin again. Every Tuesday. Every Thursday. Because the couple had long ago given up on holidays. Heaven had so far refused to bless their union.

It wasn't for lack of trying. Goodwife had choked down potions of all the wild herbs supposed to be medicinal, picked in the deep woods and distilled in the cauldrons of alchemists, charlatans, necromancers, and general practitioners, and had prayed to the harvest and fertility gods every night without fail. Even Goodman had tried them, but . . .

"Good for nothing!"

And the words continued to jam in his throat.

How long did this go on? Time passed, years went by. Leap years have a kind of hypnotic appeal. Goodman had already seen thirteen of them, and his wife . . . but his wife had sworn — sworn, mind you — to hold on to her forty years with both hands and not move an inch. And on she held, like the stubborn mule she was, not letting go, braying to the universe and all her neighbours that when she's forty years old a mother can finally deliver to the world a product that will make the wait worthwhile. And you will see what you will see what you will see.

Well, they waited, but they didn't see much. Secretly, they didn't expect to see much until the next time Halley's Comet came by, and they weren't holding their breath for that, either. So?

"So what? So you don't think I'll do it? Have this child of my old age? Well, I'll do it, and I'll do it alone, if I have to, and leave you standing there with your fly at half-mast. And what's more, it'll be a boy."

And giving her husband, whose nose had strayed a little too close to her bread dough, a sudden, brusque shove, she sent him flying arse over teakettle into the flour bin. Let him get himself out of that if he can, she chuckled. I've got my baking to do. Twice a week I make the dough, knead it, set it to rise on top of the warming oven. One of these days, though, you'll see . . . But her husband didn't see anything, having picked himself up out of the flour, dusted off his backside, and taken himself off grumbling to his carpenter's shop, which was attached to the barns.

He saw and heard nothing. Not even the sighs of his wife as she kneaded the dough, worked it, and shaped it into the form of a little man about the size of her fist, giving it a string of names: Tom Thumb, she would say, spitting into the flour, Thumbkin, Big-as-a-Fist . . . If only I had a child, oh my, no bigger than this, but a rascally, mischievous, wily boy, twenty times foxier than his father. He could help me chase away all these chickens that flutter around me and keep me from my baking. Oh, how she sighed. But Goodman didn't hear her.

He had gone back into his workshop, his "cabinetmaker's studio," as he called it, for he was the kind of carpenter who insists on calling himself a craftsman — an artist, in fact, in board and brick and mortar. With jackplane or trowel in hand, he could transform the world for you in three strokes flat. From his back pocket he produced a mickey that he kept handy for the bad days, and took a drink. Ahhh! And another. Mmm . . . And told himself that life wasn't so bad after all, and the earth wasn't as flat as everyone said it was, and the world was only empty if you were blind and deaf, and . . . but enough bellyaching! . . . and he set to work on a block of rough-cut wood, a roof-beam that Tom had ordered, or was it Dick, or Harry, it didn't matter; he felt strong enough to lift the heaviest oak trunk he had, all by himself, grab it right around the middle . . . Here, hold still. Let me round off your waist and sides, old son . . . good old Goodman's son, eh? And on he rambled. If only I had a son, he muttered, tall as that, and strong, handsome, loyal, and brave, who wouldn't say no to a bit of hard work, and who'd never tell lies . . . hic!

Goodwife recoiled in horror. Her husband was drunk and raving. He had hewn a horrible little giant from the trunk of an oak, and there he was talking to it in some strange language. Giving names to the monster: John-Bear, he was calling it, John-the-Strong, Strong-as-a-Dozen. Then Goodwife remembered her bread on the warming oven, about to overrise, and she hurried to wipe the grin off her husband's face.

"Come to bed, you old lush. You've had enough foolishness for one day."

"Wait, I'm not finished, I haven't given him a belly button."

Goodwife took a knitting needle out of her apron pocket and jabbed it into the statue's stomach, which quivered as if it had been tickled.

"There, he's finished — your trunk of oak, your son of a jackass. Now you can sleep in peace."

And that night husband and wife snored away, side by side, in the same feather bed.

Towards midnight, the weathercock crowed.

"Not the weathercock, you idiot. The cock."

"The cock? Why should the cock crow at midnight, imbecile?"

"The cock crows when the hen lays, you nincompoop. Did you leave the lamp on in the henhouse again?"

"You old fool!"

And Goodman turned his face to the wall and went back to sleep.

"Humph," said Goodwife, "that numbskull could have forgotten to close the door to his workshop and it wouldn't surprise me at all. A giant in a tree trunk . . . of all the idiotic . . ."

And she buried her head in her pillow and went to sleep, dreaming of her little doughboy no bigger than her fist.

Now, Goodman and Goodwife's closest neighbour was a woman whose name was Clara-Galante. People said she was something of a witch because instead of sleeping at night she did her spinning, and during the day she scoured the woods for plants and herbs, the virtues of which were frowned upon by the parish priest.

"That evil woman is corrupting the good fathers of our good families," he would mutter under his biretta. "God will punish her."

But God didn't seem to be listening to his servant's prayers, for the witch went unpunished, and the good fathers of good families became more fathers of a good many more families. And everyone felt better and better for it.

That night, Clara-Galante spun long threads of silk and sheep's wool from her spindle, uttering strange and jumbled spells — sesames and abracadabras and step-on-a-crack-and-break-your-mother's-back, all mixed in with *aves* in the purest Church Latin. Then, squinting towards the dwelling of Goodman and Goodwife, she let out a hideous cackle that descended an entire octave and woke up an echo hidden in the hills. The echo, in turn, set a flock of crows to flight and a gaggle of geese to gabbling and bashing their beaks against the manure spreader. "What's going on?" neighed the horse, but the mare calmed him down and led him back to his stall. "If you're going to jump up every time you hear a whimper from the barnyard!" she chided. Eventually, peace was restored. Except for the cuckoo, who kept it up for a bit, sniffing suspiciously at the stars . . . "My, my, the comet!" . . . and then crowing twelve times.

In the kitchen, the stove was still heating up, because our brave carpenter — our artist in plank and plaster — had forgotten to turn down the damper in his hurry to drown in sleep his impossible dreams of the day. And as everyone knows, when a stove gets too hot the oven begins to tremble and the grates start to rattle and dance, and before you know it the warming oven is shaking. A country kitchen really needs to be spread out over half the house, and even then it's too small to suit the needs of a busy housewife. Which explains the precarious balance of the utensils hanging on the cooking pots above the warming oven. One cry of a cuckoo and oops! There went our little doughboy no bigger than a fist: down he tumbled, landing on his head, rolling over, banging into the table leg — and waking up.

"A strange way to come into the world, falling on your head," mumbled an old housefly who had himself been born in a manure pile. The spider looked at him and shrugged his eight shoulders, as if to say that no matter how you're born it's better than staying down there, a lifeless lump at the bottom of the mixing bowl, stuck in the dough. At any rate, the two agreed on one thing: No one chooses his origins, not even a dinner roll. And the insects lapsed into silence, leaving the newcomer to come to whatever terms he could with his own destiny.

Which is exactly what our hero hastened to do. First he spat into his palms — a bad start, my lad. Spit turns flour into a gluey paste, and now he was all stuck together. Not a good way to begin life. Flailing about, rolling on the floor, swearing by all the devils in Hell, and aiming several swift kicks at the cooking pots, which gave back as good as they got: Ouch! Lesson number one: His feet were attached to his legs, which hung down from his little bum and were part of him. He appeared to be made of the same stuff all over. Funny, wasn't it? And he laughed, and clapped his hands, and spun around on his heels to get a better sense of his surroundings, and banged his head against a roasting pan, which emitted a horrible groan. Instinctively he covered his ears with his hands, and suddenly the noise stopped. How strange! He tried it again, hitting the roasting pan with his head; it groaned, he plugged his ears, and light dawned: he possessed a strange power, he could impose silence on the kitchen's percussion section simply by putting his hands over his ears.

"Aha," he said to himself. "With a gift like this, I dare the world to get in my way."

And, puffed up with his new importance, he got to his feet, found his balance, tossed a final glance at the corner where his half-baked brothers lay forming their crusts on the warming oven, cocked his eye in the direction of life, and banged head first into the door which for the moment barred his way to the world outside.

"All right," said he to himself, clenching his fists and pinching his nose. "The door is blocking my way. But life is full of doors, so I may as well bang my head against one somewhere else." And, turning his back to the exit, he gave it a solid backhanded kick that caused a little trap door at the bottom to swing open on its hinges. This, he would learn the next day, was for the private and exclusive use of the cat, a bilious old bachelor tom. But tonight the world belonged to the newborn, who feared neither cat nor devil and who strutted out into the wide world with his head (which was shaped a bit like a cabbage) planted squarely on his shoulders, ready to conquer the earth and all its planets.

Our hero's first discovery was the workshop of his father, the carpenter known as Master Goodman, who had dreamed of having an heir since the first days of his marriage and who . . . well . . . who had remained disappointed. This time the doughboy didn't bother trying to break down the door — you learn quickly at his age — but looked around right off for the cat's entrance. You don't just breeze into a workshop, however, especially not the workshop of the best cabinetmaker in the township. And cats are particularly *non grata* in workshops — because of the sawdust, you see — so there was no trap in the door of the Master Carpenter's studio.

"Now what?"

So he cast about and clambered up a stump and shinnied up a hazelnut tree and swung onto the roof and slid down a ways but managed to grab hold of something and landed in the eavestrough and said Shit! and scrambled back up by catching at the shingles and finally reached the chimney and stuck his head into it and lost his footing and toppled over and went Yiii! . . . Boompf! . . . landing, luckily, in a pile of sawdust at the base of an oak trunk that seemed as tall as a church tower.

No, that image can't be right: Our hero is such a newcomer to the world that he's never seen a church, let alone a church tower. He hasn't seen much of anything, really. But he has a good head on his shoulders, and he learns quickly.

Craning his neck and raising his eyes as high as he could, he found himself staring into two immense, rolling orbs stuck in the forehead of his opposite number, who was standing stock still before him, as if ashamed that he had not yet emerged from his wood.

Without stopping to think, the doughboy called out:

"Hey, you big dummy! Can't you bend over a bit so I can get a good look at you?"

He just blurted it out, really, in his haste to get acquainted, to understand, to make a friend. But once it was out he began to feel afraid, and he backed away until he was up against the far wall. From there he was able to take in the whole astonishing picture:

a boy about his own age, if age has an age at that age, a big, tall lad carved out of a tree and standing there like a blockhead, not moving a muscle and not saying a word.

"Maybe he isn't born yet," said the little one to himself, suddenly filled with compassion and pity for the big oaf.

Forgetting his fear, he drew closer: "What's your name? Mine's . . ."

But it was then, while trying to introduce himself, that the little devil realized the full extent of his predicament. For it suddenly dawned on him that he hadn't been named yet, that he'd come into the world naked under his crust, without a name, without anything — no past, no doughty deeds to recount to others . . . who probably wouldn't be listening anyway, preoccupied as they always were with problems of their own.

Chapfallen, the bread-boy aimed a couple of great kicks at the flanks of the oak-boy . . . who started to wriggle and emit a string of he-he-he-he's and ho-ho-ho-ho's, and finally yelled, "Stop! You're tickling me!"

And that's how the second son of Goodman and Goodwife first saw the light of day — kicked awake by his brother.

The two twins began by introducing themselves to each other, which meant the dwarf invented for himself a past overflowing with adventures and ancestors descended from the House of Danish, all very upper crust, who'd allied themselves with some Kaisers in order to invade the southern Dutchies, whilst their first cousins the Crullers frittered away their inheritance tanning themselves in the warming oven. The giant, on the other hand, dazzled by the illustrious origins of his brother, completely forgot his own branch of the family tree. Gazing nostalgically upon some lifeless, unfinished beams, he simply said how happy he was to be alive, even though he found it embarrassing that such a humble person as himself could occupy so elevated a place in the world. He was trying, you see, to reduce his own stature as much as possible in order to be more on a level with his brother, who, for his part, was busy puffing up his own importance. In the end, the two felt themselves to be more or less of a size, and they both decided it was high time they set off in search of their parents.

It was the eighth day of the week, and everything in the household of Squire Goodman and Lady Goodwife was peaceful and normal. The couple took their time getting up, washing and dressing and filling their pockets — one with his pipe and tobacco, the other with her thimbles and knitting needles — and coming down the stairs making them creak as they did every morning. When they reached the kitchen, they both went straight for the stove to fill it with kindling and to put on the kettle, when . . .

"What's this?" said Goodwife to herself. "Looks like something strange went on here last night. Who might you be, you little scamp?"

And the little scamp scampered about the kitchen, leaping from chair to chair and singing:

List, mother, list,
I'm Big-as-a-Fist,
And 'twas you made me so
Out of leftover dough!

And grabbing a feather duster, he gave a few good whacks to some chickens who had wandered into the house.

Goodwife didn't waste time slapping her forehead or trying to understand what had happened — as many disbelievers would have done in her place. Instead, she burst out laughing.

"Well done, my lad. Come here and let me wipe your nose."

And taking the corner of her kerchief, she rubbed the still-soft crust of her little manikin no bigger than her fist.

Meanwhile, Goodman had fallen back on a chair, his legs spread out before him, his mouth hanging open, his hand clapped to his forehead, his breath caught in mid-gasp. His joy was inexpressible; he couldn't utter a single word to tell his wife to look, over there, in the doorway, a son! All one piece, carved out of number-one oak, and already six heads taller than his old man.

"John-Bear!" he finally managed to whisper. "My child, my boy!"

"John-Bear?" said his wife, blind to her husband's raptures. "It isn't John-Bear. It's Big-as-a-Fist!"

And it took a good quarter of an hour and a lively quarrel before each spouse finally recognized the other's son, and both realized that their longed-for child had finally arrived — in duplicate.

This scene took place on what you might call the eighth day, but Goodman and Goodwife preferred to call it the most beautiful day of their lives.

Every Sunday it was the proud parents' custom to stand on the steps of the church bragging about their offspring to the neighbours — the labourer, the barber, the shoemaker, the grocer, and the fresh fishmonger. John-Bear, the giant, came right out of an oak tree that was at least a hundred years old, and Goodman, his father, carved him with a few strokes of his chisel and without a lick of help from anyone, thank you very much. And Mother Goodwife shaped her son Big-as-a-Fist with her own hands while singing lullabies to him and calling him by his name. Miraculous children who would go on to do wonderful things.

"And end up disowning their father and mother, like all premature babies," laughed Tom, Dick, Harry, Mary, and Jane.

Since all fathers pride themselves on the prowess of their sons, and all mothers on the beauty of their daughters — Tom is stronger than So-and-so, Mary is prettier than Such-and-such — every child ever born, to listen to its parents, is headed for greatness. Goodman and Goodwife were furious: How dare anyone compare every Tom, Dick, and Mary to their own two prodigies of the bin and the barn!

"Born from wood and bread dough!" scoffed their neighbours.

Ever since the world began, they said, children have been born in exceptional ways. Don't be daft, Goodman! And you, Goodwife, you're making a mountain out of a mole hill! So you've brought two children into the world, so what! There are children born every second, yellow ones, redskins, woolly-haired black ones . . . even white ones, occasionally. Siamese twins in Siam, Mongoloids in Mongolia. Why not a giant in your workshop, carpenter? And why shouldn't a baker make a dwarf out of bread dough? Send them to school, like everyone else, and when they're old enough, kick them out into the world. Let them earn their own keep like the rest of us mortals, and let the world be the judge of their merits.

"Bull-roar," growled Goodman, wounded in his love for his son as well as in his love for himself. Some people have eyes but they see nothing, ears though they're deaf as doorknobs. It's as plain as the nose on my face that ours are no ordinary kids. How can this lot ever be made to understand that our sons came into the world on the eighth day!

All this time our two marvels were working new wonders so as not to be caught resting on their laurels. Each day revealed hidden talents in one or the other of them, and the village began to wonder if it hadn't bitten off more than it could chew, landed as it was with a pair of havoc-making egg-breakers. Until this troublesome twosome of Squire Goodman and Lady Goodwife arrived, the village — half hills, half plains, half forest, and half coastline — had succeeded more often than not in soldering the four halves into at least the semblance of a single chunk of geography. An entity that had so far held firm against hurricanes, hailstorms, forest fires, grasshoppers, and any other mischiefs the neighbouring villages might visit upon it. Against high winds and high tides, the town had saved its face and kept its crockery intact. Ever since it had been founded, in the time of the pioneers.

And then one day two children — one too small for his age, the other too big, both foul-mouthed and born at the wrong time on the wrong day in the wrong place — had come along to remind the world that Heaven is an uncertain thing that is ever at the mercy of a passing comet. Ever since Adam and Eve bit into the apple, anything in life can happen at any time in any place.

If there was one person who daily deplored the disorder of the universe, it was Goodman. He never tired of moaning and groaning to his wife that her brainless booby, Big-as-a-Fist, wasn't worth the trouble it took to feed and clothe him. To which Goodwife would reply that if anyone in the house took up more space and ate more food than his fair share, it was that big oaf, John-Bear, who was his father's son all over.

"He can't sit on a chair without smashing it to smithereens," Goodwife grumbled. "And every time he takes a drink from the creek he dries it up. When he crosses the yard he crushes every duckling or chick in it. He's all ten plagues of Egypt rolled into one, that's what that son of yours is."

Goodman snatched his pipe from between his teeth and cast a baleful eye at his mate.

"John-Bear? My son, a plague? How can you talk that way about our own boy? I tell you, woman, one day he'll conquer the whole world with his bare hands. He can already run across the garden, through the yard, to the edge of the woods in three giant steps. Imagine what he'll do when he's bigger!"

"Bigger! Do you want him to break through the ceiling? I'm already worried about my good china."

"You'd do better to worry about that little pipsqueak of yours — he'll be lucky to get a job in a thimble factory. Big-as-a-Fist, monkey dwarf, fingers into everything — he'll never be able to earn his daily bread."

"Earn his bread? Him? Why would he have to? He was born in a bread box! Don't worry about him, he'll know how to make his living. Having big muscles and a lot of blubber under your hide isn't everything, you know. It helps to have something upstairs, too, something to keep your ears apart."

"Huh!"

"Huh yourself!"

"The dwarf will never amount to anything."

"The giant will never take his first step in life on his own two feet."

"You wanna bet?"

"Anything you like!"

"Name it!"

"I bet you . . . ," hazarded Goodwife, "I'll bet that Big-as-a-Fist, also called Thumbkin, also called Tom Thumb, will be the first to reach the edge of those woods, and the first to climb to the top of that oak you can see there, the one with all the crows circling around it."

"Done," replied Goodman, sure of his bet. "The first one to touch the sky will be my legitimate heir, and he'll inherit this house and all my lands."

"It's a deal," Goodwife signalled by nodding her head.

The two brothers watched this first quarrel between their parents with the kind of misgivings felt by immigrants waiting in the customs office. They held hands without saying a word, eyeing first their father, then their mother, already trying to shape their destiny and force the world to make room for them both, fair and square and no sides taken. John-Bear, also called John-the-Strong, also called Strong-as-a-Dozen, sighed deeply, as if to tell his brother that he was leaving everything up to him, that he'd bow to his superiority, which he couldn't explain but which was plain to see in his sharp eyes and in the set of his jaw. But Big-as-a-Fist played deaf, gripped his brother's hand more tightly, and winked as if to say, "Trust me. I'll get us both out of this."

"Agreed then?" Goodman asked his wife.

"Agreed," she replied, then shouted, "One, two, three — go!"

Both children shouted, "Break a leg!" and took off at the same time, left foot first for luck. Big-as-a-Fist used the cat door, of course, while his brother took the trouble of lifting the latch and closing the door carefully behind him. Goodman wasn't worried, though, because he could already see his favourite son taking the six steps of the porch at a single bound, then leaping over the ox cart, the cow (who mooed with astonishment), and the hawthorns flanking the lane. As for Tom Thumb, Goodwife scoured the ground with her eyes, looking in the daisy patch and the dandelions, asking herself where the little devil could have got to. That absent-minded old mare better not have stepped on him!

"John-Bear is halfway there," shouted his father, proud as a peacock and already planning his legitimate heir's future.

"It's not over yet, numbskull. Remember the hare and the tortoise."

"Fables and lies," said Goodman. "Only reality matters. And the reality is that your dwarf is lost in the grass while my giant is resting against the oak at the edge of the forest, his head already in the clouds."

Goodwife was stricken with anguish, but not with despair. She had placed her confidence in her son; he wouldn't let her down, wouldn't betray her trust; he must have found a shortcut. But where in the blazes did he go? Suddenly she heard a shout coming from the distance, carried by an echo that dropped it at her feet.

List, mother, list,
I'm Big-as-a-Fist,
And 'twas you made me so
Out of leftover dough.

Goodwife yanked back her hair to hear better, scanned the four horizons, then tore off towards the oak tree — followed by her husband, who couldn't believe his eyes and ears. There they were, both of them, the small one perched on the big one's hat, leaning against the tree trunk that was itself outlined against the vault of the sky. By jumping onto his brother's boot, Big-as-a-Fist had been able to climb up his pant leg, his spine, and his neck, and he was resting comfortably in his woollen cap by the time John-Bear reached the top.

"We both win!" cried the dwarf, while the giant, proud as could be of their first adventure, laughed with all his might.

And it was party time at the Goodman household.

A party that went on well into the night.

The next day, however, the bickering was taken up again. The cause was unimportant, even forgotten. Goodwife claimed it was all John-Bear's fault, the clumsy oaf: trying to stick his huge head in his mother's lap, he'd managed to crush a dozen eggs she'd been carrying in the pocket of her apron. Goodman, for his part, accused Big-as-a-Fist, the idiot: trying to act like a grown-up, he'd snuck off with his father's pipe and filled the whole house with smoke. But once they'd parcelled out the blame and forgotten the origins of the dispute, there was nothing left but a mutual and visceral rancour. For each of the parents, the house wasn't big enough for one or the other of the children.

Things came to such a pass that one morning John-Bear made up his mind. If the house wasn't big enough for both of them, then the one to leave should be the one who took up the most space. He would sacrifice himself and quit the family hearth and home forever, forsaking his inheritance and making his brother the legitimate heir.

"I'm going off to seek my fortune somewhere else, Big-as-a-Fist, and peace will return to the household. You'll be happy, you'll see. I'm big enough to take care of myself."

Big-as-a-Fist turned his back on his brother and aimed a tremendous fart at his feet.

"That's what I think of your plan, you big lummox. You? Take care of yourself? You wouldn't have found the oak tree at the edge of the woods if I hadn't shown you the way. You stay here at home and help your father haul logs from the forest to his workshop. I'll go out into the world myself, and I'll come back one day with sacks of gold to share with my brother."

John-Bear wiped tears the size of ostrich eggs from his eyes and said:

"I won't let you go off on your own. You'll get yourself stepped on by a cart horse."

Meanwhile, Big-as-a-Fist was sniffling himself, though he tried to hide it behind a sneeze:

"Don't you worry about me, little giant. I've got a few tricks up my sleeve."

"You don't even have a sleeve. Just a crust."

"Take care of Father and Mother. I'll be back."

"No!"

"So long!"

"We'll go together!"

The idea was John-Bear's, and he didn't get too many of them. And this one didn't come from his head, but from somewhere between his heart and the seat of his pants.

So there was nothing to do but submit themselves to their fate and search the four corners of the world for the route to their destiny — a task whose importance and difficulty our heroes had not yet begun to suspect. But off they went without a backward glance, one hopping on one foot, the other on two.

In search of Life.

2

How our two heroes developed an Adam's apple, a rough voice, and three chin-hairs

I must say that Life, when it saw them coming, was a little startled. It isn't every day you come across a pair of twin brothers, one a dwarf and the other a giant, one born from an oak tree, the other from a batch of bread dough. But Life quickly took hold of itself; if anyone is used to seeing strange sights . . .

Still their departure was less smooth than they had hoped. Before leaving for good, they made a few false starts, a matter of getting off on the right foot. The first time they headed for the woods, Big-as-a-Fist — who was the smarter of the two and who knew the tales of Little Red Riding Hood, Sleeping Beauty, and Thumbkin (his favourite hero) by heart — had filled his pockets with grains of wheat which he meant to sow along the way in order to find the true road to adventure. Unfortunately the birds ate every grain, obliterating our would-be adventurers' route to destiny and returning them somewhat shamefaced to their parents' house. Big-as-a-Fist, who didn't know a great many things yet but who had a good head on his shoulders, realized that the next time he'd have to sow pebbles. Which he did. But the pebbles also brought them back to their own house.

"Idiot!" the dwarf said to himself, slapping his forehead. "If you want to leave, you don't sow anything; burn your bridges behind you and never go home again."

John-Bear, to show he was on his brother's side, started setting fire to the nearest bridge, the one that joined their cow path to the main road. Big-as-a-Fist appreciated the gesture, but he held his brother back and made a suggestion: "Why don't we ask the advice of someone older, as we should have done in the first place?"

"We could ask our father, Goodman, or our mother, Goodwife," said John-Bear eagerly.

"Oh well, parents, you know . . ." said Big-as-a-Fist, making a face.

"We can tell them we're going off to fight evildoers and defend the downtrodden."

"And that we'll be back one day loaded with riches and glory to brighten their old age."

"And that we'll all live happily ever after . . . with dozens of children."

Then John-Bear blushed at the words that had escaped unbidden from his mouth.

When Goodman and Goodwife heard the news, first they tore out their hair, then they weighed the advantages of getting rid of one son against the sorrow of losing the other, and they ended up repeating with a sigh the words first uttered by Adam and Eve: We bring children into the world only to watch them leave.

Bright and early the next day, Goodwife began to make some travelling clothes and spare linen for her sons. For the dwarf she fashioned a pair of trousers, brown so they wouldn't show the dirt; a full jacket with a lining and plenty of secret pockets; a pair of soft shoes with good soles for climbing; and a brightly coloured cap, decorated with tiny bells so that passersby wouldn't accidentally step on him. As for the giant, she fitted him out entirely in green, so he would blend in with nature and not frighten everyone; then she covered his head with a wide-brimmed had with an ostrich feather for Big-as-a-Fist to hang onto; for his feet she made a pair of seven-league boots from the hide of a cow that John-Bear had tossed over the clock tower the day before, trying to get it to go into the barn.

Thus attired, the two travellers presented themselves to their father to receive his paternal blessings. Goodman took John-Bear aside and told him that he had a godmother by the name of Clara-Galante, who lived in a cabin deep in the woods near a bend in a small stream:

"Go to her place," said the old man. "Tell her you're going on a trip. I'm sure she'll have some gifts for you."

Goodwife meanwhile caught her little manikin up in her skirts and whispered into his ear:

"Go to your godmother's house, Clara-Galante's, near the stream. Tell her you're going away and ask for your inheritance."

Now the two children were deeply embarrassed. Did only one of them have a godmother, then? What about the other one? But then each came conscientiously to terms with his own conscience, according to how much of it he had been given at birth: John-Bear promised himself that he would share whatever he got with his brother; Big-as-a-Fist swore that he would spend his as fast as he could, and in no time at all be back on an equal footing with his twin. But before they could do anything about sharing their godmother's gifts, they found themselves sharing their surprise at arriving neck-and-neck — or rather, neck-and-navel — on the porch of Clara-Galante's cabin.

"It's not locked, my dears. Just lift the latch and come in."

The phrase rang a bell with Big-as-a-Fist, who had a fine memory, but because he was as impetuous as he was intelligent, he ignored the warning and went in. Followed by his brother.

Clara-Galante, bent over a huge cauldron, was stirring a steaming yellow soup. Big-as-a-Fist was spellbound; he clung to John-Bear and remained as silent as a donkey.

"Heh, heh!" said the witch. "Not exactly a matched pair, are you? But made of sound enough wood and a good dough. What can I do for you?"

Uh, well . . . it's like this . . . since you ask . . . Finally, Big-as-a-Fist took a deep breath and blurted out:

"We want our presents, Godmother."

Clara-Galante looked up from her cauldron and eyed them from head to toe. A right pair of gallants . . . too small, too heavy . . . and yet . . . There are dwarfs and giants born every day, malformed, misshapen, and the world finds room for them all — being none too well put together itself.

"Make your wishes," she said. "Three. Not one more. And they're for life. So think carefully."

The two brothers looked at each other in consultation. They hadn't counted on having a choice.

"Health?"

No, no, not that, they burbled.

"Wisdom?"

What's that?

"Long life?"

Come on, life isn't a gift. You get it when you're born, you don't even have to think about it, it comes with.

Then Tom Thumb grew bold and, with his hands planted on his hips, said:

"First off, I want to hear and understand the language of animals."

And he doffed his cap and made a deep bow.

Clara-Galante raised an eyebrow in surprise, started to smile, and with her head made a sign in the direction of a large spider, which dropped a stitch in its web.

"Next, I want a flute that will make everyone dance for three miles around."

The witch opened her mouth to protest, but closed it again. She looked fiercely at the bold little fellow, then plucked a straw from her broom.

Then Big-as-a-Fist lost his head completely; throwing caution to the wind, he broke into laughter and shouted:

"And I want the gift that . . . every time I sneeze . . . the person standing nearest in front of me — farts!"

And in a split second, confident in his own genius, the young knight sneezed full in the face of John-Bear, who let loose a fart proportional to his size right in Clara-Galante's nose. Their godmother covered her head with her hands and shrieked out a string of curses: "You little demon! You weathercock! You devil's dung!" But Big-as-a-Fist, bent over double and holding his sides, didn't hear her; he put his flute to his lips, sneezing and taking aim at the flies and the huge spider.

John-Bear was so ashamed of himself he didn't know what to do. His godmother saw him trying to look down at his Adam's apple and felt sorry for him. Her anger subsided. She took her magic wand, stuck its tip into the soot at the back of her fireplace, and on three dried maple leaves she scribbled phrases that rolled across the leaves from right to left and from top to bottom.

"Off you go, my lad," she said to John-Bear. "Your wishes are written there. Use them wisely."

And shaking her tangled hair to rid it of all the parasites that had taken up residence there, she returned to her cauldron, sending our heroes, her godchildren, out into the world to follow their curious destiny beyond the hills on the horizon.

The two brothers' noses were no sooner out the door than they tried with trembling hands to decipher the enchanted maple leaves . . . Chinese! They were written in Chinese! No periods or commas, no accent marks, nothing but little stick men and square boxes: Chinese! They bit their tongues in vexation. No gifts for the giant.

"It's not fair! It's not fair!" burst out Big-as-a-Fist, whose bile had risen just about up to his nose.

No godmother had the right to treat his brother this way. Furious, he gave a kick that sent the leaves flying up and flipping over, landing upside down and back to front and revealing to the astonished eyes of John-Bear letters with crosses on all the t's and dots on all the i's:

Never pick on anyone smaller than yourself.
Come to the aid of those who are weaker than you.
Always finish what you have started.

Big-as-a-Fist couldn't hide his disappointment. This was too much! Maxims! What kind of inheritance was that? School lessons! Honour thy father and thy mother . . . the truth, the whole truth, and nothing but the truth . . . never pick on anyone smaller than you . . . erk! He was about to launch into a harangue against his godmother out of sympathy for his brother when he noticed that the latter was smiling broadly, his head thrown back to the wind and the sun, his eyes glowing.

"Now," said he, "I am no longer afraid; now I know I will never be the giant who eats little children."

Big-as-a-Fist, moved and amused, looked up at his brother for a moment, just long enough for a little devil like himself to understand, make a note of, and then completely forget the meaning of the words he had just heard.

Our heroes, who had spent so much time preparing for their departure, took everything into account except the fact that they were actually going to leave. Right up to the last minute they projected, plotted, and planned their journey as if it were a game. Not until their feet were actually on Clara-Galante's porch, after she had so ceremoniously sent them out into the future, did they notice that the stream they'd been following had suddenly become twice as narrow as it had been the day before.

"What happened to it?" Big-as-a-Fist asked nervously, always the first to pose the questions and always the first to answer them. "Do you think the spring is drying up?"

"Let's go see," suggested John-Bear, the more courageous of the two.

And each one, clutching his gifts in his heart or in the palm of his hand, set off with a firm tread along the path that followed the stream, left the village, passed through the edge of the woods, and took them gradually up into the deep forest.

"Hoo-oo!"

No, Big-as-a-Fist, that wasn't a wolf; it was just an asthmatic old hoot-owl clearing his throat.

They advanced slowly, bumping into tree stumps, stumbling into an old cart abandoned in a ravine. They changed direction, wandering between trees that grew bigger and bigger and closer and closer together. Several times they lost track of the stream and then found it again, jumped over it, keeping it in sight until finally it ducked down underground and disappeared forever from their view. They tried looking up to the sky to consult the stars, but the forest there was too dense, and the canopy of trees too high.

"I think, dear brother, that we are well and truly lost."

It was John-Bear who made the statement, in all its clarity, cruelty, and frankness. He had never learned how to lie — not even for show, not even to give himself courage. Courage was one of the facets of his nature, and he had no need to borrow it. Tom Thumb, on the other hand, found his courage in the depths of his imagination, where he saw himself as a bold and fearless fellow, out to conquer the world even if it cost him his life. In a foreign land, laying siege to castles and walled towns, Big-as-a-Fist wouldn't hesitate for a minute to shed the last drop of his blood. In his own country, though, on a run-of-the-mill day of the week, shedding the first drop wasn't so easy . . .

But if the dwarf lacked a touch of valour, he had no shortage of pluck, and there are circumstances in which one compensates for the other. Not to mention the fact that he held a trump card, which, though it might at first glance seem a little unethical, was unquestionably useful for extracting himself and his brother from sticky situations: the art of saying the opposite of the truth without even a hint of a lie.

"Lost?" he said with a nonchalant air, responding to the giant's uneasiness. "Bah! Twice lost, thrice found!"

He didn't know how close he was to the truth. And here was another of Big-as-a-Fist's character traits: he never came so near the truth as when he imagined he was furthest from it. He was closest to discovering his true self when he was dreaming. To regain his poise, he added:

"We're not lost, you big dummy, because all rivers run to the sea. All we have to do is find the spring that feeds the streams that turn into rivers that flow gently towards the ocean. Then, when we're there . . ."

Then what?

But Big-as-a-Fist had said enough for one day. He had a good head on his shoulders, but he couldn't be expected to solve everything at once. Sufficient unto the day is the evil thereof. And the night brings good counsel.

And without knowing that this would be the last night in the first stage of their lives, they went to sleep in a nest made of twigs and leaves, their heads full of apprehension and their hearts overflowing with anticipation.

But when they woke up early the next morning, they were surprised to find that, during that night, each had been given an Adam's apple, a rough voice, and three hairs on his chin — not to mention a small *ne plus ultra* that neither hero dared to reveal to the other.

3

How two companions became three

That same morning, Clara-Galante went out onto her porch to scan the north-northeast. Then she pulled back her head, squared her neck, looked down at the ground, and called out to the world and all its quarters that it could go blow its nose.

The world blew its nose. And ate three meals a day. And lived fifty-two weeks and four seasons a year. And sent its travellers out on the road as if they would last forever, little bothered by the thought that, through the ages, stars have been extinguished and volcanoes have erupted. Spit out your lava, old friend, there's more where that came from! The earth can belch, erupt, split its sides, tomorrow isn't the eve of destruction. So giddyup! hyah! mush! Every week has its eight days, always has had, eight days that only count as seven in real life, the eighth . . .

The eighth has just crossed the horizon and is under full sail, headed due north.

To sum up, then:

When John-Bear and Big-as-a-Fist finally realized that their road had closed up behind them during the night, and that they could never follow it home, they set off in search of the creek, their only remaining link with their memories of the distant past.

"We can always follow it upstream."

"How would we go about that?"

Big-as-a-Fist looked his brother up and down.

"By rowing against the current, idiot!"

John-Bear smiled. The dwarf could always be counted on to come up with solutions, then it was the giant's job to carry them out. And off he went to find two of the biggest oak branches to make a pair of oars. Fear not, little one, your big brother doesn't sulk when there's work to be done; he'll build you a raft and a set of sculls such as no stream has ever held. Alas! Such as no stream *could* ever hold: for John-Bear's boat was not a raft, it was a galleon, and the little stream trembled with fear at the very sight of such a monster.

"I'm afraid we'd be better off swimming," said Big-as-a-Fist.

But no sooner had he spoken these words than he began to regret them. It was all right for a dwarf to splash about in the shallow waters of a stream. But a giant? So before they let themselves be swept away by the current — come what may! — the two brothers shook hands, spat three times on the ground, and vowed eternal fidelity against wind and tide . . .

The wind and tide that would soon swallow them whole.

And in this way — from stream to rivulet to mighty river — our two companions reached the ocean, which welcomed them home like lost waves.

"John-Bear, my brother, listen to me!"

"Big-as-a-Fist, where are you?"

And splish! And splash! And shit! It's too salty! The dwarf was reminded of the big tub of soapy water his mother, Goodwife, used to dunk him in when he was a child, to clean out his nose and his belly button. And the memory would have made his mouth water, if his mouth could have held another drop.

Suddenly he felt himself lifted up and thrown into the air on a jet of water composed of thousands of droplets so dense that they formed a soft liquid cushion under the mystified bum of an even more mystified Thumbkin. Looking down, he was just able to make out the rounded back of a whale, which he at first mistook for his brother:

"John-Bear! John-Bear!"

Hearing his name, John-Bear rushed to Big-as-a-Fist's aid without stopping to think where he was going, and came up face to face with the whale. Which was when his maxims flashed through his memory . . .

Never pick on anyone smaller than yourself.

. . . and he sized up the whale.

"John! . . . Bear!"

He looked up and saw, just above his head, the pompom of a multicoloured cap rolling and bouncing in the whale's spout. He didn't wait for the other maxims. Whale, prepare yourself for combat!

The scene that followed has never been reported in detail and in its entirety. Mainly because there were no witnesses to it except Big-as-a-Fist, who in his epic tales always got tripped up over details; and John-Bear, who never got around to telling the whole story of any of his mightier feats; and the whale himself, who didn't know, until he met up with the dwarf, that he had the power of speech. It was a grand battle, no doubt about it, and probably deserved a long ballad of its own, like the ones they still sing at some house parties. All battles are grand, of course, to the victors. But as far as Big-as-a-Fist was concerned, the most important element in a story was its uniqueness. And though all wars have their heroes, their defeats, and their victories, very few of them take place in the water, between a giant and a talking whale.

Don't get me wrong: whales have always had their own language, just as we have ours. Otherwise, how would they have been able to communicate with each other for as long as they've been in the world? But it would be unique if we were all able to understand each other in our respective languages. Of all the heroes I know, only Big-as-a-Fist has that ability — a gift he snatched, as we've seen, straight from his godmother's bag of tricks. And on this day, the first morning of his new life, he put it to good use.

"Sit!" he shouted to the whale, who froze in astonishment.

Now, the whale had never before been addressed in his own language by a stranger of another species, and of such a small size. Not only that, but he really didn't know how to obey such a bizarre command; sitting down is a most uncomfortable position for a whale. But poor Big-as-a-Fist, who was only in the first stage of learning to use his gifts, multiplied his blunders, more from inexperience than from malice. Gifted though he was, he still hadn't spoken to anyone but his cat and dog. So he ordered the whale to pull in his claws.

The whale obeyed. The largest mammal in the world, who a moment before had been tossing in his waterspout a dwarf he could easily have lodged in his nostril, bent his back and lowered his head before the marvellous gift of so small a personage.

Which was why no one could say for sure whether it was John-Bear's strength or Big-as-a-Fist's intelligence that defeated the monster. But because the brothers were as inseparable as two fingers of one hand, neither wanted to claim the whale for himself.

"We could both climb up on his back," the little one suggested. "I'll tell him to take us down to . . ."

But Thumbkin had no time to finish his sentence. At the words "take us down" the whale dove, surfaced, dove again, and lifted his head out of the water, taking our two floundering, flousing, flabbergasted newcomers to the crests of the waves. Each time he came up for air, Big-as-a-Fist tried to talk to the beast in order to assert his authority, but the wind's talk was louder than his, and was about rain and fair weather, the only truly serious topic of conversation on the high seas. Plague, cholera, war, business, republics, being and nothingness, the gods — these questions inspire not a smidgen of interest in the universe of whales. But rain and fair weather!

Big-as-a-Fist translated for John-Bear:

"We'd better get ready for snow."

"What?"

"Snow! He says there's a storm to the north of us."

The storm didn't wait to be asked twice: at the sound of her name, she descended in a swirling and twirling that encapped our heroes' heads in snowy peaks, turned their eyelashes and whiskers white, and plunged the barometer hanging from John-Bear's nose to well below thirty degrees. Ooof! And Brrr! And chattering teeth!

"Hey! Whale! Take us to land so we can dig ourselves a tunnel!"

But the land must have melted last spring, along with everything else. Nothing on the horizon. Not the tiniest island. And now the whale was fighting the wind and tiring. John-Bear looked at him with compassion. Let's let him get his breath back. But how? Whales usually warm themselves in the depths, down where the water never freezes. Alas, no rest for the steed as long as he's carrying two chevaliers like our heroes on his back; they may be extraordinary, but they haven't learned yet how to breathe through anything but their mouths and noses.

"Maybe I can give him a hand," suggested the giant.

So saying, he lay down on his stomach, plunged his arms into the waves, and started to row. Big-as-a-Fist clapped his hands. Then he began to think. He wanted to do his bit, too, but he was smart enough to know that his little arms were not much longer than toothpicks and wouldn't move the flotilla ahead an inch. He tapped his forehead; that was where his strength lay. Suddenly he smiled out of the corner of his mouth and said to the whale:

"Piss!"

The beast obeyed his master.

"No, no! Through your nose!"

The whale caught on and redirected his jet. And a superb geyser shot up from his blow-hole, climbed high into the air, and froze. Big-as-a-Fist drooled with pleasure — not a good idea, because he'd have a stalactite hanging from his chin for the rest of the day — and called to his brother to look at the superb mast above his head that had transformed their boat into a sailing ship.

"All we need now is a sail," he said.

John-Bear started to scan the horizon for an imaginary sail, then finally understood and took off his jacket. The two companions had barely had time to admire their handiwork when a strong southeasterly wind swelled their sail and took over the job of delivering them to the end of this first expedition of theirs, which would soon reveal itself to be of the utmost importance in the unravelling of their history.

To think that Goodman and Goodwife, back at home, bent over the workbench or the breadboard, hadn't yet used up the eighth day.

The whale, meanwhile, had come to a stop. Grounded. The explorers, at once elated and anxious, searched through their pockets, pulled out a sounding-line, and felt for the bottom. They had landed on a wreck. Impossible! In the middle of the ocean? John-Bear stuck his foot in the water. Believe it or not, Thumbkin, it's wood. If anyone could tell wood when he felt it, it was this son of an oak trunk.

"Wood, Big-as-a-Fist, the bridge of a ship. And I think it's frozen."

Tom Thumb lost his head in his excitement and jumped overboard. His brother grabbed him just in time, just as the water was up to his neck. The dwarf then climbed the mast and sat in the shrouds. From there he called down orders to his imaginary deckhands, who paid him no heed; for of all the stout-hearted crewmembers from days gone by, the only one left was the ship's figure-head, his face turned forever north. John-Bear went up to the bow and studied it, amazed, transfixed. The captain called out his Starboard! and Larboard! and Hard by north-northeast! But the giant stayed where he was, silent, his eyes riveted on the sad, distant face of the figure-head, frozen under its varnish of ice. Searching in his heart, John-Bear came up with his second maxim:

Come to the aid of those who are weaker than you.

Softly, with all the tenderness of a midwife drawing the first cry from a newborn babe, he breathed on the frozen face, using every bit of air in his lungs: breathe in, pump, breathe out . . .

Big-as-a-Fist felt he should warn his brother not to get his hopes up too high.

"It's a figure-head, John-Bear, a man made of wood . . ."

But the giant didn't hear him. Through the ice, his eyes had encountered a wild, pleading look, a look full of longing for life. And he pumped, and blew, and Big-as-a-Fist could say what he liked — though Big-as-a-Fist was no longer doing or saying anything, for he, too, had seen the face of the man at the bowsprit; but he's dead, John-Bear, departed this life — frozen for centuries, to judge by the shape of his hat, a tricorne, and his jacket, a doublet, and the ruff around his neck . . . you can see for yourself that he comes from the olden days and is, alas, quite dead. Dead as a doornail, John-Bear.

"Are you sure?"

"As sure as I'm my father's son."

John-Bear cocked a sceptical eye at his brother and kept blowing. And pumping, and breathing, and working on the ice — which, drop by drop, began to melt.

"He's dead, John-Bear. Stop it!"

Even if the giant wanted to stop, he couldn't, because from deep down in his chest came the words:

Always finish what you have started.

He no longer had a choice. You couldn't disown your maxims any more than you could your wishes. So he went on pumping and blowing. And the last drop fell from the wide-open eye of the figure-head.

"He's crying," said John-Bear.

This time, he stopped.

Both brothers doffed their caps, the dwarf standing at attention, the giant kneeling on the ground. And with no further ceremony, as if their whole lives had been spent waiting for this happy event, they introduced themselves.

"John-Bear, also called John-the-Strong, also called Strong-as-a-Dozen, my elder brother. And my name is Tom Thumb, also called Thumbkin, better known as Big-as-a-Fist. We are both sons of Squire Goodman and his lady, Goodwife."

They waited.

Slowly the lips of the ice-man parted, clouded over, and a stream of air escaped them in the form of white smoke. An eyelid moved and caused the lashes to tremble. A rictus . . . a smile . . . a word.

"Friends?"

The two brothers looked at each other, then gave a shout of joy. He spoke their language! They'd be able to understand each other. More important, his first word was one of cordiality.

"Friends!" they hurriedly answered in unison.

As soon as the last splinters of ice had fallen from his eyes, the newcomer snorted, flexed his arms and legs, and tried to approach his rescuers. But his feet were still encased in blocks of ice, and he tripped. John-Bear caught him and placed him upright again, then rubbed his feet in his gigantic palms, all the while murmuring gentle, unintelligible words. The thawed man contemplated him with curiosity, as if searching in the depths of his ancestral memory for the thread of his interrupted life. Little by little, words returned to him:

"Be this the new-found land?"

"— ?"

"Thou art o' th' New World?"

Big-as-a-Fist cleaned out his ears with his little fingers and tried to comprehend. The figure-head spoke his language, all right, but it was an antique, unused form of it. And he shouted to make himself better understood:

"This here's the middle of the ocean. Your ship's been wrecked. Don't know when, though, milord, or on what iceberg."

This time it was the figure-head's turn to wring out his ears.

"Sir René Renaissance, your servant," he said, making a deep bow.

John-Bear protested. This man looked no more like a servant than John-Bear looked like an acrobat. He had to be saying that to bring himself down to the level of his hosts. But Big-as-a-Fist burst out laughing when he heard the name of this returnee from the sea:

"René the Well-Named!" he said, forgetting that he himself sported a name that described him perfectly from head to toe.

Little by little, Sir René, also known as Figure-Head, recalling to his memory the last images registered there before his great plunge into oblivion, saw again the ship battling the furious waves in the northern seas, in search of an estuary to the New World. Then the memories came tumbling into his head. His ship had left Saint-Malo, in Brittany, many weeks earlier, following in the footsteps of the explorers Christopher Columbus and John Cabot. He had signed on as a volunteer, out of ambition, curiosity, and a taste for adventure. And partly to prove *de facto* that the earth was round. He turned to his new companions:

"'Tis truly round?"

"What?"

"The earth? 'Tis round?"

The brothers looked at each other, then laughed out loud:

"Round as anything!"

"Thou hast encompass'd it?"

"Well, not yet, but . . ."

The dwarf explained to the newcomer that it wouldn't be too long before they did, that it fell right in with their plans.

"Then say, prithee, how thou knowest it?"

"But we learn it at school, the same time as two and two are four."

The figure-head opened his eyes wide. Before him was a strange little gallant, no bigger than his fist, who was giving him in a broken language and without a shadow of a doubt the answer to one of the most serious questions of all time . . . of all time . . . Suddenly his eyes released a final drop of melted ice.

"Can it be that I have slept such a long night? What is the day o' th' week?"

"Thursday," replied John-Bear quickly, happy to be able to show off his knowledge. He knew all the other days of the week, too, and the months of the year, and . . .

Big-as-a-Fist began to understand just what the unfrozen frozen one's questions were leading up to.

"I'm afraid," he said, "that you've been asleep for a very long time. Years, in fact. Do you remember what day it was when you perished in the ocean? . . . I mean . . ."

And he bit his tongue.

The figure-head looked at Big-as-a-Fist as if he'd just descended from the clouds. Or worse: risen from the nether regions. And it came to him that he was returning from a strange adventure, the lone survivor of another era.

"Praise God thine is an amical land, and these be favourable times!" he exclaimed, throwing himself to his knees before the two brothers, who were as moved as a young couple before the cradle of a newborn babe.

When the initial surprise had been swallowed and digested the three companions fell over themselves trying to exchange information with each other. John-Bear exhausted his knowledge of the world and himself in three sentences; Big-as-a-Fist took three hours, and only managed to skim the surface of his favourite topic, which was entitled Big-as-a-Fist; and three full days passed before they began to get an inkling of the height, breadth, and depth of the treasure that had been hidden in the ice of the far north. Because first they had to adjust their ears to his language. It had the same roots and radicals as that of our gallants, but was adorned with prefixes, suffixes, and terminations with a multitude of variations. More s's and th's everywhere.

Once he'd stripped the ancient language of its surplus consonants, Big-as-a-Fist was able to make some sense of it. He and John-Bear then learned that their new companion, named René, sprang from sixteenth-century soil, and that he had first seen the light of day in the good city of Paris, the capital of France. His early childhood had been spent four hundred years before, when his father had laid the cornerstone of a huge church in the heart of the city. This same René, son of Jacques, son of Antoine, for reasons that seemed important at the time but trivial four centuries later, had broken with his father, left the stonemasons' guild, and taken to the sea. Just as some people today take to the road.

"The road to the New World. But lo, we attained not our end. We ne'er set foot on land."

Because, while skirting the coast of Newfoundland, the prow of his ship had struck an ice floe.

"The eve of the day of th'evil hour, saw we in the sky a witch bestriding her broom, crossing the Milky Way, slipping 'twixt Sagittary and the Goat and sweeping stardust from the horns of Taurus as she passed. 'Twas then we saw the comet."

"Halley's Comet!" cried Big-as-a-Fist, still filled with memories plucked from the land of their father and mother.

But the name awakened no echo in the otherwise infallible memory of Sir René, the explorer who'd set off to conquer a world that he didn't actually meet until four centuries later, and that he didn't recognize. Big-as-a-Fist, remembering his school lessons, sighed inwardly. Just think: if the ship hadn't prevented it, René could have been the grandfather of the grandfather of the great-grandfather of Goodman and Goodwife, the parents he'd left behind in the stream of his childhood. And from that moment, Big-as-a-Fist felt his lot in life tied to that of this possible ancestor, who had disappeared before he had time to establish his lineage.

While the dwarf was dreaming about the distant past of the revenant, the latter was amazed to receive, albeit so late and in such a small school, the answers to questions that had tortured the greatest minds of his day.

But his companions left him little time to ponder; they couldn't wait to hear the rest of his extraordinary story.

"The end, Sir René, the end!"

They little knew how true their words were: the end! It was 1531, in February or maybe March, when the ship — running due north-northwest — beheld the long plume of the comet in the sky. The crew saw it sweep the heavens with its forked, splendid, wild, terrifying, mysterious tail. They should have been more on their guard. Suddenly the ship changed course — complying with every warning in the almanacs, all of which predicted strange happenings when a comet passes.

He fell silent. His companions understood that it was a good time to observe a moment of silence.

Slowly, painfully, the narrator picked up the thread of his story.

The ship, wishing to hook itself to the comet's tail, forgot the most elementary laws of navigation and rammed its hull against an iceberg as big as a continent.

Beyond that the castaway remembered nothing, except that at the moment of collision he had been at the prow of the ship.

And that is how the first existence of our explorer from sixteenth-century France came to an end. A temporary end. Because our hero had not entered the kingdom of the dead, only of the forgotten. He had simply stopped breathing, in ideal conditions for freezing. By thawing him out with his breath, slowly, John-Bear had brought him quite naturally, and very gently, back to life. Four centuries later.

With that breath, this son of a former age had recovered his memory and all the faculties that went with it. Big-as-a-Fist understood very quickly the enormous use he and his brother could make of this well of knowledge nourished directly at the primal source. As for John-Bear, he was as transported as Pygmalion before his statue, watching the figure-head of a ship of ice begin to move, speak, laugh, and recount and recall everything that had taken place since time immemorial.

"Figure-Head," he said timidly, "how'd you like to join us? The day before the day before yesterday, we left our paternal home, and now we're going . . ."

He wasn't exactly sure. And Big-as-a-Fist, who wasn't sure either, came to his rescue anyway.

"To adventure," he said, his hands on his hips.

And that's how two heroes became three. Before a year had passed, though, the three would have become four.

4

How three companions discovered a fourth at the centre of a vicious circle

The new heroes, whether born of the same parents or someone else's, decided — after many promises of friendship, loyalty, and vassalage for life, until death do them part, come what may — to book passage on a floe that had brushed against their ship of ice and luckily was setting sail that very day for the south.

The giant began by releasing the whale; the dwarf by thanking him in his own language for his good services; and Figure-Head by showing him how to find the best east-by-east-by-southeast currents: Look out for ice pans, beware of the comet, and above all . . . But the whale had already disappeared into the vasty deep, blowing one last jet of foam in the face of the explorer for trying to give a fish a lesson in navigation.

Our heroes wended their way south, sometimes by iceberg, sometimes by dolphin, and finally stepped onto solid ground. Good old terra firma, just what the doctor ordered. The three adventures stretched their arms and legs, breathing in the sweet, spruce-scented air.

"I believe winter's over," said John-Bear, who had recognized the smell of wood-sap.

"It's the time when nests are full of eggs," recalled Big-as-a-Fist, his mouth watering.

But under the reproachful eye of his companions, he stopped

licking his lips and realized that from now on . . . he was too old to go around sucking eggs. To avoid thinking about that, he suggested that they all explore the territory, walking in single file.

"I'll go first," he said.

Which was not a good idea. Because it wasn't long before the explorers realized that they had gone off their path. Or rather, that they couldn't get off their path. Sir René was the first to notice that they were going around in circles. Somehow, at some point, they had stumbled onto the circumference of a vicious circle, and now they were unable to escape. The farther they went, the tighter the circle became. At the speed at which their universe was contracting, they'd soon run out and reach the end of it . . . The end? Big-as-a-Fist's face lit up. The end of the road could only be the centre of the circle, consequently the centre of the earth. We're walking straight towards the centre of the earth, my friends!

Sir René felt his skin go cold with goose bumps. Four centuries before, he had stuck his head out over just this kind of maelstrom, and he was in no hurry to repeat the experience of the diminishing circle. At the nether point of the last circle, my friends . . . but his friends weren't listening. Thumbkin, perched like a feather atop the giant's hat, had just spotted a wall on the horizon. A wall encircling a village. A village as round and enclosed as an egg.

"Go on, John-Bear. Go all around it. Look for an opening."

And the giant dashed off in his seven-league boots, circled the entire length of the wall, and rejoined his brothers, disappointed. Nothing. Not a door, not a drawbridge, not even a gunslit. A fortress cut off from the world.

How strange! A dead town!

Come on. Let's get out of here.

But Big-as-a-Fist dragged his feet, eaten up by curiosity. What if we just had a quick look? Just to see if anyone's alive behind these walls? Or maybe there's some old junk from the past lying around. You never know.

At the words "some old junk from the past" his ancient companion ground his teeth; he still felt young enough under his Renaissance clothing and manners. But Big-as-a-Fist was too preoccupied with his future discoveries to worry about putting his foot in his mouth *vis-à-vis* his elders. For him, the future lay full speed ahead, and at the moment was hidden behind an opaque, solid, and apparently unbreachable wall.

"Why unbreachable? What do we have a giant for, anyway?"

The giant understood, and without hesitation or forethought he lifted his two companions up at arm's length and tossed them over the wall. That done, it occurred to him to step over the wall himself, just as he had learned to step over the one that had surrounded his parents' yard when he was a baby.

Once in the village, he looked around from right to left.

"Big-as-a-Fist! Figure-Head! Comrades! Where are you?"

So eager was he to find his friends that he didn't notice the crowd of people at his feet, looking him up and down with some malice — and not a little fear. For if John-Bear had never before visited a closed village, neither had the citizens of this bizarre burg numbered a giant among their acquaintances. And our corpulent chum nearly crushed a few of them before realizing that the square and streets were swarming with people.

"Excuse me," he hastened to say, blushing, holding his hands behind his back and shuffling his feet.

Such a humble and well-meaning attitude emboldened the populace to stand up for its rights, and it pushed forward a little despot of a magistrate who, with grand airs and gestures, addressed the giant from his full height.

"What are you doing here, trespasser? Who gave you leave to effect an entry into these premises?"

Here was another language our hero wasn't used to. He'd been quick enough to catch on to Sir René's Middle French, but his comrade spoke to him, gently and without rancour, using words that, though strange, slid sweetly through his ear canals.

"I'm looking for my friends and brothers," he said simply, inadvertently revealing to these crafty people and their leader that other trespassers had penetrated their walls.

This time the magistrate decided to try a little cat-and-mouse:

"Your brothers and comrades?" he said, with an exaggerated rolling of his r's. "Are they all as big as you? And as . . . pleasing to the eye?"

And he winked in the direction of the general of the army, who was scurrying to get his men at the ready.

Throughout this scene — in which John-Bear grew more and more agitated about the fate of his brothers, and the crowd interpreted his agitation in quite a different way, and each party misinterpreted the intentions of the other — Big-as-a-Fist and Figure-Head increased their efforts to catch the eye of the giant from their perch on the side of the belfry where the two had become stuck when they landed in the village. Luckily for them. Because the truculent citizenry of this closed town would no doubt have shown a good deal less politeness towards two small- to medium-sized beings than they had to the giant.

"Pssst! Shawn-Bear!"

Had he heard something? Had he imagined it? He lifted his head, turned it in all directions, opening wide his nostrils and ears. Where were they? "Big-as-a-Fist, my brother. Sir René, my friend . . ." And he was about to start overturning walls and buildings when he was struck by the sound of a bell coming from the belfry. Thumbkin, fearful of watching his big idiot of a brother get them all in the soup, had lost his footing, slid down the great tenor bell, and grabbed onto the smaller bell, making it swing against the bigger one. Bong!

Well, there was chaos in the streets. A general chaos, complete, splendid! The most beautiful chaos Big-as-a-Fist had seen since he'd thrown a cat among the chickens in his mother's backyard. He was tempted to whistle and applaud. But he felt a hand on his collar, and his elder by four hundred years signalled him with a raised finger to keep still and silent. And if anyone knew what was what in such a perilous situation, it was Sir René Renaissance, also known as Figure-Head, who had the disquieting impression of having been here before.

Suddenly Big-as-a-Fist saw the head of an old man raised towards the tower, and two piercing eyes staring into his own. One of the villagers had calmed down and had thought to look up at the clock. Against the general opinion — which held that the bell was announcing the end of the world — one of the village's rare wise men had said to himself that clocks might after all be mistaken, it wouldn't be the first time, and might ring out of caprice, or even whimsy.

And that's how the two other trespassers on the "premises" were discovered and brought, along with John-Bear, before the supreme court of the town.

The giant who had not discerned in the swarming crowd a single opponent his own size, had allowed himself to be captured without putting up a fight. His maxims kept him from taking on anyone smaller than himself, and try as Big-as-a-Fist might to convince his brother that it was as plain as two-plus-two that a whole crowd of little people equalled one big person, John-Bear just went on juggling his maxims about in his huge head.

And now the court was in session.

As always happens in such cases, the prosecution went well beyond the initial charges, and managed to make the effects appear to far outstrip the causes. Within three witnesses, our heroes had heard themselves described as traitors to the cosmos and accused of introducing bad-time into the village. At which point the explorer from the sixteenth century, who was used to suffering through puerile, idiotic, and interminable trials, began to find this one amusing.

"Methinks we have falne into the court of King Pétaud," he said.

And Big-as-a-Fist, who never missed a joke, burst out laughing.

But not for long. For he and his brothers were beginning to understand the weight of the charges brought against them. They were accused of growing old. In all innocence, by entering the village, these intruders had brought with them a current of air that had altered time. And time was the mortal enemy of this walled circle of a village that for centuries had been protected against the ravages of the hourglass. The citizens of this fabulous village at the heart of the vicious circle had voluntarily cut themselves off from the world in order to keep their lineage and traditions intact and, above all, to escape the effects of time: time past, time killed, endless time; time that changes, runs out, flies, weighs heavily, and reduces everything in its wake to dust.

"Ah, so that's it!" Big-as-a-Fist let out, thinking he understood what was going on.

"By penetrating our walls," said the judge, "you have contaminated our ways and our customs. You have opened a fissure in our fortress through which an extra day has slipped."

It was true. The chronologists, metachronicians, and astronomers all agreed: their instruments confirmed that one day too many had been introduced into the millennium, and in one fell swoop their almanacs and calendars had become outdated.

"Everything has to be done again," moaned an aged savant, an anachronist in his own time, above the other voices. "Let one day in, and pretty soon you'll be invaded by a whole new concept of time, from the four corners of the earth!"

And he slapped his forehead and beat his chest, bewailing the loss of the good old days.

Sir René, who was learned in the fields of law, logic, and astronomy, raised a finger and courteously asked if he might have the floor. And then, in a peroration beautifully garnished with quotations from the Greek and Hebrew, which Big-as-a-Fist and John-Bear couldn't make head or tail of, he expounded on the Theory of the Extra Day. The earth, being round, as he had recently learned, must therefore have an axis upon which it turned. "Prithee, gentlemen, to place in motion a child's top: allow it to spin, and you will observe that not only does it rotate upon its axis, but also it leaves its accustom'd place and orbits about the table. In just such a way must the earth travel about the sun."

The speaker lifted his head to savour the effects of his words, and was taken aback by the general impassiveness of the audience.

"Well?" asked one of his more acerbic auditors, who had learned on his grandpappy's knee that the earth revolved around the sun.

Sir René, a trifle behind in his science but able to leap across centuries in a single bound, pursed his lips and concluded that the earth, by force of habit and profession, had gained a fraction of a second on each of its journeys about the sun.

"And that is how, gentlemen, after a thousand years, your great and noble village has on this day gained its extra day."

This time, Figure-Head was satisfied: his theory had the effect of a bomb. His discovery incited panic. Sheer anarchy. One extra day every thousand years struck the villagers like one handful of sand in a gearbox. Imagine the state of our calendar in ten millennia, in a million years! The astronomers and chronologists mopped their brows. How could they correct a calendar that gained time? The way things were going, the days would end up dovetailing into weeks, the weeks into months, the seasons see-sawing into each other, the planets plunging into the Milky Way, and God knew where it all would end!

The magistrate rocked on his pedestal and imposed silence on his people and on the three accused, the causers of the decay in time. Because without the awkward revelations of these outside agitators, the village would have carried on in the lee of time, ignorant of the flaw in the stars, happy and carefree. But now that they'd shown them the true state of affairs, the newcomers had forced a peace-loving people to become aware of the evil hour hanging over their heads.

"The outside agitators should be put to death!" he cried, striking the plinth with his crook. "To death!"

"To death!" shouted the peace-lovers at the peak of their fury.

For the first time since their arrival in the village, Big-as-a-Fist felt the floor giving way under his feet. No time to lose. He had no choice but to try his own luck, since his older brother had failed to get them out of this mess. And out of habit, he followed his instinct and shouted out the first thing that came into his head.

"Our lives versus the extra day!" he crowed from the height of his perch — from the feather on his brother's hat, that is.

Silence. The magistrate, the judge and jury, the wise men, the citizens living out of time, all shut up. Then they scratched their heads. Then they searched through the mountain of usages and customs for a precedent for this timely proposition.

Sir René smiled at Tom Thumb. Then, in an attempt to strike the iron while it was still hot, he explained to the perplexed villagers that a day could sometimes go by without leaving a trace; he himself had known scores of them. One simply eliminated it, consigned it to oblivion, out of sight out of mind, don't give it another thought.

The village surged around its magistrate, who was blown up like a bladder and round as a balloon, and consulted with him. Not a bad idea. We don't have much choice. Why not, in effect, eliminate this niche in time right off the bat, before it's too late? But how do we go about it? Who'll do it?

An old man dressed in the tattered garb of a former era, a man even more outdated than the others, suggested to his compatriots that they sleep it off; thus drowned in sleep, the extra day would disappear all by itself. But an ageless hermit, who long ago had learned how to kill time in the desert, said it would be nobler and more fitting to declare a day of silence and give the thing a first-class funeral. Yet a third, one of those young whippersnappers fresh out of school, proposed that they simply ignore the deuced thing and let it go away. Others, more bellicose than the rest, presented themselves armed to the teeth, ready to provoke it into a fight and cut it to pieces.

"We'll give it a hard time, all right," they shouted, shaking their swords and cudgels.

The magistrate turned his round and crafty head towards his captives and made them an offer:

"Rid us of this extra day, and you will be given safe conduct from our village and returned with your lives into time-that-flows."

Anxiously, the three comrades considered his proposal: John-

Bear rested his eyes on Big-as-a-Fist; Big-as-a-Fist studied the face of Sir René; Sir René returned the gaze of Big-as-a-Fist. Suddenly the dwarf lifted his eyes to the lofty forehead of the one who had returned from ancient times and asked him, in an Old French that traversed two centuries, if he remembered much about his former life. His comrade didn't hesitate; memory was his strongest suit. At that, the lad planted himself squarely before the magistrate and made his suggestion:

"A holiday!"

"A what?"

The round village was nonplussed. A holiday? What's a holiday? Never had the people from out of time given themselves over to such an activity. They didn't have a clue how to go about it. The old hermit finally conceded that, after such a useless waste of time, they could at least be sure nothing would remain.

"The extra day will be completely extinguished," he said, "down to its last candle."

And so it was that for one day our three comrades were appointed Ministers Plenipotentiary of Holidays and Recreation, with full authority to organize the Carnival of the Millennium. Purpose: to get drunk, to get fuddled, to pass out, and to forget!

Big-as-a-Fist was at the top of his form and the height of his genius. From Sir René Renaissance he learned the ancient lore connected with the rites and traditions of the holiday: the symbolic struggle between Good and Evil, the confrontation between Rex, the King of Mardi Gras, and the Shrovetide Reveller, the Parade of Fools, the Procession of the Flagellants, the masques, the plays, the songs, the dances, the bonfires . . .

Shrove Tuesday,
Don't run away,
I'll make you some pancakes,
If you'll only stay!

. . . until John-Bear hoisted the firmament at the end of his arms.

What ecstasy! Never before had the walled village seen time pass so quickly. And to stretch the festivities out until nightfall, Big-as-a-Fist played his magic flute and raised hell and high water for three miles around. So dance and leap, break wind, my beauties, every time I sneeze! By evening the village was exhausted, begged for a reprieve, and trailed away with a final burst of belching and laughter that betrayed the extent of the massacre. Never again would that extra day break upon a scene of such carnage: it was erased from the calendar forever. There was nothing left of it.

Except.

At the very end of the day, just when the three comrades were saying their goodbyes to the round village and getting ready to step back onto the road to time-that-flows, at the first stroke of midnight, who should emerge from the bowels of the mock holiday but the giantess Gargamelle. And there, in the courtyard in front of the town hall, at the foot of the bell tower, the pregnant giantess spread her legs and delivered a new baby into the world. The festival was over. Nothing of the day's tumult and shouting remained but a male child, very much alive, born outside of time, on the extra day.

When they got out of bed the next morning, the citizens of the round village expected to be able to hook their tomorrow onto their day-before-yesterday. Instead, they were astonished to find a fatherless, motherless child, a surplus babe born in the wrinkles of time, running about in their streets.

"Where does this strange individual come from?"

They had been promised that nothing, but nothing, would be left of the extra day. So the child was immediately condemned. Unanimously. Call the police, call the army, get the executioner. No healthy village can let a single germ of rot stay inside its walls. Kill it!

Kill it!

Our three comrades hardly had time to open their eyes and close their yawning yaps before they saw the executioner's hooded figure, preceded by his double-bladed axe, appear from the basement of the town hall. The crowd saw it, too, and fell in behind the executioner, who led them to the centre of town, where a block had been hastily erected. There they placed the child, who was smiling and playing with the cords dangling from the executioner's belt. Gathered in a circle around the platform, the villagers broke into prayer, craning their necks to get a better view. The axe was raised, poised at the ends of the executioner's arms . . .

Suddenly John-Bear remembered his maxim:

Come to the aid of those who are weaker than you.

He leaned his head over the child who had seen the extra day — poor thing! — and closed his fist over the handle of the axe. There it stayed, outlined against the sky, suspended between two mighty arms like a heraldic emblem.

John-Bear's courageous and spontaneous action gave his comrades time to think. Which is to say that wise old Sir René racked his brains, digging deep within his infallible memory for a similar situation, while the impetuous Big-as-a-Fist, without thinking at all because there was no time, raced as fast as his legs would carry him towards the platform. The baby was sitting calmly, blissfully unaware of what was taking place over his head. He was perfectly beautiful, perfectly formed, already fully grown, and neither small nor big, casting his innocent gaze over the citizens of the village from which he had sprung as if saying to them: I am not one of you.

He's not of this world, if you ask me, thought Big-as-a-Fist to himself; but in situations like these, such questions are a luxury, a waste of time. The dwarf gathered his wits about him and began to assess the extent of the danger. The axe was hanging just over his head. He swallowed hard; what the devil was he doing up there on the platform?

"Get down," he whispered into the ear of the child, who looked at him without understanding his urgency. "Hurry up, get out of here, follow me!"

The baby born on the extra day seemed perfectly delighted to hear Big-as-a-Fist addressing him personally, speaking to him like a playmate, even like a lifelong friend. He raised his arms to the dwarf, who didn't know where to turn and who cursed the day they'd ever set foot on the circumference of the vicious circle. The axe dipped, was about to fall on their heads at any moment, and Big-as-a-Fist had little time to save the child's skin without risking his own; better to get out of this himself than to lose everything, to turn his brother into an only child and his future children into orphans — get out of here, Big-as-a-Fist, jump off the platform, save your skin, you big dummy! The blade swam before his eyes, was about to strike him . . . no, it swung back up, returned to its place against the heavens, held there by two gigantic fists like a bejewelled coat of arms. Thumbkin heard:

Always finish what you have started.

His brother was breathing hard, really panting, and all his gnarled joints were cracking like knot-holes in an oaken plank. Never had he met such a foe. Where did this executioner get his strength?

"From the nether regions."

It was Sir René who spoke the words. He had elbowed his way through the thick of the crowd to join his brothers and loyal friends. At the hour of death, the comrades would stick by each other and either save themselves or perish together. And if anyone knew the true stakes in this unequal battle, it was René the Reborn. Only he knew how to speak to Death in Death's own language.

The word hit Big-as-a-Fist's ear like a bullet. Death? Was this Death? Come so soon? And he glanced at Sir René with eyes filled with sorrow, but also with a thin thread of hope. His wise elder brother tried to console him by explaining to him that, sooner or later, everyone must pass through Death's door, and therefore one day more or less didn't have a great deal of significance as far as the stars were concerned. Maybe not for the stars, but in the eyes of Big-as-a-Fist, sooner or later made an enormous difference, because between them lay his whole life.

"Speak to him if you know who he is," he cried to the returnee from the polar seas.

Because Big-as-a-Fist was certain, without understanding why, that from now on they were four comrades, and that no one among them would escape the clutches of the Grim Reaper alone . . . either all four of them would get away, or none.

"And if he doesn't listen to reason, insult him, call him a good-for-nothing, rotten, filthy, piece of stinking . . ."

Stinking? Big-as-a-Fist repeated the word to himself; it sounded like a fart . . . it even smelled like a fart. Well, there was nothing to lose. And everything to gain. He jumped to his feet, passed the newborn to the old man, climbed up onto John-Bear's head and winked at him in passing, as if to say: All right, big fella, I'm here! And doing an about-face towards the cowled figure, he sneezed full in his hood.

"Prrrt!"

Death had farted. A fart straight out of Hell that took only one second to stink up the entire village.

Let me out! Out of my way! Give me air!

The crowd scattered like ants from an anthill.

Open the gates!

And through a secret door with rusted hinges, closed since time immemorial, the citizens of the walled village fanned out into the surrounding meadows and fields. After an hour, not a soul was left at the centre of the vicious circle but a puzzled and embarrassed executioner, and three comrades, who had just become four.

Big-as-a-Fist was doubled over and holding his sides. Even the wise old René sniggered behind his hand, as pleased as he was surprised by the turn of events. As for the unconquering but unconquered John-Bear, he was still trying to figure out how to finish what he'd started when he heard, from the mouth of the child who was still standing on the platform:

"Hello! What's my name?"

Well, said Big-as-a-Fist to himself, here's someone who likes to ask his questions back to front.

"You're Extra-Day," he said.

To which Figure-Head added:

"Born-Out-of-Time."

Passing the battered-down door of the village, the newcomer lifted his arms and cried:

"Oh what a beautiful world! Is it all ours?"

The other three looked at each other nonplussed, then broke out in a burst of good, refreshing laughter. Oh yes, my boy, it's ours, all right! Why not? Until the end of time. Then Sir René collected himself and signalled for silence.

"Don't turn around," he said. "He's taken off his cowl and he's trying to see your faces. Don't let your eyes meet his. He must not be able to recognize us if by chance our paths ever cross again."

Big-as-a-Fist covered his eyes with his cap in case he was tempted to peek between his fingers. John-Bear obeyed without understanding why, placing all his faith in his brother who was four centuries older and knew so many things. As for Extra-Day, the future was still too new for him to be bothered with the past. He was surrounded by life: buds were budding, blossoms blossoming, streams streaming through the moss, the cry of geese responding to the woodcock, who snuffled and snorted at everything. The newborn couldn't stop looking and listening and letting life invade him from all sides. It invaded him so well, in fact, that he was soon as high as a kite. And before long he was singing like a drunkard. His comrades, watching him with compassion, told themselves that their little brother born out of time would always keep the stars from going out and the streams from drying up.

And arm in arm in arm in arm, our four heroes left the walled village and the vicious circle by the back door.

5

How our four heroes discovered the universe in a drop of water

As they left the round village, the two comrades who had become three and were now four realized that their number was complete, and that they had succeeded in squaring the circle. All that remained was to initiate the newcomer to life in the world — beginning by finding him some clothes.

"You're naked," observed Figure-Head.

"He's right," said Big-as-a-Fist. "Naked as a jay-bird. We have to get you dressed."

At this John-Bear tapped his forehead, trying to imagine what Extra-Day would look like clothed from head to foot. What a pity, he said to himself, to hide such a beautiful child under a bunch of old hand-me-downs that time will just fade and spoil anyway.

"Time is going to spoil me?"

The other three exchanged amused glances. Then the old man nodded his head:

"Time is mankind's greatest enemy," he said. "When all else is finished, time is still there, at the end."

The child didn't reply, and allowed himself to be dressed like everyone else: shoes, socks, trousers, suspenders, shirt, jacket, cap, just like everyone else. But to the other's amazement, the more they clothed him, the more transparent he became. Even when fully dressed, their new number didn't look like any of the others. His jacket slipped over his body without so much as a wrinkle;

his buttocks and thighs looked as if they'd been poured into his trousers; his shoes seemed moulded onto his feet; even the colours of his clothes took on the hues of his skin, hair, and eyes. In fact, when dressed from head to toe, Extra-Day still looked as though he were wearing his birthday suit. His three brothers decided to cover the youngster up with an overcoat to protect him from bad weather and the stares of the curious. But they soon realized that nothing — not even bad weather — could tarnish their comrade's raw nature.

"You are Beauty itself," exclaimed his distant ancestor.

"Beauty itself," repeated the other two, each secretly claiming his share in the child's paternity.

For his part, the newcomer treated all three of them with an equal and impartial tenderness. The world was so big, and contained so many things, that the child could not choose among them. To solve the problem, he chose everything, and in so doing he showed himself the true son of Big-as-a-Fist. From John-Bear he took his unclouded soul and generosity of heart. As for Sir René, the ancestor torn by his roots from the very loam of History — search as he might through his prodigious memory, he could find no line of parentage to connect him with this child born Out-of-Time, who had no recollection at all beyond the present moment. And yet . . .

"He is the son who was denied me by my four centuries of silence," he sighed.

And saw again his potential progeny, aborted on the very threshold of the New World — which he'd been on his way to discover, and which had been left to rise out of the waters without him.

Big-as-a-Fist ended the discussion by observing that four centuries was long enough for a baptism, and it was time they set out on their adventures. From now on, the four comrades would be inseparable.

"Here's to Life, and here's to Death!" he shouted, believing like all people his size that he had to shout in order to be heard at all.

He would have done better not to yell, because his voice hit the hills along the horizon and bounced into the ears of the hangman, who had left the village-out-of-time and was casting about for the tracks of his enemies. The dwarf's exultant cry put him right on their trail, unbeknownst to the four comrades who were happily leaving the vicious circle by placing one foot directly in the shadow of the other. For his sins, the hangman, dressed in black from head to foot, couldn't tell his shadow from his real person, and ended up tripping head first over the circle's circumference.

Ooof!

The brothers turned in a split second. Figure-Head recognized him first and immediately alerted the others: "Whatever you do," he told them, "don't hang back, just keep walking and don't look around . . . Oh-oh, too late." His three younger brothers were already gleefully watching the unfortunate executioner, whose arse was sticking straight up, and they burst into laughter. The giant and the baby were also laughing at Big-as-a-Fist, who was doubled over and holding his sides. They'd never seen anything so funny! The ancestor begged them to stop, to get away as quickly as possible; warned them that some truths were not to be known, and some tricks were not to be played; we must not laugh in the face of danger or toy with Death. But it was no use. The young greenhorns didn't want to listen; instead, they called out to Destiny by his several nicknames:

"Hey, Plague! Scabies!"

"Scourges!"

"Calamities!"

"Yoo-hoo! Catastrophes!"

"Cataclysms!"

"Evil Eye! Evil One!"

"Bankrupt!"

"Raging Bull!"

"Wicked Old Fart from the Sulphurous Depths! Catch us if you can!"

Figure-Head was on his knees on the ground, tearing out his

hair. Didn't these idiots understand whom they were dealing with? He was right there under their noses! Any closer and they'd be touching him! And for the second time, Figure-Head, the ancient explorer of thunderous oceans, risked his life to save his brothers. He got up, loosened his rusty old sword in its scabboard, and advanced on Death with his head held high.

"Avaunt!" he ordered his siblings, his tone brooking no entreaty. His three brothers froze under his wrathful stare and regal voice. And without knowing why, they understood that they must get out of there, and fast. They jumped up on each others' shoulders and disappeared in a flash.

Then the ancestor, trying to keep a respectful distance from his adversary, addressed him in his own language.

"You must not touch them. It is not time."

"Hou . . . ou . . . ou . . ."

"If it's a victim you want, I'll go alone."

"Snap!"

"Approach now. I'm ready."

"Boom! . . . boom! . . . boom!"

The three comrades were cooling their heels in the middle of a stand of thin woods . . . Had they stumbled into some real danger? And if so, what would happen to their older brother, out there fighting by himself. Was that old-fashioned sword of his any match for the hangman, who was armed with a double-bladed axe? My God! . . . My God! . . . My God!

"I'm going out there," said John-Bear.

"No," cried Big-as-a-Fist, grabbing him by the suspenders.

"I am so!" said John-Bear, heading out and snapping off branches around him.

"In that case, you're taking me with you," said the dwarf, swallowing hard.

"No," cut in John-the-Strong. "I'll go alone and save him myself. I am Strong-as-a-Dozen."

Extra-Day slipped in between his two brothers:

"What about me?" he said, like a mouse proposing to do battle with an elephant.

"You?" replied Big-as-a-Fist hastily. "You stay here quietly behind this rock and don't go getting mixed up in grown-up business."

Extra-Day went back to sucking his thumb. Then his face lit up:

"I have an idea!" he cried, raising Peter Pointer.

The two others were surprised to see that their kid brother knew how to act like a scholar before he even set foot inside a school. Go ahead, then, what's your idea? But though they looked all about them, no idea came from the child's lips; he had disappeared.

"Where'd he go?"

Then, as if flowing from the winds of time, they heard:

"I'll be right back!"

And the two sons of Goodman and Goodwife looked at each other in amazement.

When Extra-Day reappeared a few seconds later at the edge of the vicious circle, where a mortal combat was under way, he arrived in the nick of time. The poor ancestor had just used up the last of his strength and had run out of arguments. Nothing worked: logic, science, charm, seduction, haggling, promises, brute force. There was nothing more he could do; he felt his bones cracking in a thousand places, his muscles being torn asunder. Glancing about him, he heaved a last sigh for his three brothers, his sons, to whom he was bequeathing life . . .

"Up here!" The voice came from just above his head.

The death-bound battler just managed to open his eyes, and looked into those of his youngest brother, the last but not least, born on the surplus day.

"Save thyself," stammered Sir René between lips paler than November snow. "Go to thy brothers . . . tell them not to weep for me . . . that I have had two wonderful lives . . ."

"Up here!" Extra-Day said again, fixing his innocent eyes on those of the hangman, who was unnerved by the child's audacity.

How dare so diminutive a personage appear barehanded before so formidable a foe? The hangman raised his axe and, before bringing it down, let loose a shriek that uprooted cypresses and weeping willows. Then he sliced the air with huge strokes. To his shame, however, he saw his weapon slash through nothing but the winds of time. Where was that impudent poltroon hiding?

"I'm here!"

Where? Where are you? Where the devil are you?

"I'm over here!"

And the hangman turned, spun around, made a few about-faces, and, twisting back on himself, tied himself in knots; he ended up looking to the four brothers — who were once more reunited — like a nasty ball of snakes.

A short while later, when they were dressing Figure-Head's wounds (he had received a doughty blow, ow, owww!), Big-as-a-Fist pressed for more information about the vagaries of the battle, and received only an enigmatic response from Extra-Day:

"I played hide-and-seek with the villain," he said, "and he didn't find me."

"But where did you hide?"

"Between two seconds."

"But how — ?"

For the rest of the day the three comrades said nothing. But when the setting sun had empurpled the hilltops, Big-as-a-Fist raised his eyes to the wrinkled brow of Sir René and read his thoughts: their younger brother, born on the extra day, possessed the invaluable gift of being able to withdraw himself from the sight of mortal eyes by taking refuge outside of time. At which point John-Bear, the only one among them who liked to call a spade a spade, asked candidly:

"D'you mean to say he can make himself invisible?"

Figure-Head didn't answer, because his mind was once more surveying the field of battle . . . Just how mortal was this cowled and single-minded hangman? And to distract his brothers from questions far too serious for their tender years, he contented himself with sighing:

"For a while there, I really thought I was a goner."

"No, no you weren't," Big-as-a-Fist said soothingly, covering his wounds with balm and ointment and his ears with kind and tender words. "No one passes into the great beyond as easily as that, leaving his brothers stuck here in the back of beyond. Come on! We are sworn vassals, for better or worse, come what may! None of use can so much as lift a foot without the others, swear it! May God come to our aid!"

And to seal his lengthy discourse with a word that reflected the full measure of his talents and the flavour of his genius, he shook his fist at the sky and cried: "Shit!" The epithet so inspired the rest of the company that they adopted it as their motto. And so the heroes shouted out in full chorus:

"Shit on the hangman! Shit on our mortal enemy!"

After which they felt sufficiently restored to set out again on the road to adventure.

As they walked along the highway with a confident tread, they chatted away about this and that, supporting their theories with the opinions of sages, proverbs, back-fence gossip, and — Big-as-a-Fist's preferred source — their own personal experiences. Sir René philosophized at large on everyday life, drawing grandiose moral conclusions from the merest incidents that crossed his path along the way.

"It's a curious fact, is it not," he said, using language that he hoped would approximate the usage of modern times, "that in four centuries, things have changed but mankind has not. Look at that woman over there, placing all her eggs in one basket. And there's a fellow burning his candle at both ends. And another putting his scythe in his neighbour's corn. And all of them feathering their own nests. Nothing has changed but the shape of the nest, the candle, and the basket."

Fine speeches, especially when delivered by someone else,

always made Big-as-a-Fist hungry. He now proposed to the company that they stop at the first inn they found, huddled at a corner in the road. When asked by his friends what he intended to use for money to pay for all the good food he was already ordering in his imagination, the bold little devil snapped his fingers in the air and said haughtily, "Are the flowers in the fields not clothed? Do the birds in the sky not receive nourishment? And yet neither bird nor flower fret about the morrow." This he tossed off with an air of having invented it himself.

If he could have foreseen which exit he and his brothers would use to leave the inn, the dwarf might have been less eager to enter it. But he was hungry. And an empty stomach makes a poor counsellor.

The comrades chose the best table — facing the window, so they'd miss nothing of the day's passing parade — and ordered vegetables served in cream, fish in a cream sauce, creamed meat, fruit and cream, and the cream of the cream: at their age, our heroes would settle for nothing less than the cream of the crop. All of which stirred the blood of the gods. But drink up! It isn't every day we raise a glass to Master Fate!

That worthy must have heard his name mentioned.

"There he is!" shouted Figure-Head, choking on an artichoke leaf. "He's tumbled to us this time. And he has a score to settle with each one of us."

And each of them saw again his own battle with the hangman: the giant, who had come to grips with him on the scaffold; the ancestor, who had grappled with him hand to hand; the infant, who had hovered just out of his sight; the dwarf . . .

"He hasn't forgiven me for humiliating him in public."

And Big-as-a-Fist, yesterday so proud of his victory, now felt suddenly and personally threatened. Too much success, he thought, makes a man vulnerable. How stupid life was to get in his road like this, stopping him from going wherever the blazes he felt like going, and doing just whatever he pleased. And shit! and shit! and shit!

Sir René, seeing his younger brother thus caught between fear and anger, tried to reassure him by stacking major premise upon minor premise upon sound reasoning. But Big-as-a-Fist swept away the whole hotchpotch of lugubrious logic. A fine time to start philosophizing on life and death when, just outside the door, on the other side of the window, a very frightening personage who had a very nasty bone to pick with him was striding down the street, crossing the square, and looking in all directions for his prey. And to give himself courage, Big-as-a-Fist shouted out the first thing that came into his head:

"He'd better not make me lose my temper, by the jumpin', or I . . . I . . . I'll lead him a merry dance!"

He said it without thinking, but as usual, the little fox had conceived of an idea by expressing it. Make the hangman dance . . . why not? Hadn't he made him fart last night? And from one of his secret pockets he took out the flute that Clara-Galante had plucked from her broom.

"Be careful!" warned wise Sir René. "You might be going too far, and gaining a mortal enemy. He knows you by sight, remember."

But the little idiot, who a moment before had been trembling with terror, had already forgotten about the danger and was throwing himself into new hijinks.

"Dance!" he yelled to the hangman, who was now no more than three steps from the inn.

And from his flute came sounds the likes of which had never been heard before by his brothers, a kind of *danse macabre* that soon had the entire company in an uproar. Passersby, layabouts, village lads and lasses, they all dropped whatever they were doing, bowed and curtsied to each other as if for a minuet, then joined arms to form a human chain around the bewildered hangman, who, having no control over his legs, allowed himself to be dragged and carried and pulled by the crowd closing in on him, tighter and tighter, rocks poised over their heads, little guessing who it was they were dealing with, when . . .

"Stop!"

The cry came from the courtyard in front of the church, where the parish priest, his biretta on sideways, was furious at seeing his entire parish given over to debauchery — and in broad daylight, when all good citizens ought to be either working at their trade or going about their business. Then, suddenly, the magic issuing from Big-as-a-Fist's flute seized hold of the priest as well, and to the amazement of his flock and to his own everlasting shame, he hoisted up his soutane and joined in the dance.

Figure-Head decided it was time to take their leave, not a second to lose, let's get out of here, brothers. But no sooner did he stand up to put his plan into action than his ancient, four-hundred-year-old limbs went all atremble and he, too, started to dance, the Devil take him! How would they ever get out of this fix? Everyone but Big-as-a-Fist had been swept up in the jig. If he stopped playing, the hangman and the rest of the village would stop dancing and turn on the source of their troubles. But if he didn't stop, his three comrades would remain prisoners of the round, which was becoming rounder and rounder and more and more macabre, circling all the way around the inn, where our little flautist didn't know whether to spit or say grace. So instead he cursed his godmother and her poisonous presents, forgetting that it was he himself who had chosen them from her bag of tricks. The next time, he told himself, I'll know better, I'll make conditions, I'll write in a few exceptions or amendments. But then he recalled the words of his fairy godmother:

They're for life. So think carefully.

Beginning to despair, he turned to his brothers for comfort, but they too were twisting and sweating, caught up in the dance. Then he saw the enraptured face of Extra-Day. Following the child's gaze, he was led to the discovery of a second inn, exactly the same as the one they were in, hovering in the clouds. At first he thought he was dreaming and started to rub his eyes. This made him almost drop his flute, and he had to begin playing quickly again, for the chain of villagers — oh-oh, here's trouble! — had begun to falter in their dance. Some of them even broke tempo, and stumbled about stepping on each others' toes. Big-as-a-Fist had to think fast and hard: A house hanging in mid-air, that was their salvation. But first off, what was it doing up there? And who had put it there? By now the ancestor, looking up through the glass, had seen it, too, and thought to himself that it must have something to do with the setting sun, because certainly no inn had been there at noon. Big-as-a-Fist opened the door to get a better look — and it disappeared! So the inn was only visible through glass. And the ingenious little flute-player concluded that if he and his company were to reach the shelter in the clouds, they'd have to do it by going through the window. He turned to John-Bear for help:

"Quick, brother, as soon as I take the flute out of my mouth, rush over to the window, lean out of it as far as you can, grab the tail end of the cloud, and hang onto the balcony. We'll climb up your legs."

But he had already said too much. In order to get his instructions out, he had had to remove the flute from his mouth and stop playing. The crowd abruptly stopped dancing and slowly began to regain its senses. Already the priest was storming among his parishioners, almost threatening to refuse them absolution; his flock, however, weren't paying much attention. They were looking about for the source of the witchcraft, and in the process they let the hangman go free. Sir René saw him come straight towards them, reach the inn's porch, and place a foot on the bottom step. With one hand he swept up little Extra-Day, and with the other he grabbed the heel of the giant's seven-league boot, which was about all that was left sticking out of the clouds. As for Tom Thumb, he didn't need to climb; at the last moment he had jumped into his brother's pocket, and he was now hanging tightly onto the giant's belt buckle. When the crowd looked up, there was nothing to see but a bank of cumulus clouds floating above their heads.

Big-as-a-Fist, sitting with his comrades on the balcony of the inn in mid-air, was shouting a string of insults down at the hooded figure, who was scratching his head with a bewildered look in the marketplace below. Ignoring all caution and every rule of polite behaviour, the dwarf thumbed his nose at his mortal enemy.

"See you in a week of three Thursdays," he jeered. "See you when the sky rains meadowlarks and Lent falls in August!"

Sir René, also called Figure-Head, covered his eyes and ears. When would this little idiot learn? Making appointments with Death! Even if they were for days and seasons and circumstances that would never come to pass. If he was so smart, he must realize that nothing was totally impossible or unreal down here. At his age, he should know better.

But Big-as-a-Fist, listening to this long peroration, was far from knowing better; in fact, he had jumped up and was ransacking the inn-in-the-clouds for some forbidden fruit. He wanted it all — first fruits, early fruit, green fruit, windfallen fruit — even at the risk of waking up next morning with a pain in his belly.

But Heaven wasn't about to let the belly-ache wait until morning, as we shall see. That night a second bank of clouds moved in on the first, and the two knocked into each other, mixed their cottony whiteness together in a furious sea. The walls of the inn began to crack, and chunks of plaster broke away from the ceiling and fell to the floor.

"Let us quit this place," said Sir René, who had a strange taste of salt and frost in his mouth. "I fear the approach of a new and terrifying tempest. Pray God we'll be spared."

As memories of the lugubrious events of his first life returned, the speech and accent of his childhood returned with them.

"Flee, dear brothers! The Devil is dinging his dam and wedding his daughter, and we are bidden to the diabolical wedding feast. Fly! Hie thee down to earth!"

Great God of the Holy Water, thought Big-as-a-Fist, but didn't the old man have some fine expressions. Hie thee down to earth, he says. He wants us to jump out of the frying pan into the fire!

I wish to God our wise old comrade would come up with better solutions, and put them in more reassuring words. Then he began to add his own oar to his older brother's boat:

"What if we beard the lion in his den? Grab those thunderbolts by the horns and do unto them before they can bite the hand that feeds them? What do you think?

Sir René either didn't like the young pup's tone of voice, or else didn't quite grasp his meaning, because he remained standing stiff as a board on the balcony. He was still standing there when the first hailstone hit him on the forehead, nearly turning him into a frozen figure-head for the second time in less than half a millennium.

By midnight, the strong winds had turned into a squall that had degenerated into a storm and brought on a cyclone. Our heroes had seen cyclones before — who hasn't? But no one before them had seen the rain from above. The storm, in fact, was falling on them from below. It was also falling from within and from all sides. They themselves were the storm, if the truth be told; it was as if the sky that night had decided to rain men. Even the gigantic John-Bear, Strong-as-a-Dozen, was no more than a straw tossed in the centre of the storm in full view of the stars. Ursa Major, who was in a sense a relative of John-Bear's, must have chuckled behind her hand to see her terrestrial cousin tossed and buffeted in the sky by a few drops of water.

They were having a good time of it, the little rascals. Never before had raindrops shown such zeal in whipping and flaying their victims. As if they were saying to themselves: alone and separate we're nothing, but let enough of us get together and you've got yourself an ocean. In fact, Figure-Head felt as though he had plunged back into the ocean. He kicked his arms and legs to get to the surface. But just try to find the surface of the sky! What the devil was he doing in this inn? The he remembered: the inn . . . the inn-in-the-clouds . . . it couldn't last forever . . . he should have known better, being the oldest, but what could he have done? The hangman hadn't given him much choice. Either this airy refuge, or death . . . again. And poor René Renaissance stopped trying to figure it out and concentrated instead on surviving this new ordeal.

That was when he noticed that his younger brother, Extra-Day, was as much at home as a fish in water, dodging between the raindrops, hailstones, and wind, untouched by either good weather or bad. Even the stars, from the depths of their galaxies, must have been asking themselves where this new prodigy had come from.

That night, however, the stars stayed in bed and didn't come out until early morning, when the storm had ceased sweeping the heavens. But then, oh!, the sky was filled with them, twinkling and sparkling like never before, Aldebaran nodding to Betelgeuse, who called to Orion's Belt to get out of the Milky Way. A radiant, starry sky that came out just at the moment when the Goodmen and Goodwives of the world were rubbing their eyes and saying good morning to each other.

"Good morning," said Extra-Day, pleased at finding his brothers and comrades again.

"Good morning," replied John-the-Strong, surprised to be completely covered in bruises for the first time in his life.

"Good morning," Sir René said in his turn, looking around for an echo that didn't come.

Where was he? One of them was missing — they couldn't say his name without inviting back luck. Had something terrible happened?

Without a word, without even taking time to shake off the effects of their tempestuous night, the three brothers got up and set off in search of their fourth comrade.

"You, younger brother," said Figure-Head, who suddenly felt himself promoted to commanding officer, "you search along the ground. Don't overlook the tiniest blade of grass or the smallest nutshell. And John-Bear, you look in the trees. Check out every nest, every knot-hole, every fork. As for me, I'll take the underbrush."

And so they did.

For a whole day and night.

Something terrible had happened. They'd never see him again. Never. He was just too small. The storm must have worn him down to a morsel.

John-Bear grabbed a bough from a pine tree and started demolishing the fields, then the brush, then the forest, and would surely have denuded the entire earth if his older brother Figure-Head hadn't held him back.

"John-Bear, my friend, my brother, you can't fight Destiny. If he has decided to take our friend, there's nothing you can do about it; if, on the other hand, he returns him to us, to our great joy, your efforts here will have been useless. Our brother will come back on his own one fine morning."

And another night passed. And another day.

On the third night, Sir René urged his brothers to get some sleep. He stayed up to keep watch at the prow of the earth, letting no sign pass unexamined, no star go by unchallenged. And then, to his complete stupefaction, in the deepest corner of the night, he saw the comet.

"Miserable wretch!" he heard himself say. "So it's you who took him from us."

In the morning, he didn't dare divulge to his brothers his dismal discovery. Only he, resurrected from a former time, was acquainted with the malevolent powers of a comet. It didn't show itself to him that night for nothing; it came to taunt him, he who had returned from the dead, risen alive from death's clutches after four hundred years.

"It has revenged itself on him," he moaned under his breath. "Oh, woe is me!" And he smote his breast.

John-Bear had taken himself a little distance from the others and was weeping tears as big as crystal balls; they ran down his cheeks, hung for a second on his chin-hairs, then fell to the ground and rolled away from his feet. The giant watched his own teardrops bang into each other, burst like bubbles, then join to form a stream on which he floated back to his early childhood, when he and his brother had first set out hand in hand and left foot first on the high road to adventure. And in a small voice, John-Bear begged Death to let him rejoin his life's companion.

Hey! Brother!
It's me, Big-as-a-Fist,
Our mother made me so
Out of left-over dough!

The giant froze. It wasn't possible! He heard, surely he heard . . . his little brother's voice . . . but where was it coming from? Where was he?

"Big! As! A! Fist!"

"I'm over here! Get me out! Get me out!"

"Where are you? Brother, little brother, where are you hiding?"

But it was Extra-Day who called out:

"I see him!"

"Where? Where is he?"

"In there!"

The other two looked where their younger brother's finger was pointing, and saw a drop of water slightly bigger than its neighbours. And three pairs of eyes focused at the same time on the head of Big-as-a-Fist, who smiled up at them from the bottom of his bubble.

John-Bear, carried away by a tremendous joy, let out a gargantuan Ahhh! That set the drop of crystal spinning. It rose, to everyone's amazement, floated in the air, then came to rest on the nose of Figure-Head, who was preparing to deliver a dissertation on the Law of Gravity. And so it was, perched there on his ancestor's nose, that the dwarf made his second entry into the world.

Second entry — those were the right words for it. Because, as everyone knows, Big-as-a-Fist had yet to take even a baby step towards the Great Voyage. He had survived a storm in a drop of water, and that was about it. But coming out of his glass tomb after three days, he believed — or tried to make the others believe — that he had returned from the land of the dead. And he soon began to instruct his brothers on the mysteries of the Great Beyond.

Although his younger brothers listened to him with mouths gaping in fascination, Sir René, who really had been reborn, cleared his throat loudly to bring the little braggart back to reality — and in so doing, knocked him off his high horse and onto his feet. Big-as-a-Fist, though he didn't know many things yet, nevertheless had a good head on his shoulders, and understood that life and nature harboured enough miracles without novices like himself going around looking for more. Anyone who had succeeded in penetrating to the heart of a drop of water didn't need to invent a voyage 20,000 leagues under the sea. That was Sir René's conclusion, and the young scallywag Big-as-a-Fist took it to heart.

"In my waterdrop," he began to tell his brothers, "I found other drops, infinitely small, and each of them containing other waterdrops even more minuscule, and all of them moving about as if the tempest raging outside was also stirring things up inside. I tell you this in all honesty, my friends, my brothers; the world is much richer, much vaster, and much more complex than anyone has yet imagined. It is all packed with smaller worlds exactly the same as our own, in which peasants grind their grain and sell it to bakers who feed the people who go about their business, without suspecting for a moment that I was up above watching them live a life so similar to my own. Then all of a sudden I came to my senses and asked myself whether, by chance, there wasn't someone above me, watching me as I was watching them, with the same curiosity, the same . . ."

He stopped to give his turbulent mind a rest and to order his thoughts, which came rushing into every pore of his brain. For a few seconds his comrades, too, remained silent. Then Sir René remarked that the dwarf seemed to have grown a bit of a beard in the past three days. The others looked but didn't see anything, though they realized that their brother had returned from a long journey. Then Tom Thumb, also called Big-as-a-Fist, cast about him a look meant to encompass the four corners of the earth:

"If the sky is made up of many big balls, and a drop of water is made up of many little drops, then isn't there a danger that one day someone will drop the ball?"

And to show that he was right and that he was trying to get things back to normal, he launched into two or three of his most daring pirouettes, then topped them off by walking on his hands.

And the others understood that their brother, who had just discovered a new world in a drop of water, was well and truly back among them, with both feet planted firmly on terra firma.

6

How our heroes journeyed east in search of the Occident

The day after the storm in which Big-as-a-Fist lost touch with his comrades, our four adventurers cleaned themselves up as best they could — their ears, feet, hands, necks, and belly buttons — some in a duck pond, the dwarf in a few drops of dew he found in the fields, the giant . . . Now, where did that big oaf get to? wondered his brother.

"Come and see, Big-as-a-Fist! I'm in a drop of water, just like you!"

Tom Thumb dropped the foxglove petal he was holding and tore off through the early morning fog to find John-Bear standing under a waterfall that tumbled down from a high rock cliff.

"What are you doing in there?" he shouted through the curtain of rain.

"I'm taking a bath in a waterdrop," replied the giant, laughing.

"That's a water*fall*, you big dummy."

John-Bear was crestfallen. He saw no difference between a drop and a fall. Yesterday his brother had found out that water had drops, drops had drops, those drops had drops, and those drops, and those drops . . . and the son of a tree trunk couldn't tell where the theory started or ended up. Once again, he told himself, his brother was too much for him. Sir René, who had finished his ablutions, came up to the two of them and settled the question in favour of the weaker one.

"John-Bear is right," he said. "The sea is no more watery than the water trapped in a drop. So the giant in his waterfall can experience the world just as easily as the dwarf in his waterdrop. Neither of you is bigger or smaller than the other. It's the universe that expands and contracts as it adjusts to your size."

And so they left it at that — for the moment.

Until the next day.

Because bright and early the next morning, the incurable little gallant Big-as-a-Fist, who as usual was inundated with more farfetched ideas during the night than daydreams during the day, came up and walked around his twin brother with the air of someone who was getting ready to rediscover the New World.

"You know, John-Bear, John-the-Strong, Strong-as-a-Dozen, my buddy, my brother, last night I discovered something that could very well change my whole life."

The giant, who in his whole life had never tried to find out why flies have wings while grasshoppers have springs, raised his bushy eyebrows, looked deep into his brother's eyes, and uttered a single word: "Oh?" Big-as-a-Fist, his little Thumbkin, his Tom Thumb, wanted to change Life? But what would happen to him and the others? How could they go on with their adventures? No, no, listen, John-Bear could never survive without his blood-brother, his milk-mate, his flour-child! And he finished up the longest speech he had ever made with a sob.

"I said my life was going to change, you blockhead, not that I was going to change Life."

When John-the-Strong finally understood, he pressed Big-as-a-Fist so tenderly to his hairy chest that the dwarf emerged from his grasp as wrinkled as a winter apple. Hey, hey, my friend, my brother, don't forget you're Strong-as-a-Dozen! And the little fellow dusted himself off and straightened himself up, grumbling something about clumsy oafs and being killed with kindness. Then he picked up the thread of his idea.

"I've thought a lot about my adventure in the waterdrop," he said. "And I've come to the following conclusion, so open your big ears and listen up: even the tiniest piece of life or of the universe contains the whole of life and the universe."

John-Bear was so bowled over by his brother's genius that he didn't even try to understand his words. He was content just to sit back and admire; which prompted Tom Thumb to expound on the three points — Chapter A, section b, paragraph c — of his theory of the Infinitely Big and the Infinitely Tiny, which ended up establishing the dominant position occupied by the dwarf at the centre of the universe. John-Bear, rendered more and more goggle-eyed, wanted only to know whether this dominant position was going to remain *in situ*, or if he, the giant, was about to lose everything by this great realignment of values.

"As long as you stay here with us, Tom Thumb, you can grow or shrink to your heart's content. And anyway, your height and weight don't matter a bit. You'll always be the strongest and biggest."

And the discussion declined into a huge hugging session, in which our two first heroes swore, reswore, and reswore again their eternal and mutual loyalty. And from loyalty to friendship, from friendship to shared memories, the brothers of the breadbox and the workbench swung back into a childhood stranded on the other side of the stream, where a Goodman and his Goodwife dreamed the exploits of their progeny.

"Do you think they still remember us?" asked John-Bear, wiping eyes that were wetter than the Mediterranean.

Big-as-a-Fist sniffed behind his hand so no one could see, and stifled a sob. Then he wiped his nose on his sleeve and said, without the trace of a quiver:

"They're both leaning on the porch railing, I can see them perfectly, Goodman with his hands in his pockets, Goodwife with her arms folded under her apron, both dreaming of our return."

John-Bear's eyes were now gushing more waves than the ocean at high tide.

"Do you think, little brother, that they're mad at us, and that if they never see us again it will be too soon?"

This time Big-as-a-Fist, rather than be seen with a runny nose, took out his handkerchief like a man of the world. But when he saw his initials, B.a.a.F., embroidered on each of the four corners by his mother, he could no longer swallow his emotion. Much against his will, he let fall a tear that rolled between his fingers and onto his hat and rang the little bells that Goodwife had sewn there.

When the young babe and the old man, one born out of time and the other reborn from a former time, rejoined their comrades seated on the dewy grass, they stared at them with their mouths hanging open: there they were, two brothers, a giant and a dwarf, sitting side by side, hands stuck in their belt or under their braces, bawling like a pair of homesick calves.

Figure-Head worked it out after a long cogitation full of first premises and *distinguos*: Extra-Day jumped to the conclusion straightaway. It was the ancestor, though, who first cleared his throat and broached the subject of going home. In fact, he was playing devil's advocate, because he himself was in search of a distant future. Big-as-a-Fist tried gently to make him understand that they were really facing in different directions, since he and his brother were pining for a distant past.

"Verily, 'tis true," replied the ancestor, reverting to his dormant tongue. "But that your past is my future, or equipollent to it."

Which is when the others realized that they were all more or less escapees from different times, that their paths had crossed by the merest chance, and that fate had done them an enormous favour by letting them meet in the same time.

"Should we set forth in quest of our point of departure," proposed Sir René, with a sudden flash of insight, "we might find two things: our common origins, and proof that the earth really is round."

". . . ?"

"Absolutely," pressed the philosopher. "Because our point of arrival would be the same as our point of departure."

"You mean," said Big-as-a-Fist, "that to meet up with the west again, we have to head towards the opposite horizon? Are you saying that the shortest way to get there would be to do an about-face?"

The ancestor launched into a tortuous dialectic involving such enigmas as the Search for the Great Unknown, the Quest for the Holy Grail, the Struggle against the Blatant Beast of Mediocrity, and the Defence of Human Dignity. After which he concluded that they must set their sights on the east.

And that was how, one fine morning, our four heroes lit out for the Levant, running counter-sunwise, heading head first into a headstrong headwind.

And they walked. And walked. And walked.

From time to time Big-as-a-Fist pulled up to point out to Sir René that the curve of the horizon hadn't changed, that at this rate they'd run out of shoe leather before they ran out of daylight — an argument that elicited no reaction at all from his comrades, who couldn't figure out what he was getting at — because he couldn't just not say anything. Big-as-a-Fist, who had never had much time for the eternal silence of infinite space, much preferred saying anything at all to saying nothing at all, and ended up saying, "I'm hungry," just to have something to say.

That argument drew unanimous approval. They made camp.

The meal, though frugal, restored vim and vigour to the hearts of the company, more rapidly to the smaller ones because they were quicker to snatch up the best morsels. And with his good mood, the dwarf also regained his dreams of glory and conquest.

He was about to expand on his most ethereal proposition when a low-flying homing-pigeon dropped him a message that landed right on his hat, hitting the little bells and making them tinkle.

"You dirty stinker!" he shouted at the bold bird. "Rotten beast!"

The pigeon, surprised at being addressed in such a way, stopped in mid-flight long enough to size up his interlocutor.

"Rotten beast yourself," heard Big-as-a-Fist.

He turned around, and turned again, and finally realized that it was the bird who'd answered him, and who was now looking him straight in the eye with the obvious intention of continuing the conversation. The three comrades, seeing the dwarf talking to himself, asking himself dumb questions, and giving himself wrong answers, finally got it through their heads that he was really and truly engaged in a deep discussion with a bird. And they remembered the gifts Big-as-a-Fist had received that day from his godmother.

"What do you mean, rotten beast myself? I didn't shit on your head, did I?"

"No, but you're sitting in my nest."

Big-as-a-Fist jumped up quickly to see if it was true. A bit too quickly, in fact, for he found himself standing knee-deep in omelette.

"Well, whadya know! Double yolks!"

The pigeon stamped his foot in anger. The dwarf barely had time to jump out of the nest and seek refuge in his big brother's pocket, for the bird was already beating his wings and sharpening his beak.

"Coo-coo!" teased Big-as-a-Fist from the shelter of John-Bear's hidey-hole.

The homing-pigeon, not knowing whom he was dealing with, thought he heard the gadabout who went around laying her eggs in other birds' nests.

"I'll get you, you unnatural mother, you!"

And off he flew in search of the cuckoo in a flurry of feathers and down, to the great delight of the four comrades who, until that day, had always thought of the carrier-pigeon as a quiet, peace-loving bird.

The pigeon incident wouldn't have left much trace in our heroes' memories if they had inherited ordinary memories. But remember, first, that the sons of Goodman and Goodwife carried their mementoes around with them in the lining of their clothes; secondly, that Extra-Day, born Out-of-Time, never remembered anything that hadn't happened just this instant; and thirdly, that Figure-Head, by way of contrast, had woken up after four centuries of silence to find his memory amazingly intact. And so from now on no adventure would ever slide off our friends like water off a duck's back. The minutest slice of life was inscribed indelibly on one of the four halves of their brains, and could be called up at will from the depths of their collective memory.

And it wasn't three days before what was called up was that carrier-pigeon.

"You again!" shouted Big-as-a-Fist, diving under a fold in his brother's jacket.

But the bird didn't deign to answer.

"You could at least say hello, if you had any manners!"

"We can't all sit around doing nothing all day," said the ill-bred bird. "Some of us have more important things to do."

Although Big-as-a-Fist could do at least fifty-six things at once, he'd never been able to satisfy the conflicting demands of curiosity and caution at the same time.

"You've got something important to do?" he asked the pigeon, venturing up to him until he was very nearly touching his beak.

And snap! He was gone.

"Big-as-a-Fist! Tom Thumb! Little brother! Friend! Come back!"

And the three comrades, their arms raised to heaven, their eyes as big as saucers, their hearts banging at their chests, watched helplessly as the pigeon disappeared with an extremely odd message dangling from his beak.

"He's not going to get away with this, that's for sure," groaned the giant, gnashing his teeth.

While his brothers were calling him back at the top of their voices, their arms waving wildly, the dwarf was flailing his legs and arms trying to release himself from the pigeon's grip. He even pounded on the bird's beak to force it open until, chancing to glace downward, he stiffened and looked away. If the bird did let go now, they'd be singing a *Dies Irae* for him at home . . . Now he prayed that the pigeon didn't take it into his head to hold a conversation with his captive . . . or decide to breath through his mouth . . . as long as he holds on until he lands . . . Lands? Lands where? God, oh God, oh God! Never mind swearing, Thumbleton, better try saying your prayers . . . What in the world did you ever do to the good Lord that he always seems to have it in for you? It's not fair! And he tried to give his usual backhanded kick, but his feet just beat the air — which didn't appear any the worse for it.

Whatever you do, don't look down, Tom Thumb. Try singing, or telling yourself a story, one of the fairytales your mother taught you when you were little . . . poor mother Goodwife! If only she could see what a precarious pickle you're in now, from her kitchen or wherever she is. And she had such high hopes for your future! Well, you're high enough. But your future lies down there, with your head bashed in between two mountains!

Without thinking, he looked down for the valley that would probably be his tomb. And his head began to spin. Vertigo, that was all he needed! Then, little by little, his heart sank from his throat and returned to its proper place in his chest, his ears stopped buzzing, and his nausea went away, taking his fear with it. His fear, in fact, went right out of his mind. For he made an extraordinary discovery: they were flying over a country that was exactly his size! A country in which mountains were the size of mole hills; the forests were hardly bigger than woodlots; the rivers were streams he could wade across; and whole villages could easily have fit in his parents' back yard. Unbelievable! He slapped his thighs: at last, a country where dwarves were kings!

"Down, pigeon, down! I want to go home. I'm the king! I'm the king!"

And he punched the pigeon so severely about the head and shoulders that the bird choked, losing his wind and then trying to get it back. But one gulp of air was enough to make him let go of his cargo, and suddenly our hero was on a free-fall flight to the country where dwarves were kings, judging from the view from above, but which was getting bigger and bigger the closer and closer he got to it. The earth seemed to be inflating, its streams turning into deep rivers, its trees soaring gigantically, its crust growing rugged and full of crevasses. And . . . oh, horrors! Big-as-a-Fist had just seen him directly below, moving about in his own shadow, his face raised and his stare fixed on his enemy from the depths of his cowl. The hangman spread his arms and enveloped the entire horizon in his black cloak. This time the dwarf would not escape; gravity was too strong a force, the air was too thin to hide him, the wind was a mere sigh in the treetops. This time the fate of the little manikin born in a batch of bread dough on the eighth day, the dream-come-true of Goodwife his mother, was surely sealed.

Mama!

Whoops! What's this? At the very instant he felt his feet touch the hood of the hangman, his deadly enemy, just when he thought . . . no, as he'd later tell his brothers, he didn't really think . . . he wasn't really terrified . . . a voice deep inside him told him that his time wasn't quite up yet. After all, he had only just started out in life, he hadn't travelled even half of a quarter of a sixteenth part of the way towards the great unravelling of his destiny! So just as he was about to dash his brains out on a little rock that was no longer a rock but a huge boulder, the bird finished a vertiginous loop and swooped down between the legs of Big-as-a-Fist, who woke up from his nightmare still in mid-flight, straddling the feathered back of a carrier-pigeon.

Well, how was that for a reversal! And before he even joined his hands together to give thanks to Heaven for all its bounties, the little devil put his thumb to his nose and gave his mortal enemy one of those signs favoured by all ill-mannered children in such circumstances — which is to say, when the plot comes to within a hair's breadth of reaching a climax.

His new position was both more comfortable and more prestigious than the old one, and, as we well know, comfort and prestige figured much higher on our hero's list of priorities than peace, justice, truth, universal equality, or any other fandango cut from the same cloth, coming only slightly behind joy at being alive. Thus mounted, the dwarf forgot the fear he'd felt a few moments before, even the present danger of flying so high, and tried to determine the pigeon's destination, as well as the nature of the important business with which he'd been entrusted.

"I'm carrying an urgent message," said the bird.

"Oh? Are you carrying it in your head, then?"

"No, no; on my left foot."

"You don't say . . . You mean it's a . . . a written message?"

"Of course it's written. What do you think — they'd draw it in pictures?"

Big-as-a-Fist ignored this impertinence, wanting to keep the volley going: "No, no, of course not. It's just that, well, a messenger could read it."

The pigeon batted his eyes and bit his tongue:

"He doesn't have to read it. All he has to do is be in the right place with the message tied visibly to his leg."

Big-as-a-Fist felt himself itching all over. He was no more than an arm's length — his own arm's length — from a secret that might affect the future of the whole world! Or its destruction. After all, he didn't know where the pigeon had come from, or where he was going. He was flying pretty high; maybe he'd been entrusted with a mission of the utmost importance. The dwarf already saw himself as the saviour of the world, benefactor of society, crowned with laurels, captured for all eternity in a statute of white marble. He stretched himself out on the bird's plumed back and slid his arm down the left leg of the messenger. He felt around, ruffled the feathers with his fingers . . .

"Look down there," said the pigeon, his attention suddenly drawn by a change in the scenery. Big-as-a-Fist sat up quickly, all innocence. Then he leaned over to study the landscape unrolling below, placing his other project on the back burner. His eyes boggled, he caught his breath, let loose a string of ah-ah-ah-ahs!, and wrapped his whole body around the bird's neck.

"You're choking me, what a ride! Sit up straight!"

Little by little, the dwarf regained his spirits and got back in the saddle, holding onto his mount's feathers for dear life.

"Let's get out of here, my pigeon . . . go west, young man . . . let's go home . . ."

The pigeon didn't seem to understand. He'd never done anything like that before. A messenger doesn't retrace his steps until he's completed his mission: it goes against his nature. Big-as-a-Fist tore his hair, but he didn't dare look down.

"Don't you see, my beautiful bird, that we're flying straight to Hell? I can hardly breathe for the smoke already. Can't you hear me coughing?"

And he gave a few coughs for show, got something caught in his throat, and ended up coughing for real.

"We'll be roasted like a couple of chestnuts if we keep this up, my pigeon, my dove. Let's go back to my brothers. They'll welcome you like an old friend, honest. I'll even make you into a companion, I promise."

And with his thumb he made the sign of the cross — lips, chest, shoulders.

The bird listened to Big-as-a-Fist's blather. The dwarf's head was buried in the bird's plumage and he was trembling like a leaf. The pigeon tried to calm him down.

"It's just a forest fire. I've seen dozens of them. Consider yourself lucky you're on my back; think of all the deer, rabbits, groundhogs, and bear cubs down there, surrounded by the flames. Today, the safest way to travel is by air."

The dwarf began to breathe more easily. Then, suddenly, he dug his heels into his mount's flanks, trying to hold him back:

"Whoa!' he yelled. "Hard to starboard! Bring her about. I'm your rider, I'll give the orders around here. And I'm ordering you to take me back to my brothers."

The pigeon's wings stopped in surprise. This dwarf, so tiny he could easily fit into a man's hand, was still a man and knew how to speak with authority. And the beast obeyed. He made a wide circle and set his course for the southwest — to the complete astonishment of Tom Thumb, who didn't know his own strength. But for once his cry had come straight from his own heart without a moment's thought. Realizing the danger threatening the forest creatures, he had envisioned his brother John-Bear, his ancestor Sir René, and his youngest brother, Extra-Day, beset by the inferno. And stretching up to his full height, the dwarf had grown an inch in an instant.

"Quick, pigeon, hurry! We have to warn them to get out of the way! Heeyah! Hyah! Hyah!"

When the four comrades were finally reunited, just before sundown, it was hard to say who had been in the most danger. Because although Big-as-a-Fist had flown to the aid of the others, the others had been getting ready to beat the flames bare-handed in an effort to find Big-as-a-Fist.

The pigeon gazed on this tender scene with a lump in his throat, thinking of the mate he'd left behind last spring by the side of a broken nest. Big-as-a-Fist noticed his mournful demeanour and decided it was time to keep his promise.

"Here's a bird who has rendered me a great service, even though we got off to a bad start. What do you say we welcome him into the company with the same rank as ourselves?"

Figure-Head lowered his fine figure of a head and whispered to the dwarf that never before in the history of chivalry had anyone knighted a carrier-pigeon. The procedure, he felt, could create an unhealthy precedent in their usages and customs; without being racist about it, he did believe nevertheless in the difference between species . . . the Great Chain of Being and all that . . .

Yes, yes, all very well, you old dotard, thought Big-as-a-Fist. All very elegantly argued and deeply thought out. But the point is, here's this pigeon, his eyes baggy and his wings exhausted and his feathers flatter than a pancake from heading back into a headwind with me on his shoulders. And for what? To return a lost brother to his family, an errant companion to his company. This, my friends, is a carrier-pigeon; he's been entrusted with an important message — which, by the way, he still has, tied to his left ankle — a top-secret message he must deliver right away.

"Pigeon, my friend, my brother . . ."

And Big-as-a-Fist rubbed his feathers the right way. The bird let his master approach without fear or trembling. A bond of friendship had been sealed up there, above the earth. But when the dwarf began to slide his hand down the pigeon's left leg, the messenger pulled his foot up under his wing. That secret had been entrusted to him, it was not his to give out. Big-as-a-Fist bit his thumb. Oh, how it itched!

"Well, I must be off," said the pigeon sadly.

"Are you so set on leaving us? Wouldn't you rather stay here with your brothers in adventure?"

"If I betrayed my mission, would you still want me for a comrade? I would lose everything — honour as well as friendship."

Big-as-a-Fist opened his mouth to crush his subaltern with a telling argument, but the argument remained stuck in his throat. It wouldn't come out. Nothing would come at all. Before a pigeon who debated between duty and love, there was no argument the little man could make, so he shut up. Then he burst into laughter and spun about on his head to restore his confidence. He told his brothers, in a narrative full of inverted subjunctives and verbal adjectives, that this self-same bird whom they saw before them, whose master had just dubbed him Marco Polo, placed himself at their service and, now that he had been made a companion of the order, had consented to lead the troupe straight to the most carefully guarded treasure in the world.

The three others batted their eyes in astonishment and joy. And in this state the four companions, led by a carrier-pigeon with mottled blue wings, set out again on the route to the Orient, singing tunes from the far side of the stream and occasionally shouting, "Shit! Shit! Break a leg!"

7

How the ancestor came within a hair of proving that the earth is flat

"The things I could teach my contemporaries," lamented Sir René, who was striding from discovery to discovery.

Oddly enough, though, it was the other three who showed the most amazement. Although the ancestor was exploring a new world born four centuries before, every morning his young brothers were discovering a whole world as it had emerged from time immemorial. Only the pigeon seemed unmoved by it all, seeing no advantages accruing to his race from the process of evolution.

"Is it really round?" Figure-Head asked for the three-score-and-tenth time.

"Round as a balloon, Sir René. With one pole up north and another down south, and an equator across the middle."

And the dwarf, who, if he used his fingers, could rattle off the whole alphabet backwards and forwards, as well as the multiplication tables up to twelve and all the irregular verbs — which in his mouth, admittedly, were more numerous than in anyone else's — shook his head sadly at the ignorance of Sir René, who could easily have hung around with Copernicus and Jacques Cartier.

Suddenly Figure-Head pulled up short: he had just noticed that the eastern horizon had disappeared. He looked north: same thing. Ditto to the south. In the west, the direction from which they'd come, the horizon was reduced to the thinnest hint of a line.

"We could always turn west," suggested Big-as-a-Fist, to avoid saying: "We'd better turn back."

"I fear," said Sir René, "that the west will soon be lost to us as well: our last horizon is already no more than a thread."

The circle of fog closed in on the last word of his sentence, and cut off the four companions from each other.

"John-Bear!"

"Big-as-a-Fist!"

"Sir René, Extra-Day — where are you?"

"They're right beside you, sir."

That was the pigeon, answering Big-as-a-Fist.

"Can you see anything, Marco Polo?"

"Just the fog moving. I can fly east for a bit to see if I can find us some solid ground, if you order me to."

"Go, my friend, and bring us back a branch in your beak. We'll wait here for you."

And then Big-as-a-Fist, who thought he knew everything, warned the homing pigeon not to forget where he'd taken off from.

"Okay!" the dwarf called to the rest of the company. "Nobody move!"

"Okay!" replied the others. "We'll stay put."

A real pea-souper, thought the dwarf to himself. He hoped the gloomy weather wouldn't outlast his patience. His legs were already itching, and his feet were starting to twitch.

"You still there?"

"Still here. No one move."

And no one did.

Hour after hour they called out to each other to see if everyone was all right. To kill time, Tom Thumb suggested that each of them tell a story about the most glorious episode in his life. It quickly became clear that no exploit in any of our heroes' lives had been more glorious than his coming into the world in the first place. But the dwarf could never be satisfied with reality, even a reality more fantastic than the hanging gardens of Babylon, and so he embellished, giving the event a long preamble in which his baker-mother rolled out the dough like a Turkish carpet, like a curtain of water, like a thick blanket of fog . . .

And that's what gave him the idea.

"John-Bear, old boy, do you want to make yourself useful?"

"Well . . ."

"Good. Raise your arms over your head . . . higher . . . as high as you can, try to touch the sky . . . that's it. Now, draw a big circle by lowering your arms to the ground, stretch them out, stretch them, good, good — good work! Do you see?"

But no, John-Bear didn't see anything, except for a slice of fog that fell to his feet.

"Roll it out like a pie crust."

Which the giant did. And little by little, the other three saw a long tunnel opening up through the fog, with fine weather at the other end. They hailed Big-as-a-Fist's genius, which had returned their horizon to them. And it was a brand new horizon to boot, much flatter than the old one, straighter, more . . .

"What the . . . ?"

Big-as-a-Fist had just realized that the countryside had changed, and that therefore he and his brothers must have travelled a great distance by staying in the same place.

"Could that be possible?" he asked, scratching his head. "Could we have come to a new place without moving?"

"Only if the place itself came to us," replied Figure-Head.

And then it was his turn to scratch his head.

"It is possible that the earth, which everyone agrees is round, is actually round like a disc rather than round like a balloon. As it revolves around the sun, there'd be nothing to stop it from turning on itself as well, flipping over like a dinner plate and — who knows? — maybe showing us its obverse side." And as usual when the ancestor got carried away by his own prodigious discoveries, he began talking in his ancient language:

"I fear, my camaradas, my brethren, that we be falne thru the thick fog at th'under-side of the world, and shall henceforth walk on the heads of our countrymen and countrywomen, who have stayne home."

After such grandiloquent nonsense, Big-as-a-Fist began to suspect that if anyone be falne on his head it was the old man; every time he became excited, he retreated into his lost childhood. But in the end he managed to decipher the elusive meaning of the words he had just heard and, slapping his forehead, said:

"Great heavens, camarada, ancestral and holy master! Let's talk turkey, here: what surprise do you have in store for us?"

Sir René tried to calm his young brother and his companions. Whether the earth is a disc or a globe, it is still at the mercy of the stars that swim in the firmament like green peas in a pot of soup. The smallest pea of all, the most fragile and no doubt the most recently shucked from its pod, is at the same time the only one who sees the others promenading about in the soup, and who knows he exists.

Life's three young apprentices looked at one anther in silence — amazed, awed, and . . . alarmed. To suddenly feel yourself balanced on a green pea floating in a pot of soup . . . it made you feel a bit queasy; but it was a delicious queasiness, when you realized that at least you were at home in your own soup pot. And Big-as-a-Fist, as if he were the only being ever born on this planet, suddenly believed he was master of the universe.

"What're we waiting for? Let's conquer this place!"

His three brothers looked at him uncomprehendingly. John-Bear was still swimming about in his bowl of soup; the other two were trying to reconcile their souls with the universe. The dwarf climbed up the trunk of a white birch to address his comrades:

"My brothers, my friends," he said, "the world and its planets belong to us. New horizons are opening up before us all the time. But we've no time to waste. One of these days we'll be careless, and the hangman will catch us."

And he bit his tongue. From his perch in the tree he jumped onto the giant's hat and climbed down to the ground. Flat or round, upside down or rightside up, for now its surface was as solid and reassuring as the worn floorboards in his father's house.

The stars could hold still, for once. Neither Big-as-a-Fist nor any of his companions had the slightest intention of giving up a single iota of their heritage, which had been handed down to them straight from Adam and Eve, the most distant of their ancestors.

And they walked. And walked. And walked.

At noon they came to a border post sitting smack dab in the middle of the road.

"Anything to declare?

"Nothing," said Figure-Head, who knew enough to keep quiet.

"Nothing," said Big-as-a-Fist, who was in the habit of lying.

"Nothing," said Extra-Day, who really didn't have anything.

The giant, however, turned out his pockets, took off his hat, and stammered:

"Well, my godmother gave me my inheritance a while ago."

Before the others could clap their hands over his mouth, they saw the gates open wide to let the giant through. John-Bear didn't quite know what to think, and he hung back.

"Welcome. Your Royal Highness. Please make yourself at home."

The comrades watched John-Bear enter. Inside, the giant was so thronged, so triumphantly borne, that he didn't even have time to say goodbye.

"Ha! Well, then!" said Big-as-a-Fist, furious at his brother, the world, and the Devil.

"Are you waiting for someone?" enquired a border guard, in his full-dress uniform.

The dwarf raised his eyebrows like two little dunce caps, then made himself so soft and small that he seemed about to disappear in a puff of time.

"We're waiting for our turn to go in and visit your great and beautiful country."

The customs officer seemed extremely puzzled.

"But whom do you want?" he asked politely. And he looked at each of them enquiringly. Finally, Extra-Day took the plunge:

"The doorman."

The barrier immediately lifted to admit the little motherless, fatherless orphan who'd come into the world all alone and naked, who'd simply come into the world.

The two more intelligent comrades, the ones with the most savoir-faire when it came to the customs of their time, didn't dare to think, reason, or reflect. They were left standing at the border like a pair of puppets propped in a closet. Having nothing to lose, they decided to say whatever came into their heads, since they'd guessed that the key to this locked door was hidden in words. Choosing their words at random, they both spoke at the same time:

"My son . . ."

"My father . . ."

And suddenly the four of them were back together again, only this time in a country that seemed to be walking on its head. Which was when they realized — after a long exchange of opinions in which Big-as-a-Fist succeeded in carrying the day — that they'd crossed to the other side of the horizon. Here everything went downside up, upside down, and against the grain. And for a moment each comrade stood there with a finger in his mouth, on his forehead, in his eye, in his nose. Once their equilibrium was restored, they decided unanimously that the best way to see things upside down was to walk with your head down. And the first to do it was Big-as-a-Fist, who managed without much effort to place the palms of his hands on the ground. That done, he was soon teasing the others:

"Let's go, scaredy-cats, lazy-bones, slow-pokes . . . c'mon, up on your hands, you clods!"

Extra-Day turned a splendid cartwheel, placing his hands on the ground and stopping with his feet in the air so gracefully that even Thumbkin was amazed and lost his balance. As for

John-Bear, each attempt to stand on his hands met with such a resounding lack of success that the earth shook and rumbled in protest. The ancestor, who was four hundred years old, resolved that age had its privileges and that now might be a good time to avail himself of one of them. Not wanting to seem to be retreating in the face of adventure, he substituted mental gymnastics for the physical variety.

"We are mistaken, my children, if we think we can see upside down properly by turning ourselves upside down. The best way to observe a thing exactly as it presents itself to our eyes, in all its bizarreness and singularity, is to envisage it rightside up. Only in such a way, by standing with our feet on the ground and our heads in the air, can we see others with their heads on the ground and their feet in the air."

Even Big-as-a-Fist had to acknowledge the justness of this proposition and could think of nothing to refute its logic. And so it was that our heroes, with their heads held high and their feet on the ground, set off to discover Topsy-Turvydom.

To the dwarf, as we have already seen, every situation offered a chance to satisfy his curiosity, to have fun, to torment all and sundry, to learn things the easy way, to experience life without running the smallest risk. His brothers, remembering their oaths of loyalty and friendship, had no choice but to follow the little pillicock through all his happy escapades.

In this way, by criss-crossing the country from one end to the other, from top to bottom, from morning to night from night to morning, the company began to appreciate the odd arrangement of its social pyramid. Unlike that of all other known societies, this pyramid sat pointed end down. Sir René, who had seen more of life than his brothers had had hot breakfasts, attested that the elite in this strange society had more people entering it than leaving it, that there were more civil servants working for the government than there were citizens being governed. And Big-as-a-Fist, every time he crossed the street, probably ploughed through a multitude of Secretaries, Under-Secretaries, Excellencies, and Right Honourables, but not a single John Doe.

To their astonishment, however, the visitors found that it was precisely John Doe who received the most attention. John Doe was, in fact, accorded all the rights and privileges of a species on the verge of extinction. "Save the People!" was the common cry: "People are the very basis of society!" The very basis of this society, then, seemed so fragile that the disappearance of John Doe would result in the toppling of the pyramid and the total collapse of the elite. Which explained all the care extended to the society's most beggarly, most ragamuffin, most John-a-Stiles John Doe in the land: he had become, by his very rarity, an extremely precious commodity.

Big-as-a-Fist rubbed his neck. "Sir René is right," he said. "These people have falne on their heads."

And that wasn't the last of our heroes' discoveries. The more they ventured into this strange country, the more astounded they became. The good citizens of Topsy-Turvydom kept their heads down, for example, because the single ambition motivating everyone in the land was to get ahead, to scale the social ladder, to ascend to the diplomatic elite, to climb over everyone else's head. To such an extent that the base of the pyramid, which was at the top, was continually expanding and dangerously threatening the tip, which was stuck in the ground.

"What's got into them?" flared Big-as-a-Fist in the face of such oddity.

What had got into them was the lust for every B.A. to become a Ph.D., every deacon to become an archbishop, every lieutenant a general, every deputy a minister, every teacher a professor, every manager a director, every director a director-general, and everyone: president.

Which caused the Chief of Protocol to tear his hair out, regularly.

And he wasn't alone. The biggest complaint came from the President of the Treasury Council. Because each contributor claimed the privileges of his office, privileges that began with contributions but ended with exemption from contributions. They had all succeeded so well in slipping themselves through some loophole or other that the country's entire tax burden rested on the shoulders of John Doe, who didn't have a red cent to his name. Which explains why the coffers of a country unimaginably rich in mineral resources, agriculture, virgin forests, fresh water, oceans, and fisheries remained perpetually empty.

And why the President of the Treasury Council tore out his hair, along with the Chief of Protocol.

But the Minister of Public Works was the most desperate of all. Because the day that the last street-sweeper was promoted to Engineer of Highways, the last stonecutter became Grand Master of Bridges and Roadways, and the last honeyman was made General Manager of Waterworks was the day that every highway, bridge, roadway, and waterworks in the country was abandoned, and John Doe moved in like a pig into the parlour.

And that was why the Minister of Public Works joined the President of the Treasury Council and the Chief of Protocol in tearing out his hair.

Within three days our explorers had found that half the country was half bald, and that the other half aspired desperately to the same condition.

"The way things are going," cried Big-as-a-Fist, "the whole country will soon be as bald as an egg!"

Sir René avoided his brothers' eyes. Crossing his hands and raising his eyes heavenward, he intoned in a sepulchral voice:

"I greatly fear that we have ventured onto the dark side of the earth, my children, and that we are now on the underside of the plate. Let us remain calm. And still. For every step we take brings us closer to the edge of the world."

The three young companions huddled closer to one another, as struck by the tone of the old man's voice as by the meaning of his words. For the first time, the dwarf questioned his own view of the world, and suspected the astronomers and geographers of his country of being frauds . . . "What if the green pea was actually a lentil?" he asked himself, startled. Then the earth would be truly flat. He and his brothers would have no choice but to stand there forever, or else run the risk of tumbling into the void. He could almost feel his feet leaving the ground, his whole body blown away by the wind, plunged into the sky and . . . and recollections of an earlier plunge returned to his memory . . .

"Marco Polo!" he shouted.

They had forgotten all about the pigeon when they had crossed the border. Good Lord! They couldn't leave him back there. He'd never find the password by himself. And even if he did give the right word, no one but Big-as-a-Fist would understand it. He could be caught, roasted on a spit, stripped of the secret tied to his left leg. And in a country that went about upside down, God knows what they'd do with it. The fate of the whole world is in the balance, my friends, my brothers, my dear comrades!

"Let's get the lead out!"

Once again the dwarf's instincts proved right and saved his company from a most perilous situation. His rallying cry flew up to heaven and into the ears of the carrier-pigeon, who had been searching frantically for his masters for days, from one end of the sky to the other.

Rejoining the little troupe in Topsy-Turvydom, the pigeon gave a little coo-coo of joy and dropped a sprig of wild rose from his beak, nearly knocking Big-as-a-Fist unconscious. But the dwarf was too happy to be hurt. So it was only for show, or to hide his true feelings, that he howled:

"Ow! Ouch! Hey, Marco Polo, my friend, does my head look like a pigeon's nest?"

Our adventurous heroes made such a fuss over the messenger that he hadn't the heart to give them anything but good news. Sir René raised an eyebrow enquiringly and said:

"Round?"

And the bird replied in his own language, translated by the dwarf:

"Seen from above, it is quite round, master."

That was the good news. The rest he kept rolled up on his left leg . . .

But Big-as-a-Fist gave everyone a good clap on the back and shouted to the pigeon to lead them out of this land with no upside down or rightside up or heads or tails.

And so they recrossed the border, happy to once again see all four horizons, properly curved, standing out clearly against a cloudless sky.

8

In which our four heroes learn how hard it is to get out of the woods

And so it was back to the good life.

Could heaven offer our four fearless adventurers any better reward than solid ground under their feet, a round, well-defined horizon ahead of them, and a clear, cloudless sky over their heads?

Well, yes, it could.

"What else is there?"

For some time now, Big-as-a-Fist had been casting a speculative eye at his friend the pigeon: the company had been promised a treasure at the end of the rainbow. The bird was the first surprise. Little by little, the dwarf recalled that it had been he himself who had invented the treasure in order to bind the company together; to spice up the bland hours with a pinch or two of dreaming and hope, and maybe to seduce reality into resembling his inventions.

"Get up!" he cried. "And let's go! The treasure lies straight ahead!"

At any rate, like it or not, once an adventurer was on the high seas or the high road he couldn't go around crying over spilt milk. Besides, the very smell of milk would make any son of a Goodman take to his heels, since he on honeydew has fed, and drunk the milk of a paradise lost. Who would have thought, griped Big-as-a-Fist — first to himself and then out loud — that at the end of our travels we'd find nothing better than the same milk our grandmothers used to give us. Not that he knew much about grandmothers, having been born in a breadbox. But Thumbkin had a good head on his shoulders, as his mother used to tell him all the time, and he never forgot a word, an idea, or an image that might one day prove useful to his quest. And the quest, for this *diablotin* dropped from the cathedral columns into Goodwife's kitchen, was nothing more than to laugh a lot, eat a lot, have a lot of fun, and do a lot unto a lot of others before they did a lot unto him. He who laughs last laughs best, and no one's in a hurry to grow old. So up and at 'em, forward march!

All the same, he'd rolled the several consonants of the word "grandmother" around in his throat, and it now seemed to be wedged between his tonsils. He wanted to bring it up, in more ways than one. Like every son of a nobody, Tom Thumb was fascinated by genealogy. And when looking into your family tree gets mixed up with your need for tenderness and your longing for a lost childhood, well, it doesn't take long for the wrinkled, wizened, parchment-like face of a grandmother to come bubbling up from the depths of your subconscious. Alas! Of the four companions, only Figure-Head could boast of having known his grandmother. Long ago, in his first life. But just imagine how much would be left of a grandmother, even a great-great-gobbledy-great-grandmother, after four centuries! So all four of our heroes had to find a single, common grandmother to mourn.

"What about Clara-Galante . . . ?" John-Bear started to say.

"Clara-Galante is a godmother. And a witch, to boot."

Then, in spite of himself, Big-as-a-Fist remembered something:

"The door's not locked. Just lift the latch and come in."

And from the door to the latch, he saw the face of his grandmother emerge from the depth of the forest. John-Bear thought of the oak tree from which he had been carved, whose roots went back a long, long way. Sir René, one of life's seasoned campaigners, knew what was on his younger brothers' minds, and shrugged his shoulders despite the weight of four hundred years.

"Before we go to join our ancestors," he started to say . . . then stopped. You can't have someone else's experiences, any more than anyone else's life can make up for your own. The elder told himself that sooner or later his younger siblings would have to learn: many of us go into the woods, and we all come out with clean hearts . . . and three more whiskers on our chins. The others, however, understood nothing of the dotard's learned divagations, and raced off into the woods to pick beechnuts and hazelnuts.

Except for the ancestor, none of the heroes could say for sure exactly when he'd left the edge of the woods. Like a schoolboy who doesn't know the precise moment when school will be let out, and realizes only later, when the fields have opened up before him, rolling by one after the other, each one fitting into the next, the gate to all of them closing behind him forever. In the same way, the woods closed behind our four comrades all of a sudden, without warning, and when they turned around to take a last look at the edge of the forest, their eyes were met by a thick wall of conifers streaked here and there by the trunk of a white birch.

"We don't have any choice but to keep going straight ahead," concluded Sir René.

That was all his brothers wanted to hear anyway: to keep heading ahead, in the direction of life, was the only way to adventure. And an adventure in the forest must perforce involve such creatures as the Three Bears, Sleeping Beauty, Renart and Ysengrin . . . Oh, tell us about them, ancestor.

Sir René dug deep into his fathomless memory and pulled out whole blocks of animal stories, still fresh and alive from his own time. To cheer up the company — and also to prepare them for the trials that must surely lie ahead in the forest — he told how, one night, the wily Renart carried off Ysengrin's smoked hams; how Tybert took Renart's back bacon and cooked it up in order to attack an old cat; how King Noble held court and Chantecler, Lady Pinte, and her three sisters attended to demand justice for Lady Copette; and how, in the end, Renart almost became a monk.

A monk? Renart? The three brothers guffawed and clapped their hands. Never had they heard such stories before! Never had the woods seemed so marvellously populated! The stories went straight to Tom Thumb's head, and already he saw himself striding into the midst of the animal assembly, ready to punch out — as he would have put it — the first ruffed grouse that spread its blue-grey tail feathers streaked with black under his nose. The dwarf, as we shall see, had to learn to let sleeping dogs lie — but let's not get ahead of our own story.

The ancestor told and retold his stories so well, instructing his brothers with such enchanting tales of life and the ways of the world, that the companions penetrated deep into the darkest part of the forest without realizing it. Not until the hour when the angelus was supposed to be rung from the church tower in their village, on the other side of Clara-Galante's stream, did John-Bear start to hear his stomach rumbling.

"What about setting some rabbit snares?" he suggested to the company.

But Extra-Day, with the assembly of foxes, wolves, cats, roosters, hens, and hares — all the animals that had gathered at the court of King Noble — still parading before his eyes, cried out: "No!" and covered his ears. His older brothers had to teach their younger sibling a few lessons about the mores of animals, who think nothing of eating each other — or even the occasional human being, if they get hungry enough — when it's a question of survival. In the end Figure-Head explained to the youngsters, whose heads were stuffed with stories, that in real life animals don't come out of the *Roman de Renart* or the fables, but quite simply out of their holes.

The first hole to trip up our companions could more correctly have been called a hill than a hole; and our heroes probably should have gone around it. But they didn't, and don't ask me why. Why do people kick over anthills? Ask the ants, who never complain, but just start building it up again, perfectly aware that the next day another foot will come along. A bear, however, has neither the resignation nor the wisdom of an ant. And so when John-Bear saw a superb animal standing before him, who could easily have been a cousin of his, he studied him carefully for a long time.

"Shawn-Bear!" whispered his brother the dwarf, his throat drier than a sheet of sandpaper. "Shawn-Bear!"

Suddenly Big-as-a-Fist felt himself snatched up by Sir René and, along with Extra-Day, stuck high up in a tree trunk. Then the ancestor stretched out on a bed of moss and played dead, though not before calling out to that big blockhead, John-Bear:

"Defend yourself, John-the-Strong!"

Only then did the giant understand that he had to fight the bear, cousin or no cousin. Though descended from the same family, they belonged to two different species. So he placed himself at the ready and sized up his adversary.

"He's smaller than me!" he said, ashamed of himself.

Big-as-a-Fist, from the shelter of his oak trunk, had had time to put his thoughts together. Listening to the mutterings of his idiot brother, though, he lost them again. Don't tell me that dumbbell is going to start reciting his maxims into the jaws of the bear! Who brought him into the world, the . . . His mother and father, obviously . . . he and I are made of the same stuff, he's my brother till death do us part. And the dwarf, puffing out his chest like a dinner roll rising on the warming oven, stuck his head out of his tree and shouted to John-Bear:

"Hang in there, brother. Be brave! I'm here!"

John-Bear looked all around him: Where had the others gone? Then suddenly he saw the ancestor lying on the ground, arms folded over his chest. Dead! Figure-Head, whom John-Bear himself had brought back to life by freeing him from his prison of ice, his brother, his child, lying so still beneath the spreading oak. And the giant turned back to his forest cousin, on the verge of tears, and said angrily:

"What did you do that for? He was our ancestor . . ."

The bear was so surprised at the giant's bravery that he forgot to duck, and before he could bat an eye he had taken such a crushing blow that he was sent back to join his own ancestors. Later, when Big-as-a-Fist had fully recovered from his fear and trepidation, he'd swear he had heard the bear whisper, as his eyes swerved heavenward: you owe me one, you asshole. But at the time he could think of nothing except hopping around his heroic brother, improvising, to the delight of the company:

He got him good, the beast is dead,
He got him good, the beast is cursed!
He conked him on his beastly head,
And made him exit asshole first!

After which the ancestor made a long, throat-clearing noise, selected his tone of voice, chose low and gravely out of respect for the loftiness of the occasion, and launched into a three-part homily on the theme of primordial Chaos over which, on this day, our beloved John-Bear the Strong, also known as Strong-as-a-Dozen, had triumphed.

Tom Thumb the Thumbkin, also known as Big-as-a-Fist, had a habit of yawning during long sermons, and on this day he did not spare his elder brother, also known as the doting preacher. The dwarf punctuated Sir René's speech with an aaah . . . which was followed by zzz . . . and he began to feel a fit of sleep coming on.

Zzz . . .

Suddenly he jerked up his head. Even when he covered his mouth with both hands, the buzzing noise continued. He stood up straight. The noise seemed to be coming from over his head. He'd better check it out. And without thinking — but when did he ever stop to think? — he applied his sure-grip soles to the bark of a wild apple tree and climbed up. On all fours he clambered up the gnarled, dried-out branch that was waving in the wind and then . . . realized there was no wind. Only the apple tree was moving — and only this one branch of the apple tree!

Zzz . . .

Yikes! Better get down, Big-as-a-Fist, go back to the others. Why can't you learn not to go around sticking your nose into everything? Why can't you just stay where you are? Curiosity killed the cat, you know that, don't you, you big dummy! . . . The dwarf repeated all these lessons to himself, but he didn't once take his eyes off the forked tongue of the serpent who was hissing with pleasure at the sight of such an appetizing morsel crawling towards him. Big-as-a-Fist had enough hidden talents to take care of even such a formidable adversary, if only fear hadn't made him lose his head. Instead of talking to himself, he should have been talking to the serpent. Two such accomplished liars might well have come to some kind of understanding. But panic never made a good counsellor: the snake struck with his murderous fangs at lightning speed, and Big-as-a-Fist, who thought he too was fast, owed his life to his diminutive size, for those venomous teeth only sank into his bonnet. The string of little bells set off such a jangling that the snake was rendered mute for a good three seconds.

Long enough for little Out-of-Time to climb up the apple tree, plant himself in front of the beast — who still had Big-as-a-Fist by the bonnet — and stare directly at him with his clear and piercing eyes. The serpent froze. Then began to coil himself up like a rope on the deck of a sailing ship, undulating with his whole body under the influence of the spell, lifting his head towards the sky — along with the dwarf, who didn't have the presence of mind to disentangle his bonnet from the serpent's teeth.

The scene that followed cannot be recounted by the incessant chatterer Tom Thumb. For once. Not that he didn't see it happen. On the contrary: he found himself in an excellent position to observe first-hand the battle between the serpent and the baby. But even he had to admit that, seen from too close, the world loses its contrasts and life loses its perspective. Anyway, soon after this adventure the dwarf lost his voice for a few hours and had to give the floor to the ancestor, who had had to listen in anguish while the innocent last-born babe, who could barely tell his right hand from his left, entered into a discussion with the serpent on such weighty themes as the Creation of the World.

"You've already caused enough trouble, you villain," he had said. "Go away and leave my brothers be."

But the serpent hadn't budged. Instead, he had tried to release himself from Extra-Day's spell. With a supreme effort, he'd hurled a final hiss in a jet of spit, but had merely succeeded in letting go of his prize, who had been overjoyed to find himself only half-dead at the foot of the tree.

And that was when John-Bear had gritted his teeth and cracked his knuckles. He had finally tumbled to the fact that, despite its size, the serpent was bigger than he was. Sir René had had to hold him back and assert his authority.

"Strength has no power over lying," he'd said to the giant, who was snorting and pawing at the moss. "Leave it to the little one; he was born out of the serpent's time, and there is no bite that can touch him. When the monster is ready . . ."

The monster was apparently ready, but Extra-Day was too fast for him, and dodged a whistling lunge that split the air and ended in the snake biting his own tail. The whole apple tree gave a shudder, dropped its dead branches to the ground, and was still.

And the earth was saved from falling into sin a second time.

But even the earth has a hard time going its own way when our heroes decide otherwise. So here they are taking it apart with the firm intention of putting it back together again to suit themselves.

Sir René — claiming the privilege of age and his superior knowledge of the past, and keenly aware of his obligation to instruct his younger brothers on all things — never missed an opportunity to begin a new lesson with the words "Well, if you want my opinion" followed by a dot-dot-dot . . .

"Okay, go ahead, give us your opinion." One had begun to know these opinions beforehand, to have a presentiment about them, and so one — which is to say Big-as-a-Fist — suspected that since he first entered the woods the revenant had known everything, seen everything, done everything, experienced every human thing that one still had to know, see, do, and experience, and that if things went on this way much longer one ran the risk of having nothing left to live but someone else's warmed-over life. What a fix! To head out for adventure only to find at the end of the road that every night the hands of the clock went back to twelve; that every year the calendar started again at January; that the four seasons went around and around; and that at the heart of their little troupe there was a memory that was alive and talking — boy, was it talking! — nipping every little discovery in the bud, and spoiling every mystery and surprise! And Big-as-a-Fist spat out his biggest gob in exasperation.

Now, the biggest gob of such a tiny Thumbkin was hardly big enough to wet an earthworm. The earthworm, however, shook his back to rid himself of the flood, and reflected a ray of sunshine that caught the eye of a sparrow in flight, who plunged down on his prey, carried it up into the air, and had to defend it against an attack from a crow who was as hungry as the sparrow and who thought, Here's a double mouthful, but who in turn aroused the envy of a vulture. The resulting explosion of feathers and beaks alerted the rabbit, who, perking up his ears above the rabbit hole, drew the fox out of his den, who was then chased by the coyote. Big-as-a-Fist, amazed, felt himself once more at one with nature: if a single drop of spit could set off such a concept of consequences, imagine what he could do with three notes from his flute!

Had Tom Thumb been able to see farther than his own nose,

he would have let sleeping dogs lie and left his flute dozing safely in the bottom of his back pocket. But how could he foretell or even have a premonition about something he had never seen before? So he played his flute, like the foolhardy son of a Goodman he was, using all his fingers and all his soul — a soul that knew a lot more than his head and his heart.

With wonder, the musician saw how the forest was caught up in his spell, and how the birds let go of their prey. What prey was left. If that braggart Sir René could stop dancing and catch his breath, he would surely comment on the subject of the earthworm's eternal renewal — even when cut in half, it is indefinitely reborn from its second part. But the old man just jumped, and whirled, and bowed to his partner.

His partner? Big-as-a-Fist raised his eyes and took the flute out of his mouth. Immediately the dancers froze, one leg poised in mid-air. The first to fall on their feet were the giant and the child, who looked about to see where the lady had come from. As for the ancestor, he knew that she'd come out of the flute, and that she was a fairy.

Fairy . . . ?

And the three youngsters rubbed their eyes. They had always believed in fairies, it went without saying, but the fairy who had just appeared before them wasn't at all like their imaginings. She was more like a good country girl from across the stream, with her hair in braids and her apron full of nuts and berries. What's got into Sir René, bowing to her like that, and making such mincing faces? Fairies like her were a dime a dozen in their parents' village: Jane, Catherine, Mary, Susan, each one more braided and dark-skinned and insufferable than the one before.

You remember, John-Bear, the one who stole all the best marbles in my collection? Or the one who pushed me face first into the daisies? Or that shameless liar who thought she was so high-and-mighty and convinced you that her father was bigger and stronger than you? You remember Catherine, Carol, Mary, and Jane? . . . Don't worry about this one, brother, she's got no more courage or sense than the others had, she's no better than the rest, she'll end up laughing in your face and tripping you up . . . What's the matter with the old man, looking at her like that? Has he lost his marbles too, or what? No, keep clear, John-Bear!

If Big-as-a-Fist had known then what he couldn't possibly know until later — just wait a few years, my boy! — he wouldn't have held his twin brother back or treated the old man as if he'd lost his marbles. But we've known since he was born that the dwarf was destined to spend his whole life being too small for his age. When his mother made him she decorated his crust with finesse, cunning, audacity, and a love of life, but she added only a pinch of yeast to the dough, and hardly worked it in at all. Master Goodman, on the other hand, was a real master-carpenter, and while he didn't whittle away too much of his oak tree, he nevertheless showed a sure hand, and fashioned a giant who lacked not a single attribute from the day he was born.

"Come back, John-Bear, my brother! This beanpole isn't a fairy, she's just Jane-Cathy-Susan! Don't you see her baggy skirt and her flat shoes? And her dirty knees? And her bitten-off fingernails? And the ribbon dangling loose from her hair? And she squints, John-Bear — that's not a smile, it's a sneer. Let's get out of here!"

Little Extra-Day heard Big-as-a-Fist going on and on and wondered what bee had got into his bonnet. Why was he yelling so loudly at his brother, who was only watching an inoffensive young woman picking wild strawberries in her flowered apron? Pretty flowers on a pretty apron full of red strawberries with bright green leaves. And the rays of the sun filtering through the branches making the berries dance on the ends of their stems. She must be a fairy, Big-as-a-Fist, if she can make so much beauty at the bottom of an apron.

The dwarf looked at his younger brother as if to say: Are you so innocent that you can't see that those strawberries and stems in the apron wrapped around her waist don't come from any bag of tricks of hers, but from your own eyes? The youngster looked at him blankly: the sentence was too long and the thought too complicated. Anyway, Extra-Day's attention was suddenly drawn away, towards Sir René, who was desperately trying to wave his younger brothers away from the danger area:

"Go back," he called urgently to his brothers. "Get away. Walk on by. Don't even look at her."

Look who's talking! And Big-as-a-Fist, who a second earlier had been doing everything in his power to get John-Bear out of the woods, now went up to Figure-Head with the firm intention of tearing him away from the talons — those long, long fingernails belonging to . . . to this temptress who was hurling such venom on the old man. But the dwarf quickly realized that the old man was not as old as everyone had thought; he straightened his back, locked his joints, unwrinkled his brow. And what fire flashed from his eyes! Figure-Head, my old friend, come down to earth, it's only a woman, a child who's barely left her mother's skirts. She's not even pretty, and she'll certainly lie to you — I know her; keep away from her, my friend, my brother, she'll only make you sad.

Sad? But he was as happy as a lark; in fact, that was the sad part. He wasn't taken in by this happiness, he'd seen it plenty of times before. But despite his devastating experiences in the past, he was ready to go through it all again. He knew himself, knew the weakness and richness of his heart. He'd stay here under the trees, plucking . . .

"But what about us?"

That stopped him. In a flash, the vision of his three brothers splashed across his retinas. He took the three of them by the hands, their six eyes peering closely into his. Why hadn't they gone away yet? What was he doing here with these children, so innocent of real life and the real needs of a man? Heaven didn't give him this second chance for nothing; it was only right that he should follow it and live it to the end, for better or for worse.

"For pity's sake, leave me. Let me have my life. Thank you for bringing me back, thank you for your friendship and for those happy days of yesteryear . . ."

John-Bear looked at him with the eyes of a cow being led to slaughter; Extra-Day with the air of a groundhog sticking his nose out of his hole to see if he could see his shadow; and Big-as-a-Fist with no air at all, no look, no nothing . . . except maybe one word — Shit! — which fell like a moonbeam and tickled the image still stuck to Sir René's retina. And in spite of himself, the ancient one let loose a chuckle. He laughed, the old man, the comrade! He smiled, then he burst into laughter before all and sundry. He was saved!

"Come to us, Sir René!"

The shout must have frightened the fairy, because she evaporated in a puff of white smoke, without a trace.

Well, not quite without a trace, for in her haste to disappear she dropped the strawberry leaves that little Out-of-Time had picked for his brothers. And believe it or not, it was Big-as-a-Fist who chose the biggest and most beautiful of them for his collection of dried flowers.

After their encounter with the fairy and her apron bulging with wild strawberries, Big-as-a-Fist was convinced that the worst was over and that the forest could hold no further danger for them. And he led his small troupe joyfully on their adventures in the woods. Break trail for us, John-Bear, spread those branches. The world is our oyster. Each comrade cleared his own way according to his size: the giant by mowing down the bushes with his arms; the ancestor by zigzagging between the huge tree trunks; the youngest by following the ancestor; Big-as-a-Fist by sitting on the giant's hat, with his feet dangling over the brim.

Thus perched, the dwarf allowed the odours of the underbrush to go to his head and invade his entire body. Nothing was more likely to send him off into a trance than the smell of the woods, and before long he was singing and telling tales and taunting all the monsters in the forest. Who's afraid of the big, bad wolf, the big, bad wolf, the big, bad wolf? Let him show us his ears so we can see, so we can see if he's white or grey. Oh, who's afraid of the big, bad wolf . . . aaa-oooh!

Figure-Head looked up at the dwarf perched on the giant's hat and begged him to keep his flights of poetry to himself. Then he took it upon himself to lecture the young Apollo on the responsibilities of art. One could not invoke the Muse with impunity, he said; to name a thing is to give it birth. Thus were born the gods and demons of ancient times. As for the wolf . . .

Yes, yes, yes . . . Well, there's no telling how long this fine lecture would have lasted if Tom Thumb hadn't cut it short by hopping from his brother's hat onto the back of his pigeon and taking to the air.

"I'm going to scout out the area," he shouted to his comrades. "Giddyup, Marco Polo!"

And he spurred on his flying mount.

"Don't go too far, Big-as-a-Fist," his brothers called after him, following him with their eyes.

"Don't worry," he shouted back. "We'll just skim the ground. Just high enough to see the wolf and warn you if there's any danger."

Too sure of himself, the little devil, too bold and foolhardy. Because in guiding his winged steed through a series of ever more risky pirouettes, he came within a hair's breadth of catching his bonnet in a poplar branch, and leaving half his britches in a nest.

"Oops!"

"It was a magpie's nest, too," said the pigeon. "I hope the mother wasn't there."

She was there, all right, and she still hadn't forgiven the two imps for their invasion of her home the last time. "Barbarians!" she shrieked, throwing herself into the chase. The pigeon didn't hang around, but shouted to his knight-at-arms to hold on tight. The dwarf felt a bevy of strong winds that set his many bells tinkling on his bonnet. Music being the surest way to wake up every nest in the forest, it wasn't long before a whole symphony of trills, tweets-tweets, chirp-chirps, and caw-caws pervaded the woods and reached the ears of the small troupe of heroes below, warning them that some sort of misfortune had befallen their fourth companion.

"I knew it," moaned Figure-Head as the two others stood in front of him awaiting his instructions before moving.

But just as the ancestor was about to open his mouth, a sound torn from the very roots of the forest drowned out his voice — Aaa-oooh!

"The wolf!"

This time they were right. No doubt about it. Some sounds cannot be mistaken. Don't move a muscle. Let's keep our wits about us . . . But John-Bear couldn't hide his uneasiness. Not that he was afraid of the wolf — he was Strong-as-a-Dozen. But he was afraid for his brother, who was flying somewhere in the sky and was no doubt unaware of the danger that awaited him upon landing. The old man had to agree: the little idiot was quite capable of bringing his steed down right into the jaws of the wolf. We have to warn him immediately. No time to lose. Speaking of time, the only one who had as much of it as he wanted was Extra-Day. And Sir René turned to the youngest member of the troupe:

"Could you make yourself invisible to the wolf?"

To the wolf and to any other forest creature — but that would include the pigeon and Big-as-a-Fist, who wouldn't be able to see him either. And the ancestor wrung his hands and trembled from head to toe. John-Bear became impatient; he wanted to go out and hunt the wolf down. But where was he hiding? They could hear him, but his howling seemed to come from all directions at the same time. Good Lord! Good Lord! Just one wolf from the pack could eat the pigeon and the dwarf for breakfast!

"Not if the pigeon stays aloft."

But he'd have to get tired sometime and come down to land, there was no way around that.

"What if we climbed up one on top of another to form a totem pole sticking up above the trees? Our brother could see us then."

Good idea! John-Bear went up the highest oak, and Sir René installed himself on the giant's shoulders, with Extra-Day perched on his.

"Can you see anything coming, my son?"

He saw a bird-battle raging in the distance, a mêlée of beaks and claws in a cloud of feathers; he heard the crying of fledglings and the shrieking of the magpie, who led the attack like an enraged shrew whose nest had been wrecked.

"Down," commanded the eldest brother. "Let's get back on the ground, my brothers. We've seen enough. If anyone has wrecked the magpie's nest, I know who it is, for he has left his sign. We must concentrate on measures to aid our friend, threatened as he is from both the air and the ground."

Never had the company been so unprepared for adversity. Never had it felt so powerless. Heaven alone could save their comrade from such peril. Implore it, my brothers. Big-as-a-Fist was now running the gravest of risks.

In point of fact, Big-as-a-Fist was now running with all his might, resembling, roughly speaking, the leaps and bounds of a grasshopper across a field of clover.

Let's go back a bit.

While his brothers, alerted by the concert of birds, were discovering the perilous situation he had landed himself in, the dwarf had also come to realize the size of the catastrophe, and he slapped his forehead and cried, "Yikes!" The pigeon, for his part, understood two things: first, that he shouldn't risk his master's life in a battle of birds; secondly, that he'd fight more effectively without a rider. So, telling the dwarf not to move, he deposited him in an unoccupied nest.

Unfortunately, this plan required the blind and total collaboration of Big-as-a-Fist. The pigeon should have known by now that a little devil like his master could never stay put for long, not even in a soft, downy nest at the heart of danger; that curiosity and a taste for adventure would end up chasing our hero from the nest and bringing him nose to muzzle with none other than his first cousin of the woods:

"Fox!" he cried, completely forgetting to be on his guard.

"Hello there, little brother," said Renard, his jaws oozing compunction.

"Hi, big brother," said the dwarf, parodying the other.

"You seem to be looking for someone; I could give you a hand."

"That's kind of you, cousin. For the moment, I'm just nosing around here in the bushes, not looking for anything or anyone in particular."

"Too bad, friend. The woods conceal many mysteries and hidden treasures."

The word "treasure" ignited a spark of interest in the dwarf. But he remained outwardly calm. He was still virginal and ignorant of the ways of nature, but, as his mother often said, he learned very quickly. Especially hanging around such excellent company. It was a toss-up who was playing the subtler game, the fox or the goose.

"As a matter of fact, I might as well tell you, I was looking for my grandmother," he said, humming nonchalantly and even going so far as to twirl his moustaches.

The fox, fresh from a personal encounter with Tybert, the tribal chief of the wild cats, didn't let the gesture go unnoticed, and offered a parley:

"I could act as your go-between," he proposed with his oily voice. "It wouldn't take up much of my time, and besides, you are my cousin."

A tiny, almost imperceptible wrinkle appeared between Big-as-a-Fist's eye and his eyelid, but nothing was imperceptible to the wiliest and most conniving rogue in the forest — as our unhappy son of Goodman and Goodwife would soon attest. Because in the wink of an eye, the dwarf divined — but barely, the merest whiff, a faint foreboding — that his woodlands cousin could toy with him and perhaps even induce him to commit some unpardonable offence. But the die was already cast, and the game was compelling enough; what was more, wasn't it he who had first mentioned the word "grandmother"? Wasn't it his idea? The fox was only offering to lead him to her.

And without even coming to a formal agreement, the two little schemers set off in step — forty steps by the dwarf to four by the fox — along a zigzagging slope that descended like a rift in the side of the mountain.

"Knock," said the fox, sliding out of his protégé's view.

Big-as-a-Fist lifted his eyes and saw a cabin rise up in front of him, exactly like the one his godmother, Clara-Galante, lived in. A tremor of apprehensive joy ran up the length of his spine.

"You think I should?"

"Do I think you should? But you must, my friend. It's your grandmother's cottage. And you know how much grandmothers long for visits from their grandchildren. Knock and go in."

The dwarf tried to look behind him, but the forest had closed in tightly. Suddenly he felt completely alone in the woods; even the fox had disappeared. What mess had he got himself into this time? And what about his companions? Where were his companions now?

"The door is open, my dear. Just lift the latch and come in."

Had he dreamed it? Had he heard right? He didn't even remember knocking.

"Well! Are you coming in or aren't you?"

This time there was no doubt about it: he had heard right. Someone had called out to him. At any rate, it was too late to go back now. What the hell, he said. It's not every day you get a chance to find the road that takes you home again.

He pushed open the door and went in.

The first thing he noticed was the smell. One sniff and his whole childhood leapt to his nose. Wild strawberry and rhubarb jam. With muffins. The full smell of his maternal home.

"It smells like our house," he said.

"Well then, make yourself at home."

When he looked in the direction of the voice, the dwarf was transfixed: She was round, pink, and chubby, her hair was tied up in a bun, she had laughing grey eyes and a mouth hardly bigger than the pit of a prune, and her whole presence centred on her bosom, softer than a feather bed. Why had he imagined he'd find Clara-Galante in here? There was nothing in this grand old lady of the soothsayer, necromancer, reader of cards. This was the perfect grandmother, the kind you get to knit sweaters for your children, or to tell them marvellous bedtime stories. And without thinking — forgetting the most elementary rules of conduct — Big-as-a-Fist jumped into her lap and said:

"Do you know the story of Tom Thumb?"

Grandmother didn't seem a bit surprised by her grandchild's lack of manners. It was as if she'd been waiting all eternity for just this to happen.

"Are you very old?" he asked her. "Did you know my parents? And my parents' parents?"

He wanted to know everything at once, tossing question after question and even posing questions inside of questions: Why did she live in the middle of the forest? And for how long? Who brought her flour for her bread and sugar for her jams? Did she have any neighbours, friends? And what about the wolf, wasn't she afraid of the wolf?

"What beautiful eyes you have, Grandmother."

"From looking at so many beautiful flowers in the forest," she said.

"And your voice sings like the birds."

"From hearing them waking up nature on so many mornings."

"And your skin is soft, and your cheeks are so round."

What a marvellous grandmother, thought Tom Thumb, who had often dreamed of just such a one. How could he have gone so long without her?

"What have you been up to, then?" she asked, taking him by the chin.

"Adventure, Grandmother. I've been off to see the world, seeking my fortune."

"Your fortune? That's good, that's good. And have you learned a great many things?"

"Oh, yes indeed. A great many."

And Big-as-a-Fist launched into a detailed account of the

many ups and downs of his voyage since he'd set out, oh so long ago, by crossing the stream that ran through his native village. The old woman listened to him tell the story of the birth of his brothers and travelling companions; their encounter with the wicked, cowled hangman; the storm in the drop of water; the flight on the back of the carrier-pigeon who later became his friend; the visit to a country where everyone walked upside down; the battle with the beasts of the forest in which his brothers, one after the other, almost lost their lives . . . The dwarf looked up and turned towards the door. But the grandmother, anticipating his move, took him by the ears and looked deeply into his eyes.

"Don't worry about them. They'll get along just fine by themselves. The big one is big enough, the old one is old enough, and the little one is bright enough to get out of the woods without you. I'm going to put the kettle on the fire. Do you like barley soup?"

"Barley soup!" thought Big-as-Fist. A meal and a word from home. And he smacked his lips in anticipation.

"Go get two buckets," said the old woman, "and fill them with kindling and dry sticks, because you're still so small."

Not as small as all that, thought the dwarf, making a face.

"And be sure you don't leave the yard — the wolf is usually about at this time of day."

But small enough, conceded Big-as-a-Fist.

So they brewed up a batch of barley soup in the cauldron, and poked the fire, and told tall tales and funny, fantastic stories in which Big-as-a-Fist heard again about his favourite heroes — Puss in Boots and Little Thumbkin — both of whom ended their days quietly at home with their families. Soon the smell of barley soup and strawberry jam filled the cabin.

"Food's ready!" called the old woman.

She pushed a small chair under the backside of the little guy. Not even his mother, Goodwife, had paid him so much attention.

"Tomorrow," said the old woman, "I'll add a soup bone to the pot. I didn't get a chance today to check my traps and snares."

Ooomf . . . ooomf . . .

What was that?

"Don't move, dear, I think someone else has come for dinner."

She had hardly finished speaking when a ruffling of wings was heard in the chimney, then plop! a pigeon crashed into the fireplace.

"Marco Polo!"

Big-as-a-Fist jumped from his chair and ran to his friend. But his grandmother was faster, and had already grabbed the bird by one leg and was uttering strange cackles.

"Here he is, he'll make a fine addition to our pot," she hissed, her fingers already wrapped around the pigeon's neck.

"No!" shouted Big-as-a-Fist. "He's my bird, my friend, my companion!"

"Your companion? This thing? Come, my boy, this is a wild pigeon, and he'll be served up for your dinner tonight."

And once against the old witch started to twist the bird's neck. But this time Big-as-a-Fist was quicker in trying to save his friend's life. With a sudden and deep inspiration, he sneezed as hard as he could. The old woman let loose an enormous fart, which shook her from head to toe and made her drop her prize, who immediately flew up to the ceiling.

"Run for your life!" Big-as-a-Fist called up to him, as the grandmother held her head in both hands.

"You little guttersnipe!" she raged, reaching for her broom. "It's time you learned some manners!"

But Big-as-a-Fist didn't give her time to exhibit her teaching methods. Straddling his pigeon, who had swooped down between his legs, he let him carry him up the chimney and out of the cabin that he'd been thinking of, only a moment before, as his ancestral home.

This time the reunion party for the prodigal sons lasted all night, as they tripped over one another trying to be the most eloquent in describing the valour with which So-and-so had saved Such-

and-such's life. In the end the laurel went to the pigeon, who had risked his neck consciously; for one thing, he'd been the only one who knew the full extent of the dangers lurking in the bush.

In the wee hours, when the company judged that they had seen enough for one day and that it was time to get out of the woods, no one could agree on what direction they should take. The woods were so thick that they could no longer see the forest for the trees.

"Well, that does it. I'm going to find a way out of here," said Big-as-a-Fist, the only one small enough to slip easily between the trunks of the trees and search out the paths on the ground. The forest was only thick at the top, he said; not at the bottom.

And that was how a dwarf got his bigger brothers out of the woods.

Alas! Later that same day, that same Big-as-a-Fist got them lost again, this time in a cornfield.

9

In which a dwarf reflects on the ecstasy and the agony of a five-legged calf

After leaving first the forest and then the cornfield, the four comrades sat down in a circle to catch their breath and collect their wits. It was certainly true that the woods concealed much more than a few beech and hazelnut trees. Thinking about how the planet could be represented by a lentil or a pea, Big-as-a-Fist tapped his forehead and assumed the air of a diminutive Newton:

"If my soup pot contains so many mysteries and so much richness," he said, "imagine what the universe must hold."

The ancestor's eyes opened wide at this, then he smiled. This time his comrades were well and truly out of the woods, even if they didn't yet know exactly how far they still had to travel to reach the horizon.

"My conscience will be clear," retorted Big-as-a-Fist to Figure-Head, without stopping to ask himself: clear of what?

He only knew that the earth belonged to everyone, and that therefore he and his brothers were as rich as Croesus. No time to lose, brothers. The future awaits us. Let's go!

And the dwarf dragged his comrades along, arm in arm, whistling songs from the good old days, calling out to every Tom, Dick, and Harry who crossed their path that they were off to count their chickens before they hatched and put the cart before the horse, and not to expect them back until there was a week with three Thursdays.

The ancestor would have been happier if the little idiot had stopped taunting Destiny and challenging Life to hand-to-hand combat. The world held enough slings and arrows as it was, without his going out of his way to sweet-talk misfortune down on their heads. But Big-as-a-Fist didn't see the world through the same eyes as his older brother. From the imp's point of view, which was roughly that of an escapee from some cathedral cornice, everything in the world had to be made over again: beginning with all those chickens running around uncounted; and the horses, who would be much better off being led about by their carts; and the week, which would surely profit from having an extra couple of Thursdays in it.

Sir René let Tom Thumb ramble on for a while under the astonished gaze of John-Bear, who envisioned an infinity of chickens, and of Out-of-Time, who was amusing himself by thinking about those two extra Thursdays. These youngsters, thirsting after the marvellous and the unknown, didn't seem to have second thoughts about anything, not even their own immortality. But the ancestor refrained from examining the matter too closely. The sun had risen so red that morning, the horizon was still so far away, why hurry to close the gap that separated them? So they went back to finding out which way the wind was blowing.

That way! Each of them cried at the same time, all pointing in different directions — with Big-as-a-Fist raising his arm straight up to the sky, which was the surest way to indicate all four directions at once and thereby assure himself of a spot on the winning side. For once, heaven gave him the right answer, for it presented to the company's eyes a superb formation of geese, who never had to ask themselves which direction they should take.

"At least they know where they're going," said Sir René, recalling that even in his day the geese used to fly that way.

Big-as-a-Fist contemplated the perfect V standing out so clearly in the sky, and told himself that so disciplined a regiment must surely be headed for a resounding conquest — its very shape proclaimed certain victory — and the four comrades would have nothing to lose by attaching themselves to the rearguard of such a splendid army.

"Why don't we follow them?" he suggested.

And without waiting for an answer from his comrades, who hadn't had time to turn around, he jumped onto the pigeon's back and shouted, "Giddyup!" and they took off straight for the head of the V. Poor Marco Polo! Knowing how to fly was all very well, but it was quite another thing for a pigeon to catch up with an in-flight formation of geese who had taken wing far to the south several weeks earlier. And he muttered under his breath that creatures should choose their masters more carefully, and that if he had it to do over again . . .

"Do what I tell you," Tom Thumb ordered. "I want to have a word with my Mother Goose."

Your Mother Goose won't be too happy to see you, my lad. This is no time for bedtime stories. This is the great migration.

All this reasonableness notwithstanding, the pigeon obeyed his lord and master and brought him to the big goose at the head of the formation.

"Is that her?" said Big-as-a-Fist uneasily. He could no longer tell one bird from another, or a wing from a foot, or a feather from its fluff.

He had landed smack in the middle of a raggle-taggle flight of geese whose great V seemed to have broken down into a disorderly array of wild birds. What was going on? Why had they all broken rank? Looking down for his brothers he saw again, reflected in the mirror of a lake far below, the perfect V of the migrating flock. The dwarf, who understood so few things but had a quick brain, soon realized that perfection — like beauty — was better viewed from a distance. But he promised himself never to reveal this discovery to anyone.

Meanwhile he had decided that being straight with Mother Goose might not be to his best interests, and that he should approach her obliquely, coming from left to right, or maybe head-on from above. And he cleared his throat with a loud gurgle — Ahem! . . . ahem! — that startled the great goose.

"Look onnnk . . . ," she cried. "You're blonnnking my view . . ."

The pigeon didn't wait to be told twice, and veered off. But the dwarf wasn't ready to give up so quickly. And, as always when he found himself at the end of his rope, he turned himself over to his instincts.

"Watch out for the fox!" he yelled from some distance away.

The word produced the desired effect: the great birds lost their rhythm and the V began to waver and unravel. Their leader made a rapid dive and came up behind the pigeon and his rider.

"Did you say fonnnks?"

Big-as-a-Fist inwardly begged the pardon of his woodland cousin, then plunged ahead:

"In those bushes, right below us."

"Thank you, young man. And since onnnk good turn deserves another, there's a bandits' hideaway towards the sonnnk-sonnnk-west!"

"Bandits? What are they doing there?"

Mother Goose, having regained her rhythm, got her flock back into formation. From the point of the V she shouted down to Big-as-a-Fist:

"Counnnting . . . their . . . monnney . . ."

Which was how the company came to be heading south-south-west the next morning. But before that, our four heroes spent a long sleepless night. Because you're not to think everyone shared Tom Thumb's spontaneous enthusiasm. That worthy already saw himself seated in state in a carriage encrusted with gold and silver nuggets. Sir René especially had good reason to fear highway robbers, who had more than once held him up and left him for dead in his first life. He also nourished vague misgivings about stolen money, which usually ended up burning the fingers of anyone who touched it. For his part, John-Bear felt that no treasure was worth the danger his friends would be exposed to, but he promised nonetheless that if they did go after it he would defend them with the last drop of his blood. As for little Extra-Day, he listened attentively, sucking his thumb and trying to grasp the mysterious power that money possessed, that it could sow such discord between brothers.

By daybreak, the views of Big-as-a-Fist had prevailed. He had developed them along twelve lines — including, among others, Justice, the struggle between Good and Evil, and Robin Hood — all of which could be reduced to a single argument: money buys happiness. And so off they went.

The goose had been specific about the direction — south by southwest — but not about the distance. So the troupe all but fell head first into the robbers' lair. Luckily Big-as-a-Fist had had a presentiment seconds before they got there, and had sent the carrier-pigeon ahead for news. The news, however, came of its own accord, running, cursing, and throwing rocks at the bird, who called to his masters at the top of his voice to hide themselves in the bushes — which the four startled companions hastened to do. Only John-Bear was unable to find a bush big enough to use as camouflage. In order not to give his friends away, he froze into the shape of an oak, his arms and fingers stuck out like branches. The hunter, furious at having lost his prey, cursed his luck and relieved himself on John-Bear's ten toes, which were stretched out like roots under the moss. Big-as-a-Fist, up in his crow's nest, whispered to the two others beneath him:

"John-Bear's getting such a thorough watering, he's sure to put out blossoms in the spring."

And he snorted with laughter behind his hands.

The danger past, the troupe reassembled in a circle to hold a conference. The brigands' hideout was within earshot . . . they should keep their voices down. They must proceed with utmost caution and with a carefully planned strategy. They agreed that, in the absence of the pigeon, Out-of-Time should be sent in to scout around.

"You'll know how to make yourself invisible?" Sir René asked him.

"I will," said Extra-Day.

"Above all, don't take any risks. Don't show yourself at any time. Have a good listen, and come back and tell us their every word."

"And break a leg!"

The youngster had already disappeared. The others sat down in the leaves and crossed their fingers. Silence. No one budged. Time passed. Then wise old Sir René risked a word, then another:

"Strange how slowly time passes when he's not here."

"Here he is!"

He had just come back to their time, and leapt into their view.

"Well?"

"What's up?"

"Tell us!"

And he told them.

One for you, one for me . . . one for you, one for me . . . one for you, one for me . . . hey, where's mine? . . . He had seen four brigands sitting in a squared circle, in the process of divvying up a treasure. One for you, one for me. At one point, from his hiding-place between two folds of time, Extra-Day had asked for his portion of the money to take back to his brothers. The robbers had jumped up and searched high and low; finding no one there, they'd run off with the treasure.

"Oh, that's just great," spat out Big-as-a-Fist, tapping his foot angrily under the startled eye of John-Bear and the stern gaze of Figure-Head.

"The child thought he was doing the right thing," said the ancestor. "We're not going to argue about it now. So the thieves took off with their money, good riddance! Let's shove off ourselves!"

But the dwarf wouldn't let it go at that, and didn't feel like shoving off so quickly. The child's stupidity had blown their first plan. Well, tough luck. There was no lack of plans in that nimble brain of his. Suddenly magnanimous, Big-as-a-Fist forgave his youngest brother and proposed a whole new stratagem.

"We'll set a trap for them," he said.

"A trap? But how?"

"Simple. The right bait catches the rat."

A thin smiled curled on Figure-Head's lips. He could see where astute little Thumbkin was headed: the right bait for robbers is gold. Sprinkle gold along your path, and . . .

"But we don't have a red cent."

Big-as-a-Fist turned his face and winked at the sun. The little devil was afraid of nothing. He was ready to risk everything for the thrill of the chase. Leaping and dancing about, shaking his head, he set the little golden bells on his cap to ringing as they caught and reflected the rays of the sun.

"All I have to do is find the right spot. Sooner or later . . ."

Rather sooner than later. If the fireball had only stopped to think for a moment, if he'd considered the consequences of his strategy and reflected that the bait is usually the first to be taken, he might have exercised a bit of caution, especially in the matter of those bells. But the most cunning of foxes isn't always the wisest, and our little devil, in drawing his prey into his trap as planned, fell into it himself, which he hadn't counted on at all.

A fine mess!

The bandits were the most surprised, though.

"What kind of bug is this?"

Immediately Big-as-a-Fist pricked up his ears. What kind of language was this, he echoed to himself. On further reflection, he understood. Impossible! They thought he was some kind of insect! And he planted his fists on his hips and wrinkled his nose. The gods were merciful: his anger made him forget his fear, and the extra time allowed him to regain his composure. "I belong to the same species as you, if you don't mind."

Well, he was only trying to assert his rights as a human being. But he realized right away that he was in the brigands' camp, and he bit his tongue.

"But I'm on the side of the victims, not the killers," he added.

Another gaffe, you little lunk-head. You've just gone and placed yourself in with the victims. Good heavens! . . . You should try counting to ten before you speak, nitwit!

As four hideous heads hovered over his, and a hairy, dirty paw poked at him, making him turn around on his heels, then picked him up by the seat of his pants. Big-as-a-Fist prayed with all his might to Goodwife, his mother, and all the household gods in her kitchen. Little by little, he regained his spirits and told himself that sooner or later his brothers would be coming along the path to save him.

His brothers were indeed on the path. Big-as-a-Fist had told them to keep their eyes peeled and not to stray too far from the trap. But no one had expected the brigands to come so soon and in such force. And certainly no one had thought of the possibility of a hostage-taking incident!

"Ho-ho-ho!" laughed the largest of the four robbers. "Here's something that's worth a darned sight more than gold. A talking insect! What a godsend! Think how much he'll fetch at the circus."

"There may be a whole species just like him," said the second. "Let's use him to attract the others."

"With bait like this . . . ," said the third.

"The trapper trapped," croaked Tom Thumb. To which the fourth robber added, "We'll nab the whole lot of 'em and make our fortunes at the circus! Ho-ho-ho!"

Calm down now, Big-as-a-Fist, get hold of yourself, you've been in worse jams than this . . . oh yeah? When? . . . Well, at least you're still alive. These brigands are criminals, count your lucky stars you're not dead — after all, what's more important than life, eh? Get your breath — don't stop breathing, whatever you do — play dead, maybe, but keep your eyes open . . . This'll teach you to go around sticking your nose in other people's business, you jerk!

While Big-as-a-Fist was delivering the above funeral oration for Big-as-a-Fist, his three brothers were following the cortège from a distance, from time to time sending Extra-Day ahead for news, which got worse the nearer they got to the circus. John-Bear, as chief mourner, begged their elder brother to let him go up and kill them all, the whole lot of them, these monsters who were holding his brother hostage.

"The big one has stuffed him in his pocket," reported Extra-Day.

Sir René calmed John-Bear. A pitched battle at this point would endanger the dwarf's life, he said.

"Right now he's in no danger. Let's just keep them in sight and wait for our chance."

"Dumb, dumb, and dumbbell!" grumbled Big-as-a-Fist. "I can't see a thing from this pocket . . . Arrrgh! The dirty rat's wiping his nose with my hat! I hope the bells make him sneeze his brains out, the rotten . . . Wait a minute . . . Sneeze . . . sneeze . . . ho-ho!" he said to himself. And without wasting a second the dwarf sneezed as hard as he could from the depths of his prison. Alas! These highway robbers were no strangers to farting, and the dwarf-inspired ones they let loose now were lost amid a whole gamut of belches, spits, and curses that empurpled the air around them as they walked. One more fart could hardly make them blush. Then I'll have to use my flute, the dwarf said to himself, lying flat on his back. With great effort he managed to squeak out four notes. Before long eight feet started tapping and the robbers began hopping, dancing a sort of polka that never let go of them. They looked at each other wildly, not knowing what it was that suddenly made them want to prance about and embarrassed them a lot more than farting ever did. But the loudest complaint came from Tom Thumb; jostled about at the bottom of a filthy old pocket, he ended up losing his breakfast along with his flute. That ended the polka, as well as Big-as-a-Fist's last hope. Not all gifts are for all occasions, he told himself; I should have asked my godmother for a big needle with a poisoned tip, so I could jab my enemies in the bum. The thought of a needle brought to his mind a picture of his mother, Goodwife. And for the first time in a long while, the dwarf born from a flour bin felt a river of tears course down his face, threatening to turn his whole body into a glutinous, pasty mess.

Suddenly he felt a pair of fingers hook him around the waist and hoist him out of his sticky hiding place to plunk him down on the outstretched palm of a hairy hand. The first thing he did was dry his nose and cheeks with three swipes of his sleeve. Then he squinted at the sun. When at last he could see clearly, he was able to take in the whole scene: acrobats, clowns, caged lions, a bearded lady, music, balloons, and streamers of every colour. He had landed in the midst of a circus. Just what he'd been dreaming of all his life! Dreaming, too, of glory and conquests; of being the centre of attention for thousands of amazed onlookers. So why did he feel uneasy with all these eyes fixed on him? He didn't even dare to scratch the end of his nose, which had started to itch, or pull up the waistband of his trousers, which were sliding dangerously down his legs. All sorts of emotions were tearing at his guts and — what was worse — he suddenly felt a strong urge to . . . to do something, to get out of there, to get away from this crowd of curiosity seekers who were forming a circle around his captors, who in turn were announcing the marvel of the century. What's that? Where? He turned his head from side to side, but could see nothing but a sea of laughing, staring faces; fingers sticky with caramel poking at his sides; women in their Sunday clothes cootchie-cooing him under his chin. Shit! What kind of mess had he got himself into this time? And how was he to get away from the vigilant eye of his kidnapper, who was now raising him up above the heads of the crowd on the palm of his hand, as if he were some kind of Lilliputian king on his shield? Then the bandid-*cum*-barker began to draw the crowd's attention to his prize: "Ladies and gentlemen, a Talking Insect! Come and see! Come and see!"

"Come hear the tenor voice wrenched from the throat of the tiniest little beastie you ever saw! Come and see!"

Come and gawk all you like . . . but you'll wait till the cows come home before the little beastie gives you the time of day, you silly bunch of sheep!

"Go ahead, little fella, talk. Say hello to the nice lady!"

Cow-faced old bitch! You won't get a hello out of me, you can rest assured of that.

"Don't be afraid, speak to us in your own language, use your own words, say a sentence, say anything at all, we just want to hear the sound of your voice."

You'll hear the sound of my backside, so you will, you hoodlum!

The leader of the bandits decided that the farce had gone on long enough, and hurriedly began to pass the hat around; then, whisking Big-as-a-Fist up by the collar, he pinched his neck just hard enough to squeeze from his prey the words that the crowd had been waiting for:

"Let go of me, you lout! Help!"

His yelps delighted the crowd. They clapped so loudly that they scared a flock of pigeons into the air.

Pigeons? Hey! Where's my pigeon?

"Marco Polooo!" bawled the desperate dwarf.

The crowd was convulsed with laughter; they slapped their thighs and roared, "Encore!" To the sadistic pleasure of the brigands, who had finally discovered how to make their canary sing. We'll wring your neck for you, you little scamp, we'll make you spit nickels, we'll — Suddenly the crowd fell silent. A second went by, and then the spectators felt their feet begin to tap the ground to the rhythm of music from a tiny flute that somehow drowned out the brass horns and bass drums of the circus band. Everyone for three leagues around began to dance; under the big top, up on the stage, all along the trapezes, everyone danced. Even the four bandits danced, down on all fours, as they hunted for their unpredictable beastie — who had taken advantage of the brouhaha to make good his escape.

"We'll make him pay for this!" panted the bandit leader, trying to catch his breath.

"Don't count on it," chirped the dwarf, sticking his head out of his hiding-place under a pile of straw. Luckily for him, because he was just in time to duck the jaws of a hungry calf.

"Hey! Watch it!" he shouted at the beast, who froze and stared into his trough in bafflement.

When their eyes finally met, the dwarf and the calf exchanged a few words and then settled down into conversation. In such manner did our hero seek to increase his knowledge of the world's bizarre ways, even in the direst circumstances.

"Why did you come to the circus?" Big-as-a-Fist asked him.

"To be shown," replied the calf, backing up a few steps to give the dwarf a better view of his finer points.

"A five-legged calf!" whistled the dwarf. "Now I've seen everything!"

The calf tottered into a clumsy bow in response to his audience's whistle, which he took to be a sign of admiration.

"They come in droves to look at me," he mooed contentedly. "I'm the number-two attraction."

"Really?" said Big-as-a-Fist, pretending to be fascinated. "What's number one?"

The calf rolled his huge eyes in chagrin, then conceded:

"A two-headed pig," he said.

At that, Big-as-a-Fist laughed his first laugh of the day.

And so, while the crowd was clobbering the bandits, whom they accused of spiriting away the main attraction in the middle of the show, the main attraction was nice and cosy under a pile of straw, chatting away with the calf. Meanwhile the other three members of his troupe, as well as the pigeon, were elbowing their way through the surging sea of onlookers, questioning clowns, revellers, and children:

"Excuse me, but have you by any chance seen a little man about the size of your first wearing a red jacket and a hat with tiny bells on it?"

The children, clowns, and revellers searched through their memories, but came up empty until Extra-Day added:

"He plays the flute."

Ah, oh yes, the flute. The revellers remembered the dancing, as did the clowns and the children, who nodded their heads. But he'd disappeared.

"He can't have gone far," said Figure-Head. "Let's look around."

"We'll never find him, he's too small," moaned John-Bear, whereupon his youngest brother leapt up onto a stage and said:

"*He'll* find *us* if we climb up high enough."

And soon the crowd had gathered into a circle again, this time around a giant who was making a beautiful toddler disappear and reappear on his shoulders while a third tumbler, who called the turns, looked as if he'd just stepped out of a picture book from the days of yore.

"Gather round, ladies and gentlemen," cried Sir René. "Come see the biggest man on earth, and the world's most beautiful child . . . Let me tell you, my friends . . . We're here, on a stage in the shadow of the archway, John-Bear and Extra-Day, Marco Polo and me, Sir René . . . We're here, Big-as-a-Fist! . . ."

Alas, the desperate appeals of his older brother failed to shake Big-as-a-Fist out of the deep cogitation he'd fallen into on hearing about the agony and the ecstasy of a five-legged calf.

". . . all day long in the limelight," the freak-show star confided, "being ooohed and ahhhed at by slavering crowds — 'Oooh, I've never seen anything like that before'; 'Ahhh, what a rarity'; 'How unique' — five legs, imagine that, one leg extra, never mind that it's one leg too many, it's one of a kind, never been seen before, absolutely fantastic!" And to amuse himself, the calf would preen and strut before his court, in the warm sunshine, in the dust of the arena, suppressing at each lap his desire for food and water, his desire to boot his driver in the seat of his pants — in short, his desire. A five-legged calf shouldn't be prey to such base longings, no, my dearie me! The star of the circus! The number-two attraction, nearly number one, who in two short months had made his master rich and nearly doubled the sideshow's gate receipts. Oh, what a marvellous thing to have an extra leg!

"But at night," the calf sighed. "At night I come back here to my stall, alone and miserable, hobbling along on my useless leg."

He raised his eyes to meet those of his attentive friend. "I'm a monster!" he cried.

It was at this very instant that the dwarf heard his name trickling down the octaves from the mouth of Figure-Head. But before leaping from his pile of straw, he cast a compassionate look at the star of the circus, and called to him as he hurried off:

"Don't feel too bad, my friend. Tell yourself that maybe Mozart and Einstein were nothing more than warts on the brain."

Then he filed his new discovery away in his unconscious memory, along with the lesson of infinitely small and infinitely big, of upside down that's only upside down in relation to your point of view, and of perfection that's best seen from afar.

Circus lovers who thought they'd seen everything when they saw a five-legged calf dancing were now twitching with excitement around an arena where a battle not listed in any program was in full swing: Four identical brigands were fighting it out with four very curious opponents.

"*Olé!*" shouted the crowd, ecstatic at this free and unexpected attraction.

But just when John-Bear was about to grab his nearest adversary by the ankles and use him as a sledge hammer to pulverize the other three. Sir René stopped him in mid-swing with a terrified cry:

"John-Bear!"

The giant's arm froze in surprise, and for a moment the brigand hung poised over the others' heads. It was then that the three other comrades saw, on the face of their enemy, the cowl of the hangman.

"Let him go, John-Bear. This is not a battle to be fought in a circus."

It was a battle that had to be fought, but at the proper time and in the proper place.

"Friday the thirteenth," croaked one of the brigands. "At noon."

"In the shadow of the cypress trees," added his companion.

"In the churchyard," crowed the third, under the evil eye of the fourth, who said nothing.

Our four heroes looked at each other, their brows furrowed but their eyes dry. Then the ancestor cleared his throat and accepted the challenge on behalf of his brothers:

"Friday, then, in the churchyard."

10

How Lent fell in August, and larks rained from the sky during a week of three Thursdays

The churchyard! Finally, Big-as-a-Fist understood: The bandits had arranged to meet them in a cemetery! Well, they couldn't get away with that, not on your life! In the first place, why let our opponents have home ice? Wasn't it enough that they got to choose the day and the time? Noon on Friday the thirteenth! It wasn't exactly fair, was it? It put all the bad luck on their side.

"On both sides," corrected Figure-Head.

All right, both sides. But it left the choice up to them. Not that it was any surprise. It's well known that evil-doers of every age have manifested a taste for the perverted, the morbid, and the most lugubrious, macabre, and sombre of places . . .

"The meeting is fixed for noon, the time when the sun is at its zenith."

It just isn't fair, that's all. There are four of them . . .

"What about us?"

Four bandits, big and strong as lumberjacks, and they don't play straight, either, they're tricksters, they'd slit our throats as soon as look at us . . . we're walking right into their trap.

Out of breath as well as arguments, Big-as-a-Fist flopped down on the grass, then jumped up again like a jack-in-the-box; he had flung himself onto a bed of thistles. A bad omen . . . life sure had its ups and downs! If only Time would come and get it over with, take this damned Friday away in its sack. Who'd know the difference? Let it fly as fast as it could. Oh, how lovely life had been before . . . in the good old days . . . before the fatal meeting with those bandits, those hangmen, those Four Horsemen of the Apocalypse!

The dwarf began to count on his fingers the time left to him before the fateful encounter. It couldn't come quickly enough; he would breathe so much easier later, when this great fear of his was just a memory, remembering when nothing had happened yet, when he'd pushed so desperately against Time to finish him off, when he'd thought he'd be so relieved to see the light at the end of the tunnel . . . but the tunnel was still there, just up ahead, the dice had yet to be thrown, they hadn't got through the day yet . . .

"What's today?"

"Thursday," said John-Bear at once, overjoyed to show that he hadn't forgotten the days of the week.

Thursday!!!

This time, even Figure-Head was jolted. Thursday already? That didn't leave them much time to get in shape, to practise their martial arts. Four against four was fair. But when one of the combatants was a dwarf . . .? And as for the ancestor, he feared he had reached his prime fighting trim in his former life, and could hardly see himself entering the lists again at his age. That left John-Bear, of course. He was worth four all by himself. But John-Bear was unpredictable — what if he was hit by one of his old maxims? Even assuming that their opponents were big and fought dirty, the dwarf was right. Sir René had seen the cowl on the face of one of them. The hangman would be there on Friday, in the churchyard, they'd best have no illusions about that.

"There's precious little time left," concluded Figure-Head. "Let's get to work."

Extra-Day looked up. Precious little time? But we've got all the time in the world. Is it time you want? Nothing to it. Just tell me how much you want.

Big-as-a-Fist and Sir René watched flabbergasted as their

youngest brother juggled with time like a musician with his notes. And the same idea leapt into their heads:

"Give us time!" they exclaimed.

And that's how our heroes found themselves in a week of three Thursdays.

At 11:45 on Friday the thirteenth, the pigeon came to inform the four heroes that the four brigands were marching onto the field of combat in battle formation, armed to the teeth.

Whereupon Big-as-a-Fist begged his three brothers to excuse him; he had to get down from his lookout on the giant's hat to attend to a matter that would brook no delay.

"This isn't the time," said Figure-Head, who had been promoted to commander-in-chief of the band.

"I don't care what time it is," said Big-as-a-Fist, holding his stomach. "When you gotta go, you gotta go."

What with all the gabbing back and forth, the dwarf ended up doing half his business on the way to the woods, and arrived there in a lamentable state. "Shit, shit, and double shit!" he grumbled when he saw the condition of his trousers. He decided he'd better wash himself off in a stream he could hear gurgling close by, under some bushes. And that's how the battle began without him, at the stroke of noon.

It also started without Extra-Day, who had been sent back to the woods by his general to see what was keeping the dwarf. Sticking his nose into everything the way he did, the little devil was always running the risk of being gobbled up inadvertently by one of the forest creatures. Not to mention the ones who'd do it on purpose.

"Go on, little brother, go find the dwarf. And if he's too scared to fight, both of you stay back and hide in the crook of a tree, or in the shade of a weeping willow. We'll get along all right without you little ones."

The elder brother was just saying that to save face, making as if the battle that would soon be under way might just as well be fought between veterans like himself. From the first Thursday, Sir René had known that the outcome of the combat rested squarely on the shoulders of John-Bear.

He had, however, forgotten about one of his comrades, the one that — as a former humanist — he had a tendency to underestimate: the pigeon. Remember that Sir René's mind had been formed in some very ancient schools of thought, schools in which it was gravely doubted that animals had souls. He was consequently a long way from believing that a mere bird could be endowed with the virtue of a warrior. He was about to be disabused of that notion.

As soon as the pigeon had realized the fix his master, Big-as-a-Fist, was in, he had flown to the rescue in a rather unexpected way: he had gone to recruit reinforcements from the sky. He had remembered the formation of geese drawing its perfect V-for-Victory across the firmament, as well as the bad blood he had sensed between Mother Goose and the brigands. Certainly, in a combat like the one about to begin, it would be foolish to overlook the air force.

So the pigeon took off for the clouds to carry his message of war. And in less time than it took Big-as-a-Fist to wipe his bum, and Extra-Day to spot him in the stream he was using for a washbasin, Marco Polo had overtaken the migrating birds and conscripted a whole flight of geese, cranes, buzzards, woodcocks, spindleshanks, crows, cormorants, vultures, falcons, condors, eagles, and gyrs.

"To wing!" he cried to his company. "Let us fly to the aid of our troops!"

And without bothering their heads about the reasons for the combat, the great warriors of heaven gathered in force, circled above the field of battle, and, in a cacophony of war cries, dove into the fray.

Meanwhile Big-as-a-Fist and Extra-Day had succeeded in getting themselves straightened out and had rejoined Figure-Head at the rear of the battlefield.

"I think things are heating up at the front," ventured Tom Thumb, who had recovered from his fright as well as from his crapulous adventures. "Let's sit down over there so we can get a better view of the show."

Although he wasn't taking part in the fight himself, Big-as-a-Fist had never doubted the outcome, and placed his full confidence in his twin brother.

"Go to it, John-Bear, Strong-as-a-Dozen! Show 'em what you're made of!"

Telling himself that John-Bear was doing all right without help from his brothers, Sir René sat down on a heron's nest between the dwarf and the babe. From their front-and-centre seats, the three comrades watched the contest, shouting, holding their heads, sticking their fingers in their ears, covering their eyes, clapping their hands, slapping their thighs, and hollering like spectators at a wrestling match:

"Behind you! Behind you, John-Bear!"

"Hit him in the chops!"

"In the guts!"

"Bash his nose in!"

"Give him a left, give him a right, mix up your punches!"

"Look out! Duck!"

John-Bear ducked just in time to avoid getting an eagle beak in the eye. He raised his head and saw an army of raptors flying to the defence of the combatants. But which combatants? What side is Heaven on in a Holy War?

Big-as-a-Fist saw his brother hesitate. Good Lord, surely he's not choosing a time like this to ask himself those stupid questions about his rights! . . . the idiot could jeopardize the entire outcome of the battle with his strict conscience, and endanger his own life as well as those of his brothers! John-Bear! This is no time to reflect on the nature of Good and Evil! John, old buddy, fight! You can ask your questions later.

Sir René scratched his temples:

"Whose side are the birds on?"

Because they were filling the sky. Were they all on the same side? Who could tell in that whirlwind of wings, beaks, and claws? John-Bear regained his spirits and set about to massacre everything in sight. Dear God, don't leave him now!

Suddenly, Big-as-a-Fist caught his breath:

"Marco Polo! Marco Polo!"

The pigeon had just come into his master's field of vision.

"What's going on up there?"

But the messenger was no wiser than anyone else. He admitted that he'd gone off in search of reinforcements, thinking that he was helping out. But alas, to his own great shame, he was no longer in control of his troops. What had he started? It was a classic case of an emissary trying to run things by himself. He should have confined himself to his role as a messenger, and let sleeping dogs lie.

As if to rub salt into Marco Polo's wounded conscience, a falcon brushed the group of onlookers with his wingtips, and made them feel none too safe even in their position on the sidelines. Just above their heads a group of eagles was attacking some vultures, and the woodcocks were taunting the cranes. The whole battle was taking on the appearance of a conductorless orchestra descending into chaos.

Then suddenly, from a far-off church tower, the great tenor bell announced the twelfth stroke of noon. Big-as-a-Fist listened to the silence that ensued: the battle was over. What? So soon? It had lasted just long enough for the twelve strokes of the angelus to sound. So much carnage in so short a time? Or had time stopped altogether? Had it stretched to allow John-Bear to go to work?

"Let's go see!"

And Big-as-a-Fist jumped to his feet and ran onto the battlefield, where his giant brother stood panting, his mouth open and his eyes round, surveying the extent of the massacre: feathers, legs, and wings were strewn about the ground; a thick fog of feathers floated above the trenches; beneath it, between two weeping willows, three of the brigands lay bleeding and murmuring their last words:

"One for you, one for me . . . one for you, one for me . . ."

The litany of the dying thieves reminded Tom Thumb that this entire war had stemmed from a conflict of interest between the company of adventurers and the brigands over the possession of a chicken that laid golden eggs. And the thought of the chicken brought with it the realization that he'd come within a hair's breadth of spending the rest of his life in a circus hobbling about on five legs for the amusement of a populace fascinated by monstrosities.

"There's one missing," said Figure-Head, pulling a long face.

He had hardly finished his sentence when he received a clamorous response from the sky. A shower of larks fell on the heads and shoulders of our four heroes, who could no longer conceal their dismay. What new inundation was coming to hound them on this day that had already seen such extraordinary events?

The answer came from the carrier-pigeon, via the dwarf:

"When eagles do battle, the doves are the first to get skinned."

The poor little meadow birds, whose only ambition was to sing, had taken to the sky on their way back to their nests, and found themselves caught between a rock and a hard place!

And so it was that, in a week with three Thursdays in it, our heroes saw the sky raining larks.

Energy spent doing battle is a great causer of hunger. And the first to feel the pangs in his stomach was Big-as-a-Fist. Fortunately, there was no end of good things to eat amid the detritus in the field of honour. Unfortunately, the first to close in from all sides to claim the victory and the spoils of war were — as usual — the deserters, collaborators, and veterans of former conflicts. They made a joyous carnival of it that lasted for three days and left nothing in the churchyard but a pile of lark bones. When Sir René looked up to see what time of what day it was, he was answered by a fat man with chubby cheeks and grease running into his beard.

"Tuesday," he said. "Near midnight."

For a moment, our friends didn't understand where the time had gone. Then the penny dropped: only they had been living outside time-that-flows; for the rest of humanity, the three Thursdays had in fact been a Thursday, a Friday, and a Saturday. Add the three-day carnival, and the emaciated and lugubrious face of Ash Wednesday was snapping at their heels. No one had been robbed: having gorged themselves on the sky, they were all settling down for a month-long Lent.

"What month are we in?" Big-as-a-Fist asked without thinking, biting his thumb.

"Owgust," answered the ancestor, drawing out the diphthong.

"Ow, ow," repeated Big-as-a-Fist. He had just remembered that he'd made an appointment with the hangman for a date and a circumstance that, at the time, he had thought to be impossible.

And that's how Heaven rained larks in a week with three Thursdays, and made Lent fall in August.

The ancestor gathered his troops together and addressed them thus:

"My children, on this day we have won a glorious and decisive battle. But I fear that the worm is yet in the apple. A single warrior is missing from the enemy camp. We must be vigilant."

The three young heroes — perhaps a bit less young than they'd been the day before, but no less heroic — cast apprehensive eyes over the field of honour. And there, for the first time, the hangman's naked face appeared to them.

"There!" shouted Extra-Day, pointing towards a twisted, stunted cypress.

"Ow, ow!" cried Big-as-a-Fist, jamming his hat down over his eyes.

Only John-Bear didn't flinch. He wrung his hands together in anticipation and cracked his knuckles.

In a grave voice, Sir René ordered his younger brothers to stay put. This time he would meet the enemy alone, armed with only his prodigious memory. And under the worried eyes of his brothers, he added:

"I've been there before. And forewarned is forearmed."

"But Sir René, our dear friend . . . ," began Big-as-a-Fist.

"Peace, my children," replied the ancient, raising his hand in benediction. "Do not move from this place until I call for you. Let your minds be without fear, and your hearts remain untroubled. Attend my signal."

The three comrades held themselves in check as they watched their quadruple centenarian, who for the first half of their lives had been both father and guide to the joyous company, advance towards the cypress tree. Each wondered when he would ever see him again.

The next morning at daybreak, Sir René stepped out of the mist and, with a firm tread, approached the troupe.

"Sir René!"

"Figure-Head!"

"Our ancestor, our friend! We're here!"

This time, though, the reunited friends did not indulge in their usual joyful carousings. Instead, the elder brother spent the entire day briefing his brothers and comrades on the nuts and bolts of his meeting with the hangman:

"He knew that we had him beat, the devil — that his time had run out and you three had got through your first adventures without too much damage. He's withdrawn, broken by shame and deceit. There's nothing he can do now but crawl back into his lair, under that absurd village at the end of the vicious circle. You'll never see him again."

And to support his prophecy, the ancestor showed his amazed young companions a blood-soaked cowl slashed to ribbons like an old flag.

Big-as-a-Fist immediately wanted to order up a great feast to celebrate the victory, and was just raising his arms to call on Heaven for support when his eyes, following those of the ancestor, fell upon a black dot at the exact centre of the horizon.

"What's that?"

Sir René gathered his friends to his side and wrapped them in his huge cloak.

"The Grim Reaper," he said.

And our four heroes watched in silence as a woman in a cape larger than the wings of a condor harvested a field of ripe wheat with slow, steady, precise swings of her scythe.

11

From rain, cold weather, thunder, and wind, deliver us, O Lord

Our four comrades left the churchyard alive but still at odds with each other — walking paradoxes, dragging their heels with their insides out and their upsides down, as usual, content to get through life without hurrying to catch up to their old age.

In other words: situation normal.

All four of them felt comfortably settled in their souls, their bodies, and their emotions, and asked nothing more of the age they lived in than enough freedom to fool around as much as they wanted. So far, the age had seemed willing to be a good sport about it, and had offered them a thousand chances to get in on its secrets without their having to account for it the next day to God and his father.

Nothing had changed. Or almost nothing.

Here's how we find them: one sly little devil who answers — when he answers at all — to the name of Tom Thumb or Big-as-a-Fist; one loyal and courageous giant, Strong-as-a-Dozen; a wise old Figure-Head, descended straight from his own forebears but broken away from his lineage (although it continued on without him); and, to complete the happy quartet, the well-named Extra-Day, beautiful as a god, fresh as life itself, born between two times, at the very instant when the next instant had not yet emerged from the instant before it . . . four children of earth and of time-that-flows, with nothing salvaged from Paradise but their own Adam's apples. Nonetheless, they proudly pursue the quest and conquest of their destiny, naked under their togs, carrying nothing more threatening to the earth and her planets than two or three wishes each, distributed to them randomly in their respective cradles.

But their several gifts, taken together, have let them discover that the earth is not only round but also subdivided by parallel lines, longitudes and latitudes; that it turns on its axis at set times without ever getting its cardinal points tangled up; and that in all the time we've been scratching its surface, it hasn't given up half its secrets.

Our heroes, though battered and bruised from battle, were no less noble of soul, stout of heart, or firm in their resolve to let no stick be stuck into the spokes of their wheel of fortune, and no hangman come between their dreams and reality.

"Anyway, the hangman's dead," said Big-as-a-Fist, who was the most impatient to get back on the road to adventure. "A hangman without his mask is nothing."

And to show how thoroughly he'd demystified the impostor, he waved the shreds of tattered black cloth that had once been their enemy's cowl. John-Bear and Extra-Day mockingly saluted the symbol of their victory, while Sir René searched the horizon, his eyes full of apprehension.

"Nothing can stop us now," shouted the dwarf, "because the four of us are the strongest in the world."

And hopping up to perch on his brother's hat, he delivered a long diatribe on the length, width, and height of life, which must surely go on and on till they'd all had their fill of it, or at least until our heroes decided themselves to toss it out like a shapeless old sock.

"When we're finished with these old rags and bones," he yelled, astride John-Bear's ostrich feather, "we'll just dump them into the ditch."

He was all set to launch into the metaphysics of being and existence when a sudden change of wind took hold of him and spun him around so his face was buried in the fronds of the feather. When he'd extracted himself from the cyclone, he called to John-Bear to put him back on the ground. But before he regained his footing, his eye was caught by the huge open cape of the Grim Reaper in the middle of the wheat field . . . "Who says the floozie will some day cut the grass out from under our feet?" he muttered between his teeth, for the pleasure of saying it and, even more, to give himself courage.

Sir René knit his brow.

"Stand up straight and don't move your feet," he said, in a voice that left no doubt in his comrades' minds about the gravity of the situation. "I know that creature. Her name is Mad Meg."

John-Bear and Extra-Day breathed more easily: Meg was a pretty name. And a danger you can put a name to doesn't seem so dangerous; just as a mystery is less mystifying when you can call it by its proper name. Big-as-a-Fist followed his brothers' reasoning, but was less reassured: he knew about the strength of words and their power to destroy. They don't call someone Mad Meg for nothing . . .

"In my day," continued the ancestor, unaware of the deep furrows his words were ploughing through the collective unconscious of his troupe, "she was also called Dulle Griet, and appeared in a lot of paintings and came into all our legends. Usually at the wrong time. Our artists and writers should have known that sooner or later she'd escape from the walls and books and picture frames. And here she is, roaming the earth like an insane thing, sowing scourges by the handful."

The three others were struck dumb by the ancestor's story. Then, just to be able to say something. Extra-Day made a suggestion:

"Let's send the pigeon over to ask her what she's looking for."

"Or if she needs our help," added John-the-Strong.

"Or if she wants my boot up her arse," said Big-as-a-Fist, going his brothers one better; he wasn't running much of a risk, having already measured the distance between his foot and the intruder's backside.

"Come closer, stand shoulder to shoulder," said the ancestor to his young adventurers, "and swear that you will never abandon any of your comrades in distress, no matter what comes; that you will always come to one another's aid, whatever the circumstances; that you will press on regardless of the cost, no matter how rough the road or stormy the sea, under broiling sun or driving rain, rested or weary unto death, forever and wherever, and come to one another's defence — swear this!"

"We so swear!"

Then Big-as-a-Fist raised his arm to Heaven, and called it to witness:

"And we swear to come to Marco Polo's aid too, and even to let ourselves be saved by him, if it comes to that."

The four heroes held out their hands to their fifth companion, who responded with a yellowish, gooey oath of his own that landed on Sir René's collar. It was the pigeon's way of wishing them luck.

And suddenly the world seemed far too young, life far too large, and the appetites of our heroes far too vast for any one woman named Meg — mad or not — to ease her way into it like a worm into an apple. Let earth carry them happily on its course to the very heart of the gallery of stars!

Except that, that night, no stars appeared in the sky. Bah! So we'll wait until tomorrow night. But there were no stars the next night, either. Nor the third. An empty sky. Or a sky too full. According to Sir René, who had studied a bit of astronomy in his time, the sky never seemed so empty as when it was full.

"The rebel angels are chasing the stars from the heavens," he said. "We'd better prepare for bad weather."

Hardly had he finished his sentence when a torrential downpour started, soaking them to the skin. The gods had opened the floodgates, and the ensuing deluge immobilized the troupe from its first drops, which were as big as cherry pits. It reminded them of their adventure in the clouds, back when they were youngsters, when they'd studied a rainstorm from above and inside. But it's another thing to find yourself beneath it, and to have it pelting down on your head.

Figure-Head was afraid the freezing temperature would change the rain to ice, and turn him back into a crystal statue. Extra-Day, who was playing marbles with the raindrops, watched them turn suddenly into jacks. As for John-Bear, he was terrified that the water would rot his bark and cover him with thick, mouldy-smelling moss. When you're made of wood, he told himself . . . but he didn't have time to finish his sentence before the words stuck in his throat.

Remembering his own beginnings had reminded him of those of his doughboy brother. Good God, what a mess he must be in today! If this rain was strong enough to rot an oak, what would it do to a dinner roll? And forgetting his bark, John-Bear smashed the sound barrier into a thousand pieces, and began searching through the rubble for signs of his little brother.

"Big-as-a-Fist! Big-as-a-Fist! Answer me!"

No luck.

"It's me, John-Bear, your brother. Where are you?"

Oh, my poor brother!

"Tom Thumb! Thumbkin! Big-as-a-Fist, you little devil. Come back!"

The little devil would have liked nothing better. But how to manage it? His brother's words would barely stick to the soggy surface of his eardrums. His ears were nothing more than a pair of shapeless, perforated sponges. His stomach and chest were reduced to a soft and sticky paste. Don't let your limbs become detached from your body, he told himself; most important. And don't lose face. Keep your head on your shoulders. What a disaster! It looked as if his whole body was changing shape; by morning he might turn into a crab, or a scorpion . . . "What's happening to me?" he asked himself in a thickened voice, just before his jaws stuck together and were sealed behind cracked lips. "My God! My God!" he thought from the bottom of his brain — which, curiously, had been unaffected by the rain. If only I could . . . he said, scratching his temple. His finger, however, passed right through — there was no temple there — can the mind keep its own identity and follow its own course, intact and unchanged, in a metamorphosing body? The word metamorphosis gave him back some hope: if he could keep his identity, the being that was called Big-as-a-Fist and spoke in the first person singular, what difference did it make what body it inhabited? Who knew? Maybe he would come out of this a bigger person. What was to stop him from emerging from the deluge in a new and splendid transfiguration? And he yelled to Heaven not to hold back when remaking him . . . don't spare the yeast; make the crust nice and flaky, a little more golden if that's not asking too much; and while you're at it, why not put a better brand of oil in my joints, a little more marrow in my bones? And a drop or two of blue blood in my veins — why not? We're not metamorphosed every day, you know.

While the dwarf was trying to emerge victorious from this, the greatest adventure of his life, his brothers were searching through the tiniest folds and niches of time to rescue their unfortunate comrade. They beat the bushes; they waded through swamps; they diverted streambeds and tried desperately to mop up the glass-like sky.

In the end it was the sun, coming out for its midday housecleaning, who chased away the last tatters of clouds. On every side they could see the blades of grass standing up again, hear the water chuckling in the ditches, watch flowers dancing that only a moment before had seemed quite dead. And there, sitting smack dab in the middle of Indian summer, was Big-as-a-Fist, trying to get a deep golden tan on his new crust.

"It's him!" cried Extra-Day, who recognized his brother by his piercing eyes.

"Big-as-a-Fist!" exclaimed the others, rushing up to throw their arms around his neck.

Since it's not easy for a giant to embrace a dwarf without smothering him, John-Bear merely lifted him at arm's length and . . .

"Is it really you, Big-as-a-Fist?"

"My, how you've changed!"

"What has life done to you?"

"How do you like your new skin?"

"I'd say you've grown a bit."

"At least put on some weight."

"And your beard is a bit heavier; you've got more peach fuzz under your nose."

"Your shoulders have filled out; your muscles have firmed up."

"And your dough has thickened, your crust is darker."

Finally, John-Bear gave an admiring whistle: "If only your father could see you now!"

Goodman is a good ways away from here, thought Big-as-a-Fist, who for the moment had no intention whatsoever of going off in search of his father. A whole new life in a whole new body was awaiting him. He'd learned an important lesson: the flood had not metamorphosed him into a crab or a scorpion, but had merely thinned out his dough, hardened his crust, and gently brainwashed him. He felt like a new man.

"All right!" he said. "Bring on the Mad Megs! I'll turn them inside out and show the world their rotten linings. Let her come, this Dulle Griet!"

She came.

And when she did, the first to stare at her with his mouth gaping open and his arms hanging limp was our hero, Big-as-a-Fist. For this time he was seeing her up close. She was standing at the top of the hill, and he and his brothers could see the huge skirts of her coat flapping in the wind.

"*Exeunt*," said Sir René in his hoarsest whisper. "Let us seek refuge far from these haunts."

So they hurried off to the east, towards the land of the rising sun. But had they been led astray? The next day, the sun rose later than usual; the day after that, it didn't rise at all. The Far North's endless night had chewed away at the edge of the previous day. Everything around them was black.

"But the fields are white!" exclaimed Extra-Day, who had never seen winter before.

This babe, born Out-of-Time, was destined to live his first year over and over again; every winter he would see his first snowfall; every spring his first wildflowers. His past and his future were bunched together in a present that never ended. He was rediscovering the world at every instant.

"They're all white," he said. "White as snow!"

"But it *is* snow, silly!"

And Big-as-a-Fist, remembering how in their youth he and his brother had pelted each other with snowballs and wondered, each spring, if the next winter would see the end of their childhood games, threw a huge handful of snow down his youngest brother's neck, just to keep him in line.

"Let us not tarry in this frozen place," said Sir René. "We must find the road south. No time to lose — I feel my limbs becoming numb already."

"South is that way."

"That way? Are you sure?

In reality, there no longer was any south; winter has no south, as our heroes should surely have known by then . . . We may as well do as the trees and the bears do, thought Big-as-a-Fist: hibernate, let time take us out of here. That way we can escape winter without moving a step, and come out refreshed and heartened in the spring.

But Sir René shivered at the idea of spending an entire winter without moving. How long does the season last? Wouldn't that be tempting the gods . . . or tempting the Devil? . . . Rouse yourselves . . . my brothers . . . don't . . . let yourselves . . . go . . . to sleep . . .

"Blizzard coming!" called Marco Polo, who had come back to warn them. "Shut your mouth!"

Big-as-a-Fist knew what he meant: breathe through our noses, don't let the cold pour into our lungs; keep our heads down, our eyes to the ground, our legs bent; from time to time rub our cheeks and ears; and keep moving our feet. Big-as-a-Fist was an old hand at winter, like his brother John-Bear. Not the ancestor, though — he came from the Old World. The others could hear him snoring already, and his limbs were encased in a heavy coat of ice.

"Wake him up!" cried the dwarf. "Breathe on him, John-Bear."

And for the second time in their brief acquaintance, the giant put his nostrils and lungs to work on the frozen body of his friend . . . Figure-Head, my father, my dear brother, Sir René, come back, wake up, without you we are children, lost . . . while the dwarf and his little brother rubbed his lips and eyelids, all the while whispering tender words full of the tears that ran like bitter pills down their cheeks.

Suddenly the pigeon, who had been flying back and forth between winter and spring, came down to warn his masters that the honkers were on their way back. Extra-Day dropped his arms; Big-as-a-Fist dropped to the ground. "Just in time!" sighed the troupe, at the end of their rope as well as their breath. Except for John-Bear, who, still hung up on his maxims, was finishing the job he'd started. He continued to huff and puff long after his frozen friend had thawed out and returned to life. It was the principle of the thing; if you had stick-to-it-iveness, something good was bound to come out of it. In the end, though, Big-as-a-Fist had almost as much trouble reviving John-Bear as the giant had had reviving Figure-Head.

When Sir René finally opened his eyes, he looked around the company and said, in an accent they'd never heard him use before:

"Okay then, eh? Guess I had my forty winks. Feels pretty good, too. Hey, you wouldn't have a crumb or two at the bottom of your kit bags, would you? Something to perk up an old campaigner who's dying of hunger?"

The three young campaigners stared wide-eyed at this new Sir René, who was suddenly ten years — no, ten decades — younger, almost their own age.

"Well, our René is renewed," stammered Big-as-a-Fist, casting about for some way to regain his equilibrium.

Just then, the geese flew overhead in V-formation, filling the air with their honnnk . . . honnnk . . . !

"Spring is here!" shouted the dwarf, clapping his hands and stomping his feet. "That'll teach old Meg that her stormy blasts can't hurt us a bit!"

The ancestor had regained his lost youth, but had lost none of his ancient wisdom. If he'd known ahead of time what the dwarf was going to say, he'd have sewn his lips shut. But the unforeseeable is unpreventable, as Sir René remembered too late.

No sooner did Mad Meg hear her name called than she appeared at the edge of the woods. The dwarf even thought he heard her shout something, but it was in a language he didn't understand. What did she want this time? he wondered. Why couldn't she leave them alone?

"What did we ever do to her, the beggar!"

Sir René was about to reply to the nitwit that they'd called her by her name, that's what "they" had done to her, and they'd have been better off not to have done it. But seeing how disturbed the dwarf was, he simmered down:

"Let's keep quiet, don't even speak to her. Some dogs are best left sleeping."

But it was too late. Once the ball gets rolling . . . She had started throwing insults at them in their own language. The dwarf thought be heard her call his brother a big lummox. Well, he wasn't going to stand for anyone but himself calling his friends names!

"I dare you to repeat what you just said!" he shouted, challenging Mad Meg to a duel of words.

Of course, she took up the challenge — to the great dismay of the dwarf's three companions, who realized that the cards were now on the table and there was no turning back from —

"Lightning bolts!" cried the babe. "Look out!"

Streaks of lightning shot out from under her huge black coat, striking trees, fence posts, the peaks of distant barns; a single flash sliced in two a wild apple tree standing alone at the centre of a field. Soon the sky was filled with zigzags of fire lighting up the clouds, tearing great rumblings of thunder from them, and illuminating the faces of our four panic-stricken heroes.

Big-as-a-Fist thought of the storms of his youth, which had always stuck the lightning rods his father had put up on the roof of the henhouse, and invariably killed two or three chickens just to remind Squire Goodman that nothing was safe from the wrath of Heaven. But those storms had been mere tempests in teapots compared to the tumult going on around him now, and the dwarf was at a loss to know where he could hide his brand-new skin. Having emerged from last autumn's rains with a toughened exterior, he now felt obliged to put on a calm, courageous face — but it fooled no one, least of all his brother John, who'd known him since he was little more than a ladleful of dough.

"Hop into the bottom of my pocket," he shouted.

Then the giant invited the others to come in under his sleeves. He would shelter them from the storm.

His brothers were about to protest, if only to save face, when an extra-loud clap of thunder sent the three of them diving head first into their respective hiding places.

"Don't move," said John-the-Strong. "This time, Mad Meg is going to deal with me."

And so the battle got under way.

It was a defensive battle for John-Bear, who soon understood that the odds were against him, that even a giant can meet his match. After all, lightning had felled oak trees bigger than he was. All he could hope to do was to gain time and shield his companions. Without him they'd have been ashes already. Hold on for as long as possible, long enough to let the storm blow itself out, let the lightning move on . . . hold hard . . . withstand these bolts of fire . . . burn right down to your bones, which are cracking up and down your spine . . . as long as your heart holds out, heart of oak, son of a simple carpenter who didn't make you immortal, but brought you into the world to combat evil and to help others . . . who gave you courage and loyalty when he gave you life . . . to the end . . . for another minute, John-Bear . . . think of your friends, of your brothers, think what will happen to them if your trunk splits down the middle . . .

But split it did, taking the three astounded comrades down with it, stunned by the blow. They poked their heads out of the giant's pocket and from under his large sleeves, and tried to measure the extent of the damage. That was when they saw the lifeless corpse of their brother, the biggest of them all, the only one worthy of the name John-Bear, Strong-as-a-Dozen, the one who had sacrificed his own gigantic body so that they could live.

Big-as-a-Fist felt for a pulse, but there was none. His own breath stuck in his throat. He opened his eyes wide, his mouth, his nostrils, but nothing came out. There was no air left in his lungs, no blood left in his veins, no idea left in his head. Nothing but visions dancing before his eyes, of little laughing devils who called out to him: Your brother's dead, your brother's dead! Do you want us to bring him back to life? . . . It was at that moment, precisely at that moment, that Big-as-a-Fist understood what it meant to sell his soul to the Devil.

We'll never know whether he would have sold it or not, because just as Big-as-a-Fist began debating the issue within himself, trying once more to please God and his father both, John-Bear began to stir.

It was Extra-Day who saw it first.

"He opened his eyes," he cried out. "He's smiling. He's trying to talk."

And the three comrades observed a religious silence, ready to pluck from the lips of the resurrected one the first words brought back from the bowels of hell.

"I'm hot," he said.

That was it. He stared in amazement at the sun, to which he'd thought he'd said his last goodbye. His brothers had to help him; they pinched him and finally tickled him to bring him back to the land of the living.

"Cleanse your memory of dust from the far side of the grave," said Sir René, who had yet to recover from the shock of the miracle. "Remember that you were only gone for an instant, during the infernal storm sent to us from the cloak of Dulle Griet, on market day, Monday morning."

Marco Polo halted at the peak of his flight and, diving down to the ancestor's helmet, told him in his own pigeon language that it was still Sunday. Instead of translating such an absurd statement for his brothers, Big-as-a-Fist began to argue:

"Go away, featherbrain. Get serious. Yesterday was Sunday, so it has to be Monday today."

"That may be logical," replied the pigeon, "but all the same, it isn't so."

The dwarf and the ancestor scratched their heads: a pigeon who'd abandoned logic for metaphysics! And what was more, he could be right. For just at that moment they heard bells ringing from a distant cathedral, calling the faithful to mass. But if today was Sunday, then it couldn't yet be Monday. And if it wasn't Monday, then the storm hadn't happened yet. And John-Bear hadn't been killed by lightning. And . . . that must be why he was still alive.

Instinctively, Big-as-a-Fist raised his eyes to look into those of Figure-Head . . . who had turned to look at Extra-Day . . . who, with a distracted air, was plucking the petals off a daisy. Only John-Bear seemed unimpressed. One of his brothers had made time roll backwards for him? Thanks, kid, I owe you one. The giant had forgotten that he himself had saved the lives of the other three.

"Let's take a minute," he said to his comrades, "to give thanks to the creator of heaven and earth, this Sunday, for having given us a week with eight days. Let's use the eighth to show our gratitude."

The three brothers exchanged meaningful looks: the lightning might not have wounded his body, but it sure had affected his mind.

This time Sir René got the jump on the garrulous dwarf, and imposed silence on him before he could comment further on the ways of Mad Meg — the small troupe might have thwarted her dirty tricks this time, but there was no point in tempting fate: no place on earth was safe from her scourges.

Big-as-a-Fist understood — you can save your breath, you old dotard — and he'd keep quiet, he'd keep his mouth shut, he wouldn't even drop a hint to you-know-who . . . or anyone else, for that matter . . . that it was the baby who'd beaten her out, a newborn, an out-of-time born, and extra-day born . . . that it was the little innocent, with his air of having come from nothing and nowhere, who had got the better of —

"There she is!"

What the — But that wasn't fair! He hadn't done anything this time, he hadn't called her by her name, or done anything to provoke her.

"It looks as though we'll have to hunt her down for good, the she-devil!"

And to emphasize his words, and to indulge his taste for redundancy, he added:

"For good and for once and for all."

Extra-Day placed a hand on the dwarf's trembling shoulder and said:

"It's my fault she's come back. She hasn't forgiven me for that eighth day."

Sir René moved towards the group, hoping that together they could foretell the direction of the next attack. But before he could even form the word with his mouth, the cyclone hit.

"The witch . . . !"

It was the wind-witch, as she'd been called in his day. Mad Meg had waved her arms, longer than the branches of a willow, and the wind-witch had rushed out of the Madwoman's cloak. The air swirled around the little troupe, which was clinging as well as it could to John-Bear's braces. Except for the dwarf: Not wanting to miss a show that promised to be as grand as it was horrific, he was climbing as high as he could get, and ended up hanging onto the feather in his brother's huge hat. For once he was not afraid, certain now that the Madwoman was not out to get him personally, at least not today. Today . . . the dwarf gave himself a swift kick for not having understood until now. She was after Extra-Day! From his perch on the ostrich feather, he tried to send his tiny voice piercing the wind coming from the west-northwest-by-north-northeast-by-east-southeast-by-south-southwest, to reach the ears of Figure-Head, who was hanging onto the end of John-Bear's swordbelt. The question and its answer crossed paths at the giant's shoulder:

"— Extra-Day — ?"

"— disappeared!"

As they might have expected, the winds had carried him off. Only winds working overtime could get the better of a child born out of time.

"Where is he? Marco Polo, my friend, my brother. Find out where he is. I'll take care of the rest."

Easier said than done. He had no idea how to go about it. But identifying the problem is half the solution, the dwarf told himself. If he could just figure out which of the twelve air currents had done it . . . but his shouts never reached the pigeon, who was also being tossed about by the wild, gale-force winds. Their salvation was in their size: the dwarf and the bird were such small targets that, caught as they were in the eye of the storm, the tempest could only buffet them back and forth and up and down — though it made them both more seasick than they'd ever been in their lives.

Just as he was waving about in mid-air at the end of his feather, about to heave up half his guts, the dwarf came face to face with a face that looked equally surprised to see his.

"What's this? A weathercock?"

The weathercock, surprised at being called by name, did a double take and spun away, and could barely get back into position. Big-as-a-Fist was watching it gyrate back and forth, trying to find its way between the whirling winds, when a small light came on in his brain. It was a bit bigger than a pigeon, and no doubt a lot faster; but then, the dwarf himself had come out of the flood with a steadier hand and a firmer voice.

"Come here!" he commanded in a tone that brooked no opposition.

But the weathercock was made out of wood and had no ears for Big-as-a-Fist's music. It regained control of itself and turned its face to the wind, its only master.

"Hey! Hey!" cried Big-as-a-Fist, chopfallen and chagrined. He might have the gift of directing the wills of living creatures, but over those made of wood he had no power at all. And once again, despite the peril of his situation, he filed this new bit of information away in the deeper regions of his brain.

When he opened the door of his memory, however, he was presented with an image of his father, Goodman, hunched over his carpenter's workbench, knowing just how to coax an infant out of a chunk of oak. Trees are living creatures, too, his father had said when Big-as-a-Fist was pondering the imponderable origins of life. And from father to son to weathercock, the dwarf now recalled his first pony ride — on the back of a weathervane on the peak of his father's workshop roof. The old man had shouted and cursed his mother, Goodwife, for bringing such a brainless booby into the world.

Though he didn't quite remember how he'd managed to climb on the back of the weathercock to play, he now repeated the same motions in earnest: this time he was coming to the aid of his brother in his hour of need. Before he knew what he was about, he found himself astride the weathercock, high up in the air, at the centre of a tornado.

From down below, Figure-Head and John-Bear could hear him yelling, "Hyah, hyah, giddyup!" and could see the weathercock turning left, right, all the way around, against the winds that spun and tied themselves in knots and ended up losing all sense of direction. In the face of this stampeding whirligig, Big-as-a-Fist suddenly felt the full extent of his new power. And as usual, it went to his head.

"Whoa, big fella! Hard a-port! Full astern! Steady as she goes, sou'-by-sou'west! Let the blasted winds whip themselves to a frenzy, let 'em twist each other up like corkscrews!"

The nitwit would have gone on like that all day, enjoying chaos at the expense of order, riding on the crest of nature. But when he cast a quick glance down at the ground, he saw only two of his companions there, and remembered what had happened to the third. Holy jumpin', he said to himself, Extra-Day is caught in the belly of the whirlwind! And throwing his arms around his steed's neck, he commanded it to stop fooling around and tell those winds to settle down and give up their prisoner. The weathercock, exhausted anyway, was secretly grateful for the excuse to take a breather. It pulled up, stopping all the winds dead in their tracks.

Amazed, ancestor and giant watched as the tatters of the sou'easterlies and the shards of the nor'westerlies floated in the still air for an instant, like the skins of burst balloons, then dropped lifeless to the ground at their feet. The sky became calm and steady again, not a single whisper stirred the air, the final breath of breeze sputtered and died like a spent candle. As it fled to more clement climes, a young zephyr dropped Extra-Day from under one of its wings. The child was astonished at having gone through the most perilous adventure of his life and come out of it alive.

"I never thought weather could turn into a plague," he said when he had regained his breath. "A cruel, greedy monster that tried to swallow me up whole . . . For a minute there, I truly believed Miss Meg wanted to take me away from my brothers, to sweep me across the skies and wipe me out."

The ancestor caressed the still-wet neck of the child, who had just had his first big fright.

"You got out of it without a scratch, and without a furrow in your brow. It's all over now."

Over. The hero of the day — who was none other than Tom Thumb the dwarf, also called Big-as-a-Fist — could now leap off his weathercock and rejoin his companions on the ground. They were getting ready to throw him a party at least as big as his ambitions. But when he took his foot out of the stirrup and started to come down to earth, he glanced down to measure the distance between his aerial horsing around and terra firma. And his head started spinning. His brothers climbed up onto one another's shoulders and created the tallest human Tower of Babel that ever tempted the gods, in order to pluck Big-as-a-Fist down from his skyhook. Upon which, after distinguishing himself by saving his brother's life, he disgraced himself in his own pants.

That night, there was a red sunset.

"It's going to be a lovely day tomorrow," forecast Extra-Day. After his victory in the heavens, he had been dubbed the company's official weatherman.

12

From the miseries of war, deliver us, O Lord

The wild geese had been fighting with the swallows for the glory of announcing the arrival of spring, but in the end the honour fell to the buds, who looked up and laughed in the sun's face. The sun had risen in a good mood, though, and didn't mind it a bit. Extra-Day had been right when he said it was going to be a lovely day. And the fact that Dulle Griet had been driven out of our heroes' lives, leaving the high road to adventure wide open before them, made it even lovelier.

They had triumphed over the various calamities Mad Meg had strewn in their path, but it had been a costly victory. From her vast apron-front she had drawn her arsenal of rain, freezing cold, lightning, and strong winds, with the murderous intent of crushing anyone who stood in her way.

"And why?" complained Big-as-a-Fist. "What in the name of God did we ever do to make Nature turn on us like that?"

The ancestor, listening to his younger brother arguing with himself, thought of his own past torments and experiences. Mad Meg had been harrying adventurers who dared to cross her path since time immemorial.

"She has filled her apron pockets and her cape with all sorts of natural disasters, and has taken it upon herself to sow them around the world. You understand, my friends, that the first to get in her way is the first to be knocked down, and that she remembers who that person was!"

Plucking such sombre wisdom from the lips of their elder brother, the three heroes had trouble swallowing the lumps in their throats. Little by little, though, they rallied, John-Bear raising the standard of his courage and the others taking refuge under it.

"Take heart," continued Sir René, conscious of his role as mentor and instructor to his younger brothers. "The sower of scourges never strikes twice in the same place. After yesterday, she knows that none of her weather weapons can touch us. On that point, we can rest easy."

But when his three brothers were all set to celebrate their victory over Dulle Griet, the more cautious Figure-Head poured cold water over their inflamed spirits. It wasn't a final victory, not by any means. There were worse weapons in the world than bad weather. "The abysses of the human heart are far deeper than the gyres of cyclones or the craters of volcanoes," he said, his voice resonating with four hundred years of experience.

"So what you're saying is . . . ," began Big-as-a-Fist, incapable of finishing a thought that might come to a bad end.

"I'm saying," continued Sir René, "that the world will always be a stage for violent and bloody games, and that no player can hope to cross it without running the risk of falling through one or another of its trap doors."

John-Bear and Extra-Day received their older brother's words with respect, but Big-as-a-Fist continued his interior debate between illusion and reality, trying to find in the thread of the argument the Madwoman's Achilles heel. One solution, of course, would be to retrace their steps, to go back to their parents' house where the soup was always hot on the stove and the mattresses always soft; another, perhaps better, idea was to stay where they were, camp at the edge of the world, and keep out of the way of the ogress.

"There's really no need to press on," he said suddenly, glancing at his companions from the corner of his eye. "There's no guarantee that we'll find a better climate anywhere else, with more ripe grain in the fields. What I suggest is . . ."

But his suggestion died on his lips, for his companions knew him well enough to know who'd be the first on his feet as soon as the bells pealed in the next village, or the village after that. No one guessed, though, that the call would come from a foghorn in a lighthouse perched on the very border of the sea.

The little troupe rarely rose before dawn — except for the chief, of course, the captain, God's second-in-command, a fellow by the name of Big-as-a-Fist who'd anointed himself with supreme authority. Besides him, no one knew of his kingly role; he never lorded it over his subjects, and a good thing, too, since he was smaller than the smallest of them. To such a Jesuitical observation he would have replied with a whole rosary of howevers, neverthelesses, on the other hands, that depends ons, in my opinions, and all in good times! The morning he came nose to nose with the floating islands, however, he didn't have time to reply to anyone, or to trip himself up on his own conjunctions, and had to content himself with a resounding *huh!* (Being Big-as-a-Fist, he couldn't have settled for a simple hmmm; with such a tiny throat he had to force out the maximum sound if he wanted to make himself heard at all.) Which is why, when he wanted to wake up his comrades, he would shout, "Shut up! Quiet!" at the top of his voice.

Saying that Big-as-a-Fist came nose to nose with the floating islands is just a figure of speech, of course, like saying that the ship of state sails above the clouds. Because when you have a nose as small as that of Thumbkin, it's at least as difficult to bump into an island with it as it is for any ship of state that I know of to sail higher than its accustomed level. Or for the hand of man to set foot in the virgin forest.

"Silence!" he shouted until he was hoarse, all the while whacking the daylights out of his companions. "Get out of your featherbeds, and try not to draw too much attention to yourselves."

In the first place, his comrades hadn't felt a featherbed since they'd left home, and considered themselves lucky if they could find a spot that would keep the dew off them in the morning. In the second place, though they looked all about, they couldn't for the life of them see whose attention it was they weren't supposed to be drawing. There wasn't a living soul between themselves and the four horizons. The only things they could see were a few soggy patches of earth floating on the water just off shore, which under normal circumstances would have been called islands. These, however, distinguished themselves by a certain tendency to undulate, making them think more of oil slicks than of islands.

"Those two islands weren't there last night," said Big-as-a-Fist, squinting until his eyes completely disappeared between his cheeks and his forehead. "And if you ask me, I'd say islands that go to the trouble of moving about at night aren't sleeping with a clear conscience."

John-Bear and Extra-Day were still rubbing the sleep out of their eyes, and Figure-Head was racking his prodigious memory for previous examples of such phenomena, when Big-as-a-Fist, perched on the highest branch of the tallest poplar, announced that the two large islands were surrounded by a whole fleet of lesser islets, floating subordinate satellites, and that all the land was inhabited. He could see rooftops, a lighthouse, a forest of masts, and a crowd of people moving about.

Suddenly, Sir René slapped his forehead with the palm of his hand: "Atlantis!" he cried. "Bits of the Lost Continent broken off from Europe, floating and wandering about the oceans. Tatters of an ancient world run aground on the new!"

While the ancestor philosophized on the fate of civilizations made playthings of the gods, John-Bear had already taken to the water. He splashed about, made some headway, beat the foam with his arms. If those small errant islands with their jagged coastlines harboured a people of noble sentiment, they might have need of him; if not, his friends and brothers would surely need him. And he cleft the pliant waves with his mighty arms.

Big-as-a-Fist called him back as loudly as he could: "John-

Bear! Be careful! You never can tell! We don't know where those floating lands came from or where they've been. Since they're floating, that suggests they've been cut adrift. But from what continent? And why? How do we know their intentions are honourable? And besides, it's never a good idea to go sticking your nose into other people's business. Come back, John-Bear!"

Under cover of the dwarf's protestations, Sir René continued his learned rumination: "The Atlantans, if any of them survived the cataclysm, would be little more than remnants of a more primitive, barbarous time — stuck in the ditch, as it were, beside the highway of evolution." And the son of Jacques, son of Charles, son of Charles, son of Oliver shook his head sadly in the direction of the escapees from antiquity — forgetting that he himself had just leapt across four centuries of history.

But Sir René was wrong. Before long, the troupe would learn that the floating islands had not been set adrift from the Pillars of Hercules, and did not bear a population of Atlantans drifting at the mercy of the waves. In the end, the troupe would learn the truth; and they would come within a cat's whisker of not living to regret it.

The three comrades left behind on the shore shouted themselves hoarse trying to get John-Bear to turn around, but the giant could be deaf as a doornail when it suited his purpose. As soon as he'd set eyes on the floating mass, he'd judged it to be bigger than he was and had known that sooner or later he'd have to come to terms with it. For the frothing, swirling currents around their edges suggested that the islands were not entirely peaceful. Now kicking, now doing the crawl, now floating on his back, he finally arrived at the nearest island, situated more or less halfway between an island to the north and another to the south. When he let his feet touch bottom, he became lost to his friends' view.

Big-as-a-Fist was running up and down the beach, raising himself up on his tiptoes, climbing up onto rocks and hummocks, hopping down to get closer to the shore, using his hands to shade his eyes or to make a megaphone for his mouth, or just jamming them in his pockets, then running up and down the beach again . . . and then, damn!

"She's there!"

Mad Meg, crazy as ever, shaking out her apron and cloak to the four winds and jeering at the little troupe gathered anxiously around the ancestor.

"That she is showing herself so openly," said the latter, "does not bode well for this coast. Let us not shift from this spot, my children, but pray to Heaven to save our dear brother and friend, John-Bear."

Big-as-a-Fist didn't budge, but he felt his heart pounding against his ribcage, his bronchial tubes, his esophagus, and his windpipe.

Hurry, Tom Thumb, scratch your head, rummage through that noggin of yours, find something. Some way to warn your brother that the Madwoman is at his heels. Some way to get a message . . . Marco Polo!

"Marco Polo, my pet, my comrade, go over to the island, the small one between the two big ones, where our luckless, beloved John has just climbed ashore. Find him for me, tell him that Mad Meg has come back. He'll understand."

"He'll understand what?" asked the pigeon, for this was not his first diplomatic mission. "Do I summon him to return in the name of his sworn fidelity, or because of the peril threatening his comrades left here alone on the shore?"

The dwarf realized that his servant had gone to a good school, and was even beginning to follow in the footsteps of his master.

"Bring him back in the name of everything he holds most sacred," he said.

What John-Bear held most sacred was his soul, his brothers' friendship, and their safety. In inverse order. So as soon as he heard that Dulle Griet had come back to shake out her hideous apron at their feet, he dove back into the sea — without even taking the time to empty his seven-league boots — and landed on the shore with his pant legs as big around as two buoys.

"There's something rotten on those islands," he said when he'd rejoined his friends.

The company sat down in a circle on the sand and began to weigh, counter-weigh, estimate, judge, evaluate, and dissect the situation. In the end, they assessed it to be critical to the highest degree. To be brief, the news brought back by the giant was not encouraging. Let's not kid ourselves.

"This is war," he told them, not mincing his words. He figured he might as well call a spade a spade.

Two large islands, North Island and South Island, were in a state of perpetual war, no truce, no prisoners taken. It had all started long ago — in the era of the Great Flood, according to the North, or at the time of Creation, according to the South — over a debate, still unresolved, on the question of the law of primogeniture. North Island declared itself a product of the Ice Age, extending its claim over all fire-breathing dragons, the living as well as fossilized remains; South Island, on the other hand, claimed direct descent from a branch stemming from the primordial epoch at the time of the Garden of Eden, and insisted on its exclusive rights to the Tree of Good and Evil.

"Eat your forbidden fruit!" shrieked one party.

"Take your dragons and stuff them!" screeched the other.

And so on and so forth, for centuries.

It would be a while, of course, before our adventurers learned about the origins, causes, and endless divagations pertaining to the Holy War that pitted the North against the South. John-Bear's first expedition wasn't able to shed much light on the situation, since the giant wasn't overly bothered by such details. He would gladly have thrown his gigantic self between the belligerents, right into the thick of battle, without even thinking to ask what the dispute was about, or whether one side or the other was in the right. The flimsiest excuse was enough to arouse his deep sense of honour, as expressed in his three maxims. But as he was swimming out towards the islands, he had run aground on a shoal midway between North and South islands, and on this shoal had stood a disused lighthouse.

"Disused? What's the good of a disused lighthouse?" Big-as-a-Fist wanted to know.

John-Bear hadn't thought to ask. As far as he knew, the tower wasn't used for anything . . . except as a vantage point for the contemplation of the lives that went on around it, so you could make up stories about them for your descendants.

And that was the word that finally convinced Big-as-a-First to go to war: more than honour, duty, or nobility. Little coward that he was, he had felt not the slightest temptation to expose his comrades and himself to the horrors of a war that didn't concern them. But the bait dangled so innocently before his imagination by John-Bear — the lure of stories — made him bite. Epic tales of war! Told by the keeper of the disused lighthouse! That was more like it!

"Let's go! What are you waiting for? Come on, hop to it, let's hit the road!"

And so, forgetting the colour and pitch of his former fear, the little devil took command of his company and led it to the front.

A front that was no more than an islet, a sandbar slipped in between North and South islands, a dune dominated by a lighthouse made from dozey wood. You didn't think the dwarf had screwed up enough courage to actually go into combat, did you? A war is like any other spectacle — best seen from a distance. Thumbkin had rather fixed ideas on the subject: distance creates a much better perspective, and allows fairer judgements to be made about the rights of each participant. So, in the manner of a great many of his predecessors, Captain Big-as-a-Fist directed his campaign from a judicious distance.

Here's how it happened:

When the dwarf decided that he and his brothers had to go off to the front, he tried to enlist in the Reserves. A reservist — apart from being used to protect the main army's rear — is the recruit of choice when it comes to the Great Moment: in other words, when all is lost. Which is why the hero who plucks the laurels and gathers in the spoils is often a reservist. The dwarf displayed a great talent for this type of combat; moreover, he suspected that this idiotic War of the Islands would be prolonged indefinitely, and would never even get close to the day when the Reserves had to be called in. All that, however, changed once he discovered the lighthouse, with its storytelling keeper. Rather than be a reservist, Big-as-a-Fist now felt his true vocation was that of a chronicler of war. It wasn't until he met the keeper, and saw him hobbling about on a wooden leg and staring blindly at him with a glass eye, that the dwarf realized the danger that surrounded the lighthouse, caught as it was between two islands at war.

At that moment, our hero wanted to cry.

Except that he couldn't spare the time. By then, things were tumbling over one another with such speed and fury that our four companions, along with the pigeon, found themselves more or less drawn into the fray. The battle was being fought with heavy and murderous artillery: pitchforks, cooking pots, jam jars that bounced off the noses of innocent bystanders. The war had become generalized, and spared no one, not even orphans and widows. And this was all that was known any more by the people caught up in it, because North and South islands had been at war since the beginning of the world.

"Go eat your fruits of good and evil!"

"Go burn yourselves on your own dragon skins! You don't come from the Ice Age; you come from the Fall of Man, liars!"

"And you got your land from your neighbours, who gave it to you out of charity, you beggars!"

"I'll beggar you, so I will!"

And bang! . . . and boom! . . . and biff! . . . and psss . . . kabloom! . . .

On the morning of the sixth day, Sir René gathered his small troupe on the top floor of the lighthouse and spoke to them thus:

"My friends, my children, the time has come for us to take

part, to engage ourselves in combat. We are men of honour, and there is no honour in observing a civil war from the top of a tower, without even attempting to bring peace to our fellow human beings, though it cost us our lives. We can no longer countenance such dereliction of our duty to our allies."

"Our allies?" interrupted Big-as-a-Fist. "What allies?" He liked having an excuse to remain neutral. "Neutrals don't have allies," he said. "We should remain calmly and conscientiously peaceful."

The little bluffer congratulated himself on his speech. There would be no going to war, not with speeches like that.

Or so he thought.

"Why are those islands floating like ships?" asked Extra-Day suddenly, his eye glued to the lighthouse keeper's telescope.

And they learned that these bellicose people had known exile before, a time long ago in their history, back when they were still brothers. Oh yes, brothers, descended from one stock, from the belly of a single fertile land. Too fertile, in fact; it was too tempting. And one day their voracious neighbours couldn't stand it any more, and took a bite out of it. A rather big bite, too — in fact, the lion's share. And then the lion stole the rest of it from their children. Ever since, they had wandered the world, trailing their roots behind them like seaweed, searching for solid ground in which to transplant themselves.

Our four heroes looked at each other for the first time since the chronicler of the islands had begun intoning his epic tale, and each one swallowed a lump the size of his emotions. Big-as-a-Fist tried so hard to camouflage his that it went down the wrong way and he nearly choked to death. Then, to camouflage that, he said the first thing that came into his head. And in so doing, he changed the whole course of the ocean, as we shall see.

"Roots floating like seaweed?" he said. "Then what's to stop us hooking ourselves up to them, like the tail of a comet, and dragging the islands to better ground ourselves?"

The three comrades, the lighthouse keeper, and the pigeon looked the audacious little manikin straight in the eye, both perplexed and fascinated. Then, bit by bit, they turned to the eldest to weigh the consequences of such an initiative.

"It is never a good idea for foreigners to get mixed up in other people's wars," he concluded.

Big-as-a-Fist drummed his fingers on the windowsill. Could this be the same Sir René who, a few minutes earlier, had been defending the concept of solidarity between allies? Who had evoked the dignity of man . . . ?

The dignity of man? Having been resuscitated from a former time, Figure-Head could never use these words to express a notion that hadn't existed in his day. As for this duty to our allies, it couldn't possibly extend to the transplantation of an entire people!

"History shows us," the ancestor's commentary went on . . .

Big-as-a-Fist knew he'd gain nothing by taking his adversary on on his own turf; and the ancestor's turf was history. Better to arm himself with new ideas.

"By transplanting those islands," he said, "we open the door to recolonization. We offer these oppressed peoples the opportunity of peace and security in exchange for their exhausted ancestral homeland. And peace, peace above all."

While the others lapped up his words like mother's milk — all but Sir René, who stared at the horizon with a worried look — Big-as-a-Fist nurtured the seed of his idea until it blossomed into a host of new ones. And in less than an hour, hopping from idea to idea, the company mapped out a strategy that would have made Alexander the Great and Napoleon quake in their boots.

They began by sending the pigeon on a mission of reconnaissance over each camp. Before they could put their recolonization project into effect, they would have to do their best to reconcile the warring parties through diplomatic channels. Make proposals, set up negotiations, arrange parleys . . .

"Parleys, I like that," interjected the pigeon, who was principally concerned. "But has my master considered that, since he is the only one here who can speak and understand the language of animals, he will have to come along to act as interpreter between the islanders and his emissary?"

Big-as-a-Fist was beside himself with fury . . . who did this feathered fathead think he was? The master act as a servant to his own underling? He, the strategus extraordinaire, commander-in-chief of armies, stoop to the role of interpreter to birds? And he cursed his generous godmother for burdening him with such gifts.

In the end, Figure-Head decided the matter by imposing the full weight of his authority on the debate, and common sense prevailed. The pigeon was right: a messenger couldn't deliver a message and interpret it at the same time. Certain decisions had to be made at the highest level. And under the circumstances, Big-as-a-Fist was the only one small enough to ride on the bird's back.

And that's how our little hero, after a bellyful of storming and stamping, ended up going to war.

Once again Tom Thumb was to learn that courage does not consist in having no fear, but rather — fear or no fear — in setting off for the front. And also that it's the first mouthful that's the hardest when you're drowning. In the heat of battle there is rarely time to consult your heart — you just want it to keep pumping new energy to your brain. Which is why our cowardly little dwarf always found himself in the front line of adventure, no matter how much it cost him.

As they ought to have expected, the negotiations led nowhere. The high command of each island refused outright to receive so diminutive an emissary perched on the back of a pigeon. It was a shamefaced Big-as-a-Fist who returned to his headquarters at the lighthouse, leaving the North to rage against the South, thief of their Promised Land, and the South to fume at the North, usurper of their right of primogeniture.

"Very well," concluded Sir René, "if that's the way they want it . . ."

"If that's the way they want it," fulminated the dwarf, whose pride as chief negotiator had been mortally wounded, "then let's send in our big gun. Over to you, John-Bear."

The giant, aware that he was going on a mission of peace, armed himself to the teeth. He tightened his belt, tied his seven-league boots around his neck, pulled his hat down over his ears, and cracked his knuckles to test the soundness of his muscles and bones. Then he embraced each of his brothers in turn, shook the lighthouse keeper's hand, winked at the pigeon, crossed himself with both hands, and plunged into the sea.

His dive created a tidal wave that shook the pilings of the lighthouse, to the great dismay of the keeper, who recalled other high-road adventurers and their zest for peace. For now, though, our companions had other things to worry about than the lighthouse keeper's shell collection; they tore over to the telescope in order to follow the progress of their champion. The sea had calmed down, they saw, and the swimmer moved across it without making a shadow of a wave. Giant among men though he was, on the immense ocean he was little bigger than a drifting reed.

"But a thinking reed," pronounced Big-as-a-Fist, who had not forgotten his classical training.

The old man blinked in astonishment at the dwarf's words; with a little less blather, he thought, this sly little fox could go far.

Meanwhile, out at sea, the thinking reed was doing his best not to think, having enough to do just remembering all the instructions he'd been given by his brother who, ever since their birth, had been doing his thinking for him. Big-as-a-Fist had told him first of all to steer clear of the Madwoman's missiles; then to approach the islands under water, coming up only to breathe; to untangle the clumps of seaweed at the bottom, separating the true roots from the false ones, which were dead; to take hold of the roots belonging to the North — or to the South, it didn't matter which, as long as he didn't grab both — and to tie them to his belt. The giant also recalled the thoughts of Sir René, who had told him: "Since all discord derives from prejudice, all you need do to restore order is to tow the islands like a tugboat, transporting the North to the south, and the South to the north." John-Bear didn't quite grasp the meaning of the ancestor's thesis, but he retained the bare essentials: transplant the North to the south and the South to the north.

And that's what he did. By night.

To his great surprise, he found that a floating island could be towed along without much resistance, once he got it moving. Like a boat. You know how you sometimes see quite small tugboats pulling those gigantic freighters? It's all a question of overcoming friction — according to Big-as-a-Fist, who was an expert at overcoming friction, since he spent most of his life provoking it.

Suddenly there was an outcry from the shore. From his lighthouse tower, the keeper had just called down to his guests to say that the thing had been accomplished: the position of the islands was now reversed. The three comrades left behind on solid ground could now admire their brother's handiwork. No doubt about it, North Island had been well and truly rerooted to the south of South Island. Hurray!

Before diving back into the ocean to rejoin his friends, John-Bear stared out over the water and shook his head. At school he had always been the dummy, the one who couldn't tell an isosceles triangle from a square root, or a past participle from an adjectival adverb, and yet here, using nothing but the strength of his will and his bare hands, he had just remade a sizeable chunk of the earth's geography.

And they welcomed him back like a second Christopher Columbus.

Early the next morning, while Big-as-a-Fist was standing in the smallest porthole of the lighthouse, haranguing his troops on the art of winning wars without losing a single battle, the inhabitants of the two islands were waking up and realizing that their world had changed, and that from now on the sun would be rising in the west. For each of these peoples, it was much easier to believe in a revolution in the stars than in an upset of their geographical position. The Northerners would never admit that they had all of a sudden found themselves south of the Southerners, nor would the Southerners ever find themselves north of the Northerners. Much safer to conclude that the sun had changed its course.

Big-as-a-Fist held his head in his hands — "I don't believe it! I don't believe it!" — refusing to admit to himself just how firmly entrenched human stupidity could be: "Let's go show them with *a* plus *b* that two and two make four."

And off went our troupe, leaving the lighthouse in the care of its keeper and sailing gaily across the water on the giant's back, towards the islands.

But which island?

"We'll split up. Two delegations are better than one."

They tossed coins: Big-as-a-Fist and John-Bear won South Island and said goodbye to their comrades, who headed off for North. Before leaving them, Sir René took a few moments to remind his brothers that an ounce of precaution was worth a pound of cure. And they all agreed to meet up again at the same spot, at the same time, on the next day.

We now know the gist of the arguments presented by the two delegations: That of the ancestor and Extra-Day leaned heavily on history and reason to demonstrate the evils of an all-out civil war; Big-as-a-Fist and John-Bear based their case on the size, strength, and cannibalistic reputation enjoyed by the giant. According to their various lights, the two missions undertook to demonstrate to the North and South factions that the sun still rose in the east and that therefore both camps must recognize that, over the course of time, their positions had changed.

In the end, the islands gave in. Not because of astronomy — each side continued to insist that the sun never set on their empire — but because of the herring. For millennia, the herring had followed the cod, the cod had fled from the whales, who were chased by icebergs, and the icebergs had come down from the north. Now, these inflexible islanders could far more easily believe that the sun had changed direction than that the herring had. So, thanks to the herring, the Northerners and Southerners finally had to admit that, yes, it did look as if they might just possibly have exchanged positions.

And consequently that they must now come face to face with their new destinies.

It was then that Figure-Head made use of his infallible memory and limitless knowledge of the past to instruct the new peoples on their deep roots, and to help them recover their true identity. Before their astonished eyes, he began to recount their history to them — backwards.

"In the beginning . . . ," he said.

He recounted so much, in fact, that the islanders blushed and tried to cover their faces. They learned about the volcano, which had suddenly erupted one day and spewed its lava all the way up to the walls of Heaven's vault. They learned how this lava, when it met the absolute cold of those walls, had hardened into foul cinders and fallen back down as plaquettes of earth, more or less the same size, more or less the same shape, and more or less evenly distributed on the waters. They were told how, in time, two of these plaquettes had pulled farther and farther apart, buffeted by contrary currents, and had ended up with quite separate and distinct identities, and even different names: they had called themselves North Island and South Island.

The poor islanders! The more they listened to the history of their islands' common and somewhat comical origins, the paler and more confused they became: formed from the vomit of an erupting mountain, from a stinking, hardened hunk of cinder, fallen from the sky as misshapen platelets of dirt, swilled about by contrary and haphazard ocean currents. For two proud islands that had paraded their glorious roots throughout the world since the beginning of time, this revelation was the final blow. They wanted to drown their shame in the deepest depths of the ocean.

Contemplating their dismay, our four heroes took pity on the crestfallen islanders, and each tried in his own way to buoy the populace back to the surface . . . "What is this?" demanded Figure-Head. "No one springs from the loins of Jupiter. Every town started life as a village. Every kingdom was once just an estate crowding over onto its neighbour. The North will soon discover the benefits of a southerly clime; and the South will find that the rigours of the north have their advantages. You'll see!"

"Who needs an Ice Age when they have the chance to come from the Promised Land?" added Big-as-a-Fist to the citizens of the North, now South.

Then, turning to the citizens of the South, now floating on northern waters: "You want to go back down there, dragging your eternal regret for a lost paradise with you? Look around! Have you ever seen anything more beautiful than the Northern Lights?"

And from Northern Lights to rainbows to the Evening Star, the ingenious Tom Thumb brought water to the parched lips of the islanders — and, though he didn't know it, grist to their respective mills. Because before long New North Island was turning up its nose at the miserable little sand dune that let itself be tossed about by the southern sea, and New South Island was sneering as it looked north, where such a poor patch of land was preyed upon by thunderous oceans.

"That came from the Ice Age? Hah! No dragon of theirs ever breathed fire — poison, maybe, that hardened their hearts and softened their brains!"

"Think they came from the Garden of Eden, can you beat that! Ha-ha! A paradise filled with snakes and rotten apples, no wonder they're always bellyaching! Go on, eat your forbidden fruits!"

"And you, you can go stuff your dragons!"

And so the war between the New North and the New South began once more.

Our adventurers had just enough time to dive back into the sea and regain the lighthouse, then swim back to the mainland.

"Bloody hell!" bawled Big-as-a-Fist as he left the islands behind. "Won't they ever know what peace is?"

The answer came from above their heads, running down the octaves in a cackle that set his teeth on edge.

"The witch!"

In person. With her cape spread open, her apron-front filled to the brim, Mad Meg was scattering her seeds of discord to the four winds. The four companions watched her set off for the islands, obscuring the whole horizon with her malevolent shadow.

"Well, there it is," said wise old Sir René when the grotesque image had disappeared towards the coast. "After discord comes war. The shrew never rests."

"But we can!" said Big-as-a-Fist, kicking the air behind the Madwoman as she disappeared. "Let's go back inland and find a nice corner of the country where there's nothing but order and peace."

Then, under his breath:

"I can't believe that on the eighth day . . ."

This thought led his mind back, against his will, to his childhood — where he had left Goodman and Goodwife bent over a workbench and a batch of bread dough.

13

From famine, treachery, and sluggard kings,
deliver us, O Lord

A batch of bread dough! Just where he'd started out — in a batch of bread dough. He began to envy his brother — at least the giant had made it out of the woods. In spite of his square, knobby head, John-Bear impressed people, they bowed to him, they raised their hats. It never occurred to anyone to bow to a dwarf who smelled of yeast and whole-wheat flour. His father had been right: a half-baked bun like him would never succeed in earning his daily bread.

Shit, shit, and more shit!

Looking around, he couldn't see any of his companions. No doubt they were lying in the tall grass, regaining their strength, not bothering their heads about where they'd come from or where they were going. Why was he the only one to drag around this hole in his heart, left there when his first ancestor, Adam, took a bite out of that apple? Forbidden fruit. Bah!

Ever since he'd been born he'd been told not to do this, to stay away from that, to leave this alone, the same old thing every time. Would he ever see the day when he could do what he wanted, even if it wasn't allowed?

Shit, shit, and shit again!

His mother used to tell him about his miraculous birth; he could still hear her thick accent and trembling voice. How she had kneaded him out of her bread dough, rolled and shaped him with her own fingers, a gallant little fellow with, scratched on his skin, his own name that he'd been called by since the day he came into the world — a name that was already popping up in the folktales and picture books of his native country. A prophecy come true, a child of the eighth day!

So where was it now, today, this famous destiny of his? What road should he follow into the future? His future? Would that glorious day ever come when he tasted of the true apple, the fruit of good and evil, which had been forbidden the sons of Adam ever since the Fall, which had been treated like Original Sin but might in fact be the key to all happiness?

Happiness!

The most widely used yet most indefinable word in the world. Take any two people — say, his father, Goodman, and his mother, Goodwife — and casually drop the word *happiness* between them. Each of them would leap at it, tear it out of the other's hands, turn it round and round, count its consonants, sift through its syllables. Goodwife's happiness would end up in her sewing basket and her breadbox. Goodman's would curl out of his jackplane and fall into the wood shavings on his workshop floor.

And Big-as-a-Fist's?

He thought about it, smiling to himself, snuggling up into himself, sliding into the space between the two halves of his brain. If his happiness existed anywhere, it must be in the depths of his imagination. There, spread out like a display in a shop window, were all the things that made him happiest: beauty, pleasure, power, glory, heroism, wealth, tenderness, talent, friendship, love . . . In his dreams Big-as-a-Fist could have anything, he had an infinite capacity for happiness.

Almost.

Not infinitely infinite. He'd stop, sated, every time — before he'd reached the bottom of his treasure chest of happiness. He'd change the dream, start over, pass from one pleasure to another, from power to glory to beauty to love . . . And each time he'd discover that he felt the greatest happiness of all when he was creating a new kind of happiness.

He looked up again, and this time saw his three friends sitting in a field of clover, pulling petals off the heads of daisies.

"Well, well," he said to himself. "She loves me, she loves me not, she loves me . . ."

Aloud he said, "What the devil are you up to, you lazy good-for-nothings? Picking daisies at a time like this? Get up, lazybones! Life is young, the future is still ahead of us! To hell with calm mornings, quiet times, wasted time, they're not going to trap us in a dead season. Let's go, brothers! Onward to adventure!"

Clapping his hands together to get the troupe in line, he added:

"Hop to it! Hit the road! I'm starving. Never mind the dead wheat!"

Sir René furrowed his shaggy brow. If only the blabbermouth would learn not to go around calling scourges by their proper names, he thought, his apprehensions stirring him back to life. Why did he always need to provoke destiny?

John-Bear had stood up in response to his brother's roaring appeals. Casting his gaze at the curved horizon, he saw a dark, moving profile that was no stranger to his view; he opened his mouth to warn his comrades, but Marco Polo, who could see even farther, beat him to it.

"Dulle Griet! Dulle Griet!" he chattered, borrowing for once the language of the magpie.

Big-as-a-Fist had just enough time to stifle his hunger and his impossible dreams, and to grab his youngest brother, Extra-Day, by the leg. "Hurry up, get the lead out. Everyone, find a sapling or a small bush and hide yourselves."

Sir René cocked his ear, trying to find out why everyone was in such a scuddle of confusion, when he heard the clop-clop-clop of Mad Meg's wooden shoes on the pavement. She was heading straight for them. The ancestor, arms spread wide to protect his brothers, saw nothing but the birds flying through the branches, and a few rabbits scampering out of the brush in fright. Then he bent his four-century-old spine and crawled into the undergrowth.

Had Dulle Griet seen them? Smelled them? Had she sensed their presence? They were so rooted in existence that they could hardly help but leave a distinct odour of life in their wake. Wherever our four heroes strayed, alas, the ground preserved a trace of their passing. It would have been almost impossible for them to pass by unnoticed. This spoke well of them, but it could also cause them trouble.

There were times when it put their lives in danger.

Sir René would have to fill them in later on the true nature of Mad Meg, who was not as mad as all that, my brothers, and who knew perfectly well whom she was dealing with in these four knights of the road.

Four knights of the road who for now were holding themselves mute and immobile under the trees and bushes, imploring all 365 saints of the calendar — 366 for Big-as-a-Fist, who'd been born in a leap year — to get this sower of scourges out of their hair.

But the calendary saints must have been listening to someone else that day, because she chose to sow her green seeds along precisely the same route that they had followed.

"Wait a minute," thought the giant. "That can't be right, green seeds." That was one thing that had always irked their father, who had his own sense of economy. Hadn't he always told them never to eat wheat before it ripened, and never to sow all their grain in one field? Meg would soon exhaust the soil if she kept harvesting her grain before it was ripe, he said to himself.

Suddenly, to their astonishment, the three brothers saw young Extra-Day slip out of his hiding place and start crawling towards the Grim Reaper — who calmly went on taking great handfuls of unripe grain from the large pockets of her apron-front, and broadcasting them on both sides of the footpath.

Sir René covered his eyes.

"Stop him! Don't let the little one get close to her! Her grain is poisoned."

At the word *poison*, both giant and dwarf caught their breath. Then, without thinking, John-Bear broke cover and leapt over the ditch, with Big-as-a-Fist, his mind racing as fast as his feet, following close behind. He had heard the ancestor muttering something like "If you value his life . . . ," and though he valued his own life first and foremost, he valued those of his brothers almost as much — that of John-Bear, his alter ego; that of his forebear, the leader of the pack; and now, after seeing him throw himself so unexpectedly into peril, that of his youngest brother, whose only defence was his total innocence. You couldn't abandon a young, ignorant, inexperienced infant to the wolves, could you? Of course you couldn't, damn it!

These reflections swarmed into Big-as-a-Fist's head from all directions; he wasn't their master, he had no control over them — or over his own courage and fear. Which is how he found himself at the feet of Dulle Griet: not quite knowing how he'd got there.

John-Bear had got there first, of course. When the dwarf looked up, the first thing he saw was the giant, standing at his full height before the Grim Reaper. Looking even higher, Big-as-a-Fist saw Mad Meg's cap, rising at least a head taller than his brother. It was the first time John-Bear had met someone bigger than himself, and he had no trouble standing up to her. With more passion than Mad Meg had ever excited before, Out-of-Time fixed his eyes on the front of her apron and prepared to follow them with his teeth.

"Don't touch her!" shouted Figure-Head from some distance away. He was hustling over as quickly as he could on his rheumatic, rickety legs. "Get away from her!"

Easy enough to say, get away from her. But what about the baby — who'd get him out? Big-as-a-Fist wrung his hands, tapped his forehead, conked his cranium. And a light appeared somewhere behind his temples: he had already made Death fart and dance once: you remember the hangman cavorting under the noose and in front of the inn? The dwarf rummaged through his pockets for his flute . . . where the devil was it? . . . well then, sneeze, my good man, sneeze for all you're worth — go ahead, pinch your nose, Tom Thumb, you've got the gift, hurry up . . . try it, take a deep breath, hold it, then let 'er rip . . . you idiot!

Later, Big-as-a-Fist would learn that no one can sneeze just like that, on command. Confronting the hangman in his youth, he hadn't squeezed out his brainpin to blow a tempest through his nose; he'd done it quite naturally. Now — facing Mad Meg, who represented the greatest danger and the gravest hour of his life — he came up empty, incapable of the slightest puff of inspiration.

All of which occurred to him after the fact. For the moment, he had to content himself with watching helplessly as his brothers struggled to carry the day without him.

Truth to tell, young Out-of-Time pulled the whole thing off pretty much on his own. He'd come out of his hiding place and crawled along the path to pick up some of those tender-looking grains of wheat that were lying there turning nice and golden in the sun. He was hungry. And he had seen his brothers sticking out their tongues and licking their lips at the sight of all those seeds spread out by the roadside. How could he know this wheat had come straight from Hell?

But the ancestor's warnings and the giant's scowling made him suspect that Meg was hiding something up her sleeve, and he remembered a lesson he'd learned about good and bad mushrooms. In a flash, he realized that he had dragged the whole company into a trap, and that it was up to him to get them out of it.

Without losing a second — although he had plenty to spare — he slid himself between times and disappeared from the sower's sight, much to her surprise and consternation. She looked around on all sides, sniffing the air and beating the wind with both arms. Then the others saw her turn to the east, gather up her enormous apron, and set off with giant steps towards the horizon and the rising sun.

"She's smelled him," the ancestor said tentatively. He alone had had previous experience of the reaper's machinations. "That must mean our little brother's headed that way. Let's follow her and see if we can find him again."

And off they went, following in Mad Meg's own footsteps.

The trail led them to the foot of a wall that surrounded a kingdom. Meg did not bother to step over this wall; she had already passed that way once, and had created much havoc within, as our heroes were about to discover — to their very great astonishment.

For this was the realm of King Pétaud.

Big-as-a-Fist, having barely recovered from one of the biggest frights of his young life, and being hardly over the relief of seeing Extra-Day return into time, shouted for joy when he realized that he and his brothers had arrived at the gates of the drollest, most disorderly kingdom they would cross in the whole of their adventures.

"Time for some fun!" cried Tom Thumb, not noticing that both sides of the road were lined with dilapidated hovels filled with a poverty-stricken populace. "At last, the court of King Pétaud," he laughed.

And he leapt and danced and whistled, pulling the rest of the company along in the wake of his merriment. He stopped only long enough to ask directions from some passersby, and to find out how to go about gaining entry to the court. He didn't see the grimace on each of their faces at the mention of King Pétaud, or how they merely raised their emaciated arms to point the travellers down the road, then tucked their heads hastily back into their threadbare collars and scuttled away into their shacks.

"This King Pétaud is either the poorest or the most miserly liege in the land," said Sir René, saddened by such suffering. "I've never seen such misery. Except once, when I . . ."

At which Monsieur René Renaissance became lost in thought, and said nothing further.

But he soon raised his head again at the happy welcome shouted by one of the king's heralds, dressed in brilliant livery, who was inviting everyone, citizen and stranger alike, to a banquet held by the king on the occasion of the wedding of his favourite horse.

"Hear ye! Hear ye! His Royal Highness King Pétaud has declared today a national holiday! Tournaments! Contests! Games! Come and celebrate in the palace. Hear ye, hear ye!"

"If people don't have enough bread, give them circuses," muttered Figure-Head, who was the most cynical of the troupe. "We've heard that tune before."

He may have thought he knew the tune, but in fact no one understood King Pétaud's song; it passed all understanding.

The four companions began by presenting their letters of credence at the gates of the palace; they had written the letters themselves on pieces of birchbark and sealed them with yellow daubs of birdlime issued by Marco Polo. The porter made no difficulties for the foreign guests, taking no more trouble over their documents than he seemed to have taken over his turban. As a matter of form, however, he authenticated the seal by licking it.

"Good," he proclaimed, "excellent. Please be so kind as to enter, sirs; the grand tourney is about to begin."

Big-as-a-Fist didn't waste a second. Not wanting to miss a thing, he called to his brothers to hurry up to the highest row of seats.

"Come on," he cried to John-Bear, who was embarrassed by his size and always fearful of crushing someone else's feet in trying to move his own.

The dwarf wasn't troubled by such considerations. Despite his short legs, he clambered over people's heads and installed himself in the topmost circle of the amphitheatre, and sat there as if the whole kingdom belonged to him. Let the fun begin!

And begin it did. With a vengeance.

First, enter King Pétaud.

"The king! Long live the king! Our own King Pétaud!"

Everyone shouted and yelled and hollered as if at a fair.

"It *is* a fair," ventured Sir René, "but it's the most unfair fair I've ever seen. This is a land of disorder, discord, and chaos."

Even Big-as-a-Fist was a bit put out. For his first king, he would have liked a little more majesty. Instead, he watched as a courtful of gaudy, bleating buffoons cavorted before him, hoisting on their shoulders a carved throne on which a dishevelled king sprawled with his crown slumped down around his ears. The dwarf was all for a good time, but not at the cost of his illusions. Turning to Sir René, he asked:

"Was it always like this when there were kings?"

"This is the court of King Pétaud," replied the ancestor. "Every century has one."

The dwarf filed this observation away in his collection of the axioms and statements his oldest brother had been uttering since their first happy encounter. In the presence of such a master, he told himself, he and his brothers would soon be able to tell good from evil, beautiful from ugly, and true from false. So saying, he crossed his arms and awaited further unfolding of events with the utmost patience and curiosity. Come what might!

But he could never have predicted what came next. Instead of a troupe of knights surging into the arena, wearing coats of mail, armed to the teeth, and mounted on prancing chargers, our heroes watched as a vulgar, hysterical lout leapt up onto an overturned barrel and, after five or six mocking bows to the throne, proceeded to deliver a speech that had no head, no tail, no punctuation, no logic, no sense.

"What's he saying? What's he telling us?" asked the four comrades in turn, scratching their heads and wringing out their ears.

"Sounds like a tissue of non sequiturs and a bowlful of fibs to me," Big-as-a-Fist finally confessed, settling back in his seat. "Lies!"

As he spoke, he raised his eyes heavenwards and happened to see Marco Polo passing by, on his way back from inspecting the farthest regions of the stadium — where bats abounded. It was there that the pigeon had learned the true nature of the tournament: it was, in fact —

"A lying contest!" he cooed into his master's ear.

"A what?" sputtered Big-as-a-Fist, unable to credit his senses.

"The flittermice upstairs told me this fellow doesn't stand a chance, everyone's waiting for a liar renowned throughout the land for his incredible ability to twist the truth, turn reality on its head, and inflate the merest molehill into a mountain of mendacity. They call him the King of Liars, or the International Connoisseur of Claptrap."

The four companions listened slack jawed to the pigeon's report. So that was it! Talk about a contest! Big-as-a-Fist felt something stirring within him, in spite of himself — a twinge of jealousy.

"Tall-tale tellers, eh?" he said. "Goes to show how untravelled this King Pétaud's subjects must be. If it's lies they want, real lies . . ."

And turning towards his nearest neighbour, a woman decked out in feathers, chiffon, spangles, and bangles, he asked:

"What does the winner get?"

The corpulent Pétaudite, a member of the upper class known as the Fat Cats, cast a scornful eye in the dwarf's direction. Then she let out a wicked laugh:

"His life."

"His . . . what?"

But the woman didn't deign to repeat her answer. At any rate, the dwarf's attention was drawn back to the overturned barrel, where a new contestant was strutting his stuff to the applause of the audience.

"Bravo, liar! Hurray! It's your turn, tell us a real whopper!"

Sir René signalled to his comrades to keep quiet and stay still. Given the nature of the prize, it seemed best not to get involved.

"I fear," he said, "that this King Pétaud is a cruel tyrant as well as a mock potentate. We'll get out of here at the earliest opportunity."

Alas! The earliest opportunity took a long time coming, long enough for our heroes to start getting nervous. And as we know, nervousness was always a bad sign for Big-as-a-Fist, who had landed on his head after falling out of his warming oven as a baby. Which explains why, instead of remaining quietly in his seat and keeping his mouth shut until the contest was over, as his ancestor had recommended, he suddenly heard himself shout:

"Liar!"

. . . at the last participant, who had billed himself as the foremost liar in the world.

The audience, stunned, turned immediately to the top row of seats to look for the new champion who had just tossed out so superb a challenge.

"To the barrel!" they cried from all sides. "Make way for the young liar! Bring the foreigner down!"

But the young foreign liar had curled himself up and was pressing his minuscule body into the depths of his idiotic being. The crowd swept the row with its eyes, searched around the platform — Where'd he go? Who is he? Let him show himself!

He showed himself. He had no choice, really. His fat, feathered neighbour in the spangles had recognized him and lifted him up over her head. Her former disdain transformed into ecstasy when she realized that under the little manikin's unpromising and diminutive exterior there lurked a superior brain and a blithe spirit. As she waved him aloft, the delirious multitudes surged out of the stands and crowded around their new star, practically crushing the life out of him at least a dozen times.

"Let me see him!"

"I want to get closer!"

"I was here before you!"

"You're blocking my view!"

"Don't push! Where's you manners?"

"I can feel my heart pounding!"

"Oh, I'm going to faint!"

"Give him to me!"

"No, to us!"

"Put him on the barrel!"

Placed on the overturned barrel, what was left of Big-as-a-Fist was barely worth looking at. Crumpled, crinkled, and cracking in every seam, he tried to catch his breath by sucking air deep down into his chest, which had been crushed against that of a buxom old woman who, unable to resist the wild enthusiasm displayed by the crowd, had leapt down from the royal dias.

"My hero, my jewel, my sweet . . ."

"My jewel, my nutcake, my dearie, my sweetie pie, my sugar-plum, my pet, my foot!" finished Big-as-a-Fist, who was regaining his composure as he recovered his breath. With the return of grammar came the return of words, and with words came ideas. It was lies they wanted, was it? No problem. Our little devil was a past master. He could give them an earful all right, he thought. But first he'd better introduce himself.

"Your Majesty, Your Highnesses, Your Excellencies," he began, his voice dripping with sincerity and without the slightest hint of an accent. "I come from a country across the sea and beyond the horizon — where I have left behind my father, who is a fine cabinetmaker, and my mother, who is a master pastry chef — in the company of my twin brother, who is a giant."

There was a preliminary burst of laughter and a round of applause.

Big-as-a-Fist, taken aback, looked around trying to figure out what he'd said what was so funny. Then he shrugged and went back to his narrative.

"I was born of a batch of bread dough made by my mother. She put me up on the warming oven to rise, you see, and —"

This time there was thunderous laughter, and shouts of Hurray! and More! which forced the dwarf to rethink his strategy. Was his life, his own reality, a bigger lie than any tall tale he could tell? At the court of King Pétaud, the naked truth was decidedly more unusual than any degree of invention.

Once he'd figured this out, Big-as-a-Fist launched into his story.

"Listen to me, ladies and gents, because my being born in a batch of bread dough was nothing compared to the birth of my brother the giant, who was carved from a tree trunk; or to the re-awakening of my ancestor, who slept away the last four centuries of his first life; or to that of my small-fry brother who was born outside of time, on an extra day, and has retained the ability to pull himself back inside time and disappear from view . . ."

The wild applause and laughter had died down. A hush fell over the entire arena. King Pétaud and all the Pétaudites were thunderstruck by the storyteller's charm and the marvels he was relating. Never had they heard such invention, such splendid lying. There they all were, lapping up every word, as Big-as-a-Fist took them along on his journey into the clouds, over a waterfall contained in a waterdrop, down to a world turned upside down, where the citizens walked with their heads bent from climbing up on each others' shoulders, and finally through the story of their battles with Mad Meg, who had tried to destroy them with storms and the scourges of war and, most recently, with famine and poisoned wheat. The crowd, unable to hold back any longer, burst into tears.

"Your poor brothers! Your dear comrades!"

They demanded to see the entire company. Lies like this were masterpieces; such liars were geniuses. Our four heroes were carted aloft and carried in triumph — all except John-Bear, who helped to carry the carriers — to the steps of the palace, where they were proclaimed the happy winners of the tournament and therefore awarded first prize — their lives.

"What happens to the losers?" asked Extra-Day, innocently.

All heads turned away. But one ancient, wrinkled man, more shrivelled up than a winter apple that had dried out in the sun, let a few words whistle through his teeth:

"Well, ssson, sssince they lossst the contessst . . ."

The four companions exchanged glances charged with apprehension. Sir René, trying to look nonchalant, managed to whisper out of the side of his mouth:

"We'd better find a way out of here, fast. Meanwhile, keep you eyes peeled."

For once it was Big-as-a-Fist who showed the most courage. Or was it recklessness? Anyway, he was suddenly seized by a foolhardy curiosity; he wanted to know where all this lying would lead them. When reality had intruded into imagination, he now had to admit, he had breathed in the perfume of the Muses, and he was still in its thrall. Grasping at any pretext, and swallowing his Adam's apple, he said:

"We can't just leave and let innocent people die in our place."

At the word "innocent" John-Bear and Extra-Day sided with Big-as-a-Fist, the hero of the day. Sir René realized that his own arguments, buttressed though they were with caution and good sense, would never stand up against the fanciful flights of the inspired youth. For the dwarf was already going on about saving the wretched from their wretchedness, releasing prisoners from their prisons, rescuing the famished from their famine.

"Let us feed the hungry!" he prattled, without the slightest idea how many empty bellies there were in this kingdom.

Big-as-a-Fist had forgotten that Mad Meg had recently paid a visit to Pétaudia. The ancestor felt it prudent not to remind his brother of the fact, for fear of pushing him to new heights of folly. He contented himself with warning his comrades against the dangers of dreams and illusions, and told them not to try to remake the world each morning over breakfast, as if it were a bowl of porridge.

Big-as-a-Fist congratulated the old man on the felicity of his imagery, but refused to take his warning seriously. What kind of world would it be if some dreamer didn't come along every morning to reinvent it to his own liking? If his father and mother hadn't dreamed of an eighth day, what limbo would he and his brother now be floating in? And without them, what would have happened to Figure-Head, frozen as he was in the Arctic ice, and to the babe saved from the carnival that they themselves had invented?

Figure-Head and the infant Out-of-Time were completely cowed by such blinding evidence, convinced beyond all doubt that they owed their lives to the two brothers who owed theirs to a pair of parents who had refused to believe that the impossible couldn't happen. Smiling broadly, they bowed in Big-as-a-Fist's direction.

If our hero Tom Thumb could have foreseen all the consequences of his fears and fancies, he might have been more inclined to trim his sails a bit. But when had Big-as-a-Fist ever been content to play in a minor key?

They had hardly emerged victorious from their first test when they were presented with even more formidable challenges. The tournament of liars was a game — a deadly one for the losers, but still related to amusement and celebration. But if people could be condemned to death while playing a game on a public holiday, imagine what could happen to them on an ordinary working day.

Our heroes found out the next morning, when three servants who were serving them breakfast literally fell down at their feet, having either fainted or else died from lack of food. The brothers hurried to the aid of the first, then to the second, then to the third, and finally to all the others — because they soon realized the palace with littered with corpses. People were dying like flies in the realm of King Pétaud. Of exhaustion and hunger.

"What's going on here?" asked a bewildered Big-as-a-Fist, who just the night before had thought he'd died and gone to heaven.

He was beginning to find out that Muses could have feet of clay.

"Might as well call a spade a spade," observed the wise old ancestor. "We've stumbled on a country filled with famine and chaos. The king and his court are the only well-fed people in the land. All the others, all the king's subjects, are as thin as playing cards."

Big-as-a-Fist ground his teeth. "It's intolerable, totally unacceptable. Something must be done about it."

"Something must be done about it," repeated Extra-Day, always ready to tackle the impossible.

"Something," threw in John-Bear, always ready to tackle anything.

Anything, anything at all, they chorused, each one ready to scour the land, beat the bushes, and drain the seas and oceans. They never doubted for a moment that their proposals would be carried out to the letter. That was another of King Pétaud's character traits that they had yet to learn: he was open to suggestions because he was certain that none of them would ever come to anything, and that he'd be able to wallow forever in his lazy, voluptuous state.

So when our four companions arrived at the palace, preceded by Marco Polo, who had gone on ahead to scout out the territory, they were surprised at the courteous reception that awaited them. There was much bowing and scraping, a plethora of curtsies, "if it isn't too much trouble," "if the gentlemen would care to enter," "His Majesty is in attendance," all washed down with gallons of gracious smiles and pleasantries.

"Too good to be true," thought Big-as-a-Fist.

"He who gives everything gives nothing," murmured Sir René.

The two others kept their thoughts to themselves, being too busy worrying about slipping on the marble floor or tripping over the patterned carpets.

They managed to arrive at the first step of the throne without incident, except for a throaty cry from the pigeon — who, blinded by a crystal chandelier, had flown head first into a distorting mirror. Big-as-a-Fist hastened to apologize to the king on behalf of their mascot, with whom, he said, he conversed in its own language. The bird, he explained, was gifted with an instinct far greater than reason, and moreover was the holder of a secret rolled around its left leg that was destined, one day, to revolutionize the world.

The whole court choked with laughter at this new sally by such a master inventor, and begged the king to name Big-as-a-Fist his prime minister on the spot.

"He's perfect," they cried from every quarter. "Absolutely perfect!"

The king himself was caught in a fit of hiccups, and was allowing his back to be slapped by a bevy of twenty-eight valets retained for the purpose.

Our heroes looked at each other and agreed that now was as good a time as any to convey to the king their dismay at the misery of his subjects, and to advance their proposal for remedying the situation.

To their complete astonishment, the king received their petition with his full attention and courtesy. He even went so far as to confess, with trembling voice, that their dismay in this matter was equalled only by his own, and that his ministers had already commissioned dozens of White Papers preliminary to the undertaking of a study to consider the various agrarian, social, economic, and administrative reforms demanded by the people.

"My poor people!" lamented His Majesty. "I fear that famine is wiping them out."

And the court, dripping with tears and chicken fat, echoed the sighs of their monarch with a chorus of belches that made Big-as-a-Fist wince in disgust. But he recovered his composure long enough to lay out for the assembly his plans for relieving the people of their misery, as drawn up by the four comrades.

The king and his ministers — the whole court, in fact — stopped chewing and rifling through their chocolate boxes. One plump dowager even reached into the wrong box and inadvertently swallowed two thimbles and a pincushion. Then they regained their calm, swallowed their fears, and told themselves that the plans of these newcomers were no different from all the rest, that they'd heard much better ones, and that ever since the world began and Pétaud became King of Pétaudia, society had been divided into two classes: the lean and the fat. It would take more than the passing of a single comet to change things around, their Minister of Justice told them, they could rest assured of that.

The four heroes looked at each other and decided to feign incomprehension, to ignore the smiles and whispers, the nodding heads, the chuckling behind hands, and press forward with the debate. However, Sir René had hardly mentioned the wealth of unexploited natural resources rotting in the fields and forests when his speech was interrupted by the entrance of a strange personage, a faceless, ageless courtier wrapped in a grey cloak and wearing dark glasses, who glided in as if on roller skates between the rows of ladies and gentlemen of the court. After two or three bows towards the throne — not more, just enough to acknowledge the king's presence without implying a humble servility — the rogue executed a pirouette that allowed him to address everyone at once while turning his back on them at the same time.

A full hour later, when our heroes heard him make the final points of his proposition, they realized that he was none other than their mortal enemy, and that once again they were back in the same boat. John-Bear didn't quite understand, though, and asked Big-as-a-Fist to enlighten him.

"I think we're being sent up the creek without a paddle," said the dwarf.

The dwarf was only partly right: they weren't being sent up the creek. Not exactly. Or rather, not *just* up the creek. As it turned out, the sly one's plan was to send the four reformists to the four corners of the kingdom. From there, after one year had passed, they would each bring back to court specimens of grain, plants, rocks, and fish that could be reproduced in greenhouses or factories, thereby restoring the economy and returning the country to its former prosperity.

"And then the people will eat again," concluded the man in the grey cloak and the dark glasses.

"And by then we'll be pushing up daisies," muttered Big-as-a-Fist under his breath. "We've got to get out of here. Old Tartuffe here has beaten us at our own game; we'd better beat him at his." Then, to gain some time, he asked aloud:

"Where do we begin?" As if he couldn't wait to get started.

"Why, everywhere at once," replied the cowled figure, his voice oily enough to make you sick. "You are four doughty knights. This country is teeming with four great unexploited resources, as you say — the land, the sea, the forest, and the bowels of the earth. Divide these tasks among you, and the people will see an end to their misery that much sooner."

What — break up the troupe?

Shit, shit, and shittier!

John-Bear turned towards his twin brothers with beseeching eyes; Extra-Day looked at the ancestor as if to say: our trust is in you. But neither the ancestor nor the dwarf could dredge up from his memory or imagination the slightest idea of how to deflect the sword dangling over their heads.

All of a sudden Extra-Day went up to the throne, bowed, and addressed himself to the king in reverential tones:

"With all respect, Sire, could Your Majesty outline for us in advance the kind and amount of payment we can expect to receive a year from now, when we have brought prosperity back to your country?"

The king, Tartuffe, the ministers, the court, and all those in attendance held their breath. For that matter, so did the dwarf, the ancestor, and the giant. Only Extra-Day remained calm, awaiting an answer and a promise from the king.

The silence might have lasted forever, the throats of the onlookers were so tied up in Gordian knots. Between the liar king and the truthful child — who had discovered that the king had no clothes — there was a total impasse, no possibility of contact. The silence descended upon them like a shroud. It might have lasted forever if . . .

"Hello-o-oo!"

Every head turned.

There she stood, a fairy, a princess, the king's only daughter. Like all fairy-tale princesses, she was beauty itself, beauty unsurpassed, without equal in elegance, charm, the svelteness of her figure, the pallor of her skin, the regularity of her features — she was incomparable. BEAUTY, in capital letters. Not even the ancestor, who'd lived in an era that had given birth to Anne Boleyn and Diane de Poitiers, had ever seen the likes of her, and he was panting like a rooster in rut. Imagine how the others felt, who had never seen a beautiful woman in their lives!

John-Bear was puffing hard, with no control over his emotions. He twisted back and forth, bobbed from one foot to the other, sweated drops of water as big as French cherries, and hid his face in his hands. Extra-Day remained motionless, as transfixed as an angel in one of Giotto's nativity scenes. Suspended for all eternity.

And as for Big-as-a-Fist . . . er, Big-as-a-Fist! Hey, Big-as-a-Fist! Well, nothing was heard from Big-as-a-Fist but a single cry.

"Sire!"

The king, the princess, the courtiers, his brothers — all stared at the dwarf who had dared to break the eternal silence.

"Sire," and he could barely hear himself say it, "if she is our reward, then let us not delay our departure by a single day. Offer your daughter's hand to whichever of us comes back a year from now and returns prosperity to the kingdom and happiness to the people."

Curiously enough, it was the figure in grey who signalled the king to accept, with a smile that told the monarch he'd never have to pay for an expedition doomed to failure. Death was what awaited these adventurers, death in the storm-tossed seas, in the vast, dark forests, in the arid deserts, and in the mines from whose depths no traveller returned. This was Tartuffe's chance to rid himself of his four rivals in one fell swoop. He had already tested their strength of body, soul, and mind; now he was going to test the strength of their love.

Love!

It would be some time before our heroes fully grasped the nature of the trial their destiny had set before them. For the first time, they had agreed to separate. For the first time, they were competing against each other. From now on they would be lone adventurers with no help or support from the company, no brotherly love. Big-as-a-Fist surprised even himself as he sat like a porcelain puppy watching John-Bear gazing with tear-filled eyes at their beloved princess.

Love! . . . ah!

The next morning, our heroes set out for the four points of the compass, without looking around and without saying good-bye.

A year!

Three hundred and sixty-five days during which the court of King Pétaud wallowed in orgies and idleness, never once deigning to lift their eyes towards any of the four horizons.

Fifty-two weeks for Goodman and Goodwife, down by Clara-Galante's little stream, to wend their way each morning to carpenter shop and kitchen, without the faintest idea of the whereabouts of their peripatetic progeny.

Twelve months of Herculean labours for our heroes in their contest with the elements — calming active volcanoes, purifying waters, taming wild forest beasts, exploring subterranean galleries in the bowels of the earth.

A year of sighs and stubbornness, of fear and courage, of hope and despair. But every night our four heroes slept and dreamed of beauty, glimpsed but once at the court of a cruel and foolish king. And the dream gave them the strength and courage to tackle the Augean stables again in the morning. Four little Herculeses with a single foolish notion in their heads and a single wound in their hearts: love.

And the end of twelve months they returned, filing in from the four corners of the kingdom and presenting themselves before King Pétaud. Only then — right there in the court where, a year before, the vision had appeared to them — did the four companions remember each other. Big-as-a-Fist, standing at the foot of the throne, raised his eyes and caught sight of his big lummox of a brother, John-Bear, who smiled back timidly at him and shuffled his feet; Extra-Day winked at Sir René, who blinked fondly back. Then the four comrades broke out into sudden, uncontrollable laughter as each received a sticky message on the head from Marco Polo, who cooed ceaseless words of welcome.

"Shit!" they exclaimed in joyful chorus.

Even so brief a moment of reunion, barely long enough for a smile, a wink, and a shout, was enough to reunite the company and to set the Cupid that dwelt in each of their hearts to trembling. But love is tenacious, voracious, and jealous. Before long, the princess reappeared, the sole daughter of the king who had promised her hand to the winner of the contest.

"I have won, Sire," the dwarf affirmed quickly, dropping a handful of seeds into the king's lap. After a year of toil, he had succeeded in growing grain in the desert.

"No, Monseigneur, I have," grunted the giant, depositing at the foot of the throne an oak trunk bigger than himself. He had felled the mighty tree at the very heart of a wild forest.

"Your servant, Your Highness," put in the ancestor, taking from his scrip a rare species of fish that filled the court with a strong odour of iodine and brine.

The latest born said nothing; he merely turned out his pockets and let a half-dozen pieces of gold fall to the ground. They rolled about on the palace's marble tiles, under the astonished gaze of the courtiers.

King Pétaud rubbed his eyes and looked furiously at the figure in the grey cloak and dark glasses. So the four comrades had won. They had survived the most severe tests, deportation to the four most uninhabitable corners of the kingdom. How had the traitors managed to escape their exile?

Tartuffe bit his lips and avoided the king's eyes. This was the first time a victim had ever escaped him, and he wondered what mysterious force had been bestowed on these remarkable beings. Where did their courage, their endurance, their ingenuity come from? He looked each of them over, followed their gaze — which was trained on the face of the beautiful princess. Suddenly he slapped his forehead with the palm of his hand: he understood.

But then the traitor changed his mind. Love was a two-edged sword. Any feeling strong enough to transform a dwarf into a Hercules was also strong enough to change a Hercules into a bleating lamb — especially if the feeling was unrequited. And so Tartuffe gently pushed the princess in among the rival brothers.

"My dear sirs," he said, "the king can only keep his word. But it is also true that he can give his daughter to only one of you. As soon as the most meritorious among you has his superiority acknowledged by the other three, the king will accord him the prize. In his magnanimity, he may even agree to let the losers live, and to give them and their goods safe passage out of the kingdom. I leave it to you, dear sirs, to place the crown on the head of the victor."

The odious figure in grey smothered a snicker that briefly roused Figure-Head's suspicious nature. But a languorous look from the king's daughter soon put it back to sleep.

There they were, then, the four comrades, drooling, lapping up each sigh that left the lips of the princess, hoping to catch her eye, aching to touch her heart, longing to carry her far away from the view of their rivals. But first, each had to convince the others to recognize his supremacy, to emerge victorious from this ultimate test. They had defeated the sea, the desert, the forest, and the underground mines — but which of them was the most worthy, the most needed by the country? All four looked up at the same time, and their eyes met. In a flash they saw that, alone, each was nothing; that gold was a vile, useless metal without the fruits of the earth, which required nourishing streams of water, which had their sources in the forests.

Sir René, wise in his years and in his vast experience, finally took the floor and asked his brothers to listen to him without anger and without taking sides.

"Here we are, we've fallen into the most dangerous trap that cruel, blind Destiny ever set for mankind. We must try to extract ourselves from it without doing irreparable damage or irreversible harm."

The other three were taken by their ancestor's grave tone, and in an instant had recovered their senses and their lost innocence. Sir René had time to weigh his advantage and used it to develop his argument.

"Never before has any of us tried to triumph over nature or the world's ambuscades by himself."

"Never!" echoed his three listeners.

"Never until we set foot on this cursèd soil," the ancestor continued.

"Cursèd soil!" repeated his brothers.

But in cursing the country each brother had raised his fist to the sky, and had found himself brandishing it almost under the nose of his lady love — who smiled at him reproachfully. Immediately all Sir René's fine arguments tumbled down like a house of cards, falling on the head of the ancient mariner himself. Our heroes were lower than ever, wallowing on the ground, crawling on all fours, their noses pressed against the marble that reflected their unrecognizable features back up at them. Big-as-a-Fist, in the depths of his misery, could only console himself with the certainty that he would never know a greater misery. Shamelessly, without restraint, he opened wide the floodgates of his soul and bawled like a calf.

Tom Thumb's tears flowed along the tiles and joined those of John-Bear, which were snaking across the floor like the stream left so far behind in their childhood. Then the two brothers, born out of bread dough and hardwood, took stock of their degradation, lowered their eyes, and thought of the many adventures they'd undertaken since leaving their cradles — a cupboard and a workshop, corrected Big-as-a-Fist, who couldn't keep a small smile from twitching the corner of his mouth — adventures that had led to the discovery of two new brothers, and the exploration of the earth and its mysteries and treasures . . . Such treasures . . . Could they ever find a greater treasure? And wasn't this treasure worth the risk of so many perilous exploits?

Big-as-a-Fist was all in favour of having a good, long cry over his life and his fate, of just staying there on the ground feeling sorry for himself . . . when he heard, warbling just above his head, something that sounded like "I've a message on my foot, my foot, my foot." Raising his head, he found himself looking right into the eye of Marco Polo, his faithful fowl-weather friend.

"What did you say?" he somehow found the strength to ask.

"I said, with your bum stuck up in the air like that, you're not showing the world your best part," replied the pigeon, without getting flustered and without missing a beat.

Taken by surprise, Big-as-a-Fist gathered his feet under him, straightened his legs, and found himself standing up. John-Bear, seeing his brother in an upright position, wiped his face and tried to stand up himself. Instinctively, Extra-Day crawled over to the giant and clung to his ankles, then his knees, then his thighs. Figure-Head saw them all getting up, one by one, and figured it was high time to regroup his troops and restore himself as head of the company. And picking up the thread of his last statement, left stranded in the cursèd land, he added:

"This godforsaken kingdom has enough hidden resources to turn it into a second Eden, if we join forces and share the fruits of our discoveries."

The other three wiped their eyes and noses on their sleeves and listened attentively to the wise old man's propositions.

And that's how our four heroes threw themselves head first into the biggest project of their lives: for a whole year they worked at turning right side up a country that since the beginning of time had been upside down.

Who was it who had the idea — Sir René? Big-as-a-Fist? Or possibly Extra-Day, who by asking good questions forced the others to find good answers? Or perhaps it was John-Bear, who, without a word, immediately rolled up his sleeves and went to work. Suffice it to say that the idea was conceived at the same time in the brain and imagination and soul and heart of the four companions, companions who had no idea where the combined power of their gifts might take them.

They began by withdrawing from the court. Once out of earshot, they compared the fruits of their experiences at the far reaches of the kingdom — their discoveries at the bottom of the sea, in the desert, in the virgin forest, and in the mines of King Pétaud.

"Let's toss all our treasures into a hat, stir them up, and see what kind of rabbit we can pull out," proposed Big-as-a-Fist.

"Or we could weave all the strands together," suggested Sir René, "and see what picture emerges on the tapestry."

And they set to work, weaving images, drawing plans, mixing ideas, turning and turning in their hands the four elements of nature that could bring prosperity back to the country. As they talked, they traced geometrical lines in the sand that boxed one into another and finally drew a cry of triumph from Big-as-a-Fist:

"Eureka! Look here, brothers. Follow the lines, the curve, the circle!"

And the three intrigued comrades leaned over the drawing and followed the dwarf, who was hopping about like a flea on a hot rock.

"One, the lumberjacks take the trees out of the forest and sell them to the carpenters, who, two, make boats out of them which they sell to the fishermen, who sell their fish, three, to the farmers, who use the fish to fertilize their dry fields and then, four, offer wheat for sale to the bakers who sell their bread to the miners, five, who rip gold out of the belly of the earth and make the whole system work. Which is six."

The three listeners opened their eyes wide. John-Bear asked his brother if he'd mind blowing the dust off numbers one, three, and six, which were muddling up his brain, and run over the plan again backwards so it would sink in a bit better. Just as when he was learning the alphabet and the twelve-times table, and had to do them backwards and forwards in order to remember them at all.

"It's quite simple," replied the dwarf, in the magisterial tone of someone who had just discovered the formula $E = mc^2$ and was trying to explain it back to front. "The miners produce gold to buy bread which requires wheat which grows in the desert because the farmers fertilize it with rotten fish taken from the distant sea by fishermen using boats built out of wood cut from the forest by lumberjacks paid for their trees with the king's gold, so he needs more to be taken out of the ground by the miners who buy bread which comes from wheat which comes from the soil . . . Now do you understand, you big dummy?"

No, but it didn't matter: the dummy trusted the genius of his little devil of a brother, and he knew who would eventually be the one to lead the lumberjacks into the forest.

As for the ancestor and the youngest brother, after the twelfth explanation they began to see that if two plus two made four, there was no reason why the king's gold, as it rolled from the wheat fields to the forest, couldn't rebuild the country's economy and provide work — and therefore bread — to every subject in the kingdom.

"Neatly argued," said Sir René, who was not easily impressed. "Let's go to work. In one year, if the gods are with us, Pétaudia will be a land of justice for all, in which the Fat Cats will be trimmed of their fat and the string beans will have put some flesh on their bones."

The gods must have been with them, for the reforms instituted by the four comrades bore fruit. The whole country was put back on its feet: lumbering, planting, building, sea-going, ground-breaking, bread-baking; and last but not least, joyfully eating bread paid for with the king's gold. The king himself never missed it, never even asked where the gold that made the system run so perfectly was coming from.

And our heroes were borne in triumph on the shoulders of the people, who had rediscovered happiness. A happiness too intense to be dampened by a certain grey-cloaked figure in dark glasses, who sat alone in his quiet corner, brooding.

Then, one morning, our four comrades got together and had the following conversation . . . each in his own words and his own accent, and with his own degree of logic or understanding. Big-as-a-Fist's speech went something like this:

"My brothers, we have come, we have seen, we have conquered — conquered famine and the misery of the poor. We have triumphed over the idleness, egotism, and greed of the wealthy. Now it's time for us to be paid, as we were promised by the king's sacred word."

There was a long minute of silence out of respect for the king's word.

"But, my brothers, each of us has grown during these years of challenges and battles, and we have learned, among other things, that love cannot be bought."

At this point the wise René took up the speech and instructed his brothers on the futility of being rivals in love.

"We can all try our luck, since the princess can only love one of us. One at a time, in good faith and fairness, let us see if we can make her love us."

"And may the best man win!" cried Big-as-a-Fist, who couldn't wait to get it over with and come out the winner.

"But first let us swear fidelity, friendship, and fraternity, no matter what happens or to whom it happens," interjected the wise ancestor. "Let us swear to submit ourselves to the verdict of love."

Five hands locked together to cement the agreement: five, because Big-as-a-Fist used both hands in order to keep busy.

"We swear," chorused the four brothers.

And so it was done. Marco Polo was sworn in as a witness and charged with the responsibility of seeing that the rules were strictly adhered to. Each brother would present himself to the princess and formulate his request in is own words, free to make as much of his own advantages as he felt he needed to, and to express in his own way the depth of his feelings.

"Who'll talk to her first?" asked Extra-Day.

"We'll draw lots," said Sir René.

And the shortest straw was drawn by the youngest brother.

He was the youngest, the most innocent, the least experienced in the ways of the world, but he held a trump card the three others didn't have: perfect beauty. Enough perfection to stun the sun, to seduce the moon out of its orbit, to make a stone shed tears of joy. He stunned the princess, swept her off her feet, and made her cry. Never had she seen such beauty outside her own mirror.

She fell madly in love with Extra-Day even before he had time to state his case. She wanted to know only one thing about him — his lineage.

"M-my lineage?" stammered the boy born Out-of-Time. "But I don't have one. I was born no place, on an extra day."

"You're a nobody?" said the princess, with a deep frown. "And the son of a nobody?"

How could the first lady of the court ally her house to someone who didn't have a house? The king would never countenance such a morganatic marriage.

"Nobody?" she repeated. "But surely you can find a small bit of nobility somewhere among your ancestors? A teensy-weensy drop of blue blood? A single great-great-grandfather who beat up his neighbours and stole their land and annexed it to his own?"

"No, nothing like that," bemoaned Extra-Day, who couldn't tell a lie to save his life. "I was born on a public holiday, during a carnival. My mother was a famous giantess who, immediately after delivering me, returned to her place in the collective memory of the people, and their picture books. I have no pedigree, no ancestors."

The princess looked longingly at the splendid infant and contented herself with a deep sigh bracketed by two sobs:

"Oh, how I could have loved you!"

Next, according to the order of the straws, was Sir René, who straightened his back, twirled his moustaches, and stretched his neck above a freshly starched ruff as white as milk.

"Dear lady, arrayed as thou art in such finery," began the ancient gallant. Not in vain had he studied the romances of courtly love and chivalry. "Such unearthly beauty . . . thy voice is as the song of the sirens, thy body is as tender as . . ."

"Hey, wait a minute," cut in Big-as-a-Fist, who was never one for playing by the rules. "What kind of rigmarole is this?"

But René of the Renaissance was well on his way, and had no intention of giving up his advantage. At the feet of his lady love he placed such a bouquet of sonnets, rondeaux, envois, and ritornellos, all dredged up from his cavernous memory, that the king's daughter blushed with embarrassment and pleasure. Big-as-a-Fist was beside himself with rage.

"Oh, what rot!" Worst of all, the princess seemed to be lapping it up. Calm down, Tom Thumb, your turn will come. And when you give her poetry, you won't have to go stealing it from the ancients, you'll make it up yourself. That old windbag may have a memory; but you've got genius on your side.

For the moment, though, the old windbag was sticking it to the young genius, plaiting quatrain into madrigal and dazzling the lady into such a swoon that the question barely dropped from her lips:

"Your lineage, sir?"

His lineage? What a question! If anyone could boast of a family tree, it was Sir René, who'd been suckled at the very breast of yesteryear. He could trace his ancestry back to the First Crusade without even straining his memory. And to please his lady he began sketching a whole pedigree of marshals, crusaders, and cathedral builders, all of whom had long since taken their places in history.

"That's it," Big-as-a-Fist encouraged him. "Bluff her socks off. Bore her to death with all that fatuous self-puffery!"

But far from being bored, the princess was fascinated, and begged to hear more.

"Tell me about mine!" she cried suddenly.

"Yours?"

"Yes, my noble ancestors. Tell me about my noble tree."

"Er . . . Your noble . . .?"

"Come. Your memory won't fail me. Describe my family's past."

Oh-oh!

"Please, I beg of you."

"But . . ."

"No buts. I want to know everything. Nothing less and nothing more than the truth."

"Ah . . ."

Big-as-a-Fist drew closer, intrigued. The wind was about to shift.

Sir René — who owed it to himself, to his brothers, to whom he'd sworn to be true, and to his princess, who required nothing less from him — ended up confessing just how low were the antecedents of the house of Pétaud. One ancestor had been a highwayman, another had been a lady of the night, a third had sold rotten fish at Les Halles in Paris — in short, her ancestors were a whole rogues' gallery of perjurers, pirates, pickpockets, and false priests who had stolen their lands from honest folk and built their kingdom on the domains of others.

The mortified princess blocked her ears and hid her face behind her golden tresses. Never in her life had she been so humiliated. With one hand, she signalled her admirer to go take his admiration somewhere else.

Big-as-a-Fist wasn't as thrilled with the turn of events as might be expected. For one thing, he loved his elder brother dearly and could take no pleasure in his suffering; for another, he loved the princess with all his might and shared her humiliation and chagrin. But after a day or two he observed that she was recovering her spirits, and he decided it was his turn to present his case.

This is how he went about it.

From watching the others, he had learned the pitfalls to avoid and the best path to follow. At all costs he had to divert the princess' mind from the tricky question of lineage. In any case, he realized that she was probably less anxious than he to touch on that particular point, now that it had proven even more awkward for her than it had been for the others. He decided to play it safe, relying on his shining intelligence and his flamboyant personality.

So in he went.

The princess seemed to have grasped the fact that true love didn't have much to do with ancestry, family lines, or social hierarchy, but depended solely on the person. Here, for instance, was a dwarf who, despite certain obvious lacunae in his makeup (which we needn't go into), was perfectly capable of amusing, of astounding, even of touching deeply, the daughter of a king. So rich and varied were the tricks up his sleeve, so full of sallies and interlopings was his speech, so infinite was his capacity for invention, that in his company every day was transformed into the first day of creation.

"No, not the first," he corrected her with a wink; "the eighth! I am a child of the eighth day of creation, the day when everything is dared and anything is possible. Ask me for the moon, the stars, and all the planets."

"Oh-oh," thought John-Bear, "the little devil's getting too big for his britches."

But that day nothing was too big to fit into Big-as-a-Fist's heart. He was soaring so high that even the planets were within his reach. The king's daughter was completely won over: she decided in favour of the manikin.

The wedding was fixed for the next day. The king gave his royal assent; the brothers wisely and loyally accepted the decision; the table was set for the engagement banquet. Big-as-a-Fist, as cock-of-the-walk, was all grace and magnanimity. He sat with his comrades about him and his betrothed, and even thought to toss some cake crumbs to Marco Polo, who was perched on the carved back of his chair.

Suddenly he stood up to his full height and, raising his flagon in both hands, proposed a toast to love. He spoke with such fervour, such inspiration, gliding from love in general to the love of his life to the brotherly love he felt for his comrades, whom he would never forget and to whom he wished as much happiness as he had found, a happiness that would last forever . . .

"If he doesn't finish pretty soon," thought John-Bear, "I'm going to start bawling." The giant already had a lump in his throat, and in order to help himself swallow it he looked around for something to eat, anything, the first piece of meat that came to hand, and he grabbed a side of beef and vigorously began to shake pepper onto it. Maybe too vigorously, because a few grains flew up Big-as-a-Fist's nose, and he sneezed at the very moment when he was down on one knee and about to make his official proposal to the princess.

And the princess farted!

On the day of her engagement, in front of her betrothed and the entire court, the princess had farted. It wasn't something she could take back. Instead, she slipped out of sight behind the thick, golden tapestries that were gently glowing in the light of the setting sun.

Her lover, meanwhile, was on the point of having a nervous breakdown. His eighth day had shattered into a thousand pieces. It wasn't fair. Shit, shit, and more shit! That was one gift that his godforsaken godmother could have left in the bottom of her cauldron. Shit again! What was the use of being supremely gifted? What good did it do him to be born on the eighth day? Would he never find infinite, eternal happiness? He'd never be consoled.

He took to his bed, confining his misery to the depths of his pillow, and awaited death.

He awaited it for three days. On the third day, he opened one eye. Then one ear. Then both nostrils. The smell of roasted fowl in fruit and almonds was wafting up the staircase and into his room. Then came the sound of padded feet in the hallway. It was John-Bear, who had come with his two brothers to bring dinner to his dying comrade. Big-as-a-Fist's nose could now make out the kind of fruit — greengages — and the kind of fowl — goose.

And that's how our moribund manikin was dragged out of his bed and away from death's door.

The princess eventually recovered, too, and agreed, after eight days of supplication, to receive the fourth and final claimant: the giant.

After so many trials and tribulations, the first lady of the kingdom was somewhat humbled and, like the heron in the fable, believed herself capable of being content with a snail. That's why she was so surprised to see John-Bear that she didn't even notice his knotty head or his big feet. All she saw was his fine stature and his superbly crafted body, and she sighed for the rest of him, which was hidden from her view.

And that's how John-Bear triumphed over his three brothers.

You might think that the contest was over, for lack of contestants. That the story of John-the-Strong ended there, in the triumph of love over friendship, adventure, and destiny. His three brothers certainly thought so. Even the giant himself must have given it a moment's thought. But, well, John-Bear did have his maxims, as well as a loyal and generous heart. And all of these, taken together, gave him as hard a time as they gave his brothers. One day, coming upon a gardener in the palace grounds who was weeping for love of his lost princess, John-Bear refused his challenge to a duel in the name of love, because the gardener was smaller, weaker, and more miserable than himself. Then, without saying anything to his fellow adventurers, he snuck out of bed on the morning of his wedding day and tiptoed out the door. Extra-Day saw him go and woke up Sir René, who woke up Big-as-a-Fist, who had practically kicked the stuffing out of his straw mattress.

"Let's leave this god-awful place while there's still time. Grey-Cloak visited me in a dream last night, and I got the distinct impression the old cockaballoo has plans to get his hands on this country again. Let's go while the going's good."

As the four heroes crossed the border just before sunrise, they noticed that the lumberjacks were no longer selling wood to the carpenters, but were making boats with it themselves and selling them directly to the fishermen. And the farmers, instead of selling their wheat to the bakers, were making their own bread and supplying it to the miners, while the miners . . .

"Alas!" cried Figure-Head, "we should have known this would happen. I give them four seasons of this, the schemers, before chaos and famine once again descend on the land of King Pétaud."

Big-as-a-Fist shot a glance at his elder brother and gave a little smile. This time the old dotard couldn't blame *him* for calling down scourges by name. If Mad Meg suddenly appeared . . .

Suddenly, she appeared.

"I knew it!" said Big-as-a-Fist, for the ancestor's benefit. "You didn't have to go and call her, the rotten old witch."

The little upstart would have been less eager to poke fun at his brother had he known what the Grim Reaper's ultimate weapon was, the one she'd been holding in reserve especially for these four, her most redoubtable enemies.

The appearance of Dulle Griet at the edge of the kingdom at least served to distract our heroes from their broken hearts, and to cement them even closer than they had been before King Pétaud split them apart.

"Shit!" shouted Big-as-a-Fist as he watched Mad Meg striding towards them.

"Double shit!" replied his companions, remembering their rallying cry.

And without looking back, our four heroes shook the dust of Pétaudia off their feet and fled the hideous countenance of their enemy. As for her, she just shrieked with laughter and fluttered the wings of her huge mantle, pushing them straight into the hell they should have been — and thought they were — avoiding.

14

From the plague, and from all the scourges of the world,
deliver us, O Lord

No sooner had the four brothers set foot inside the village walls than they heard the gates groaning on their hinges. The village was shutting in upon itself.

"Plague!" cried Sir René, who had survived the terrifying epidemic in his own time, but had lost so many ancestors to the Black Death in the fourteenth century that his very existence had hung on a thread. "We must leave this place; this is the worst of all scourges, and it spares no one."

Too late. The gates had been closed, and a state of siege declared. This time, our heroes were well and truly cornered.

"Oh my God, oh my God," sighed Big-as-a-Fist, as if to echo the shrill laughter of Mad Meg, whose shadow already enveloped the northern half of the village.

"We'll take refuge in the southern quarter," Figure-Head proposed hurriedly.

But alas, though they slipped like ghosts from the north to the east and south, the black shadow followed them. Finally it darkened the entire village.

Wherever they went they saw boarded-up houses, drowned rats in the gutters, litters bearing away the dying, and tumbrels carting off the dead. And there were cries, and groans, and unbearable silence. After four days, a tenth of the village lay dead; the rest of the population wouldn't last a year.

At first our companions tried to look the other way whenever a barrow or a cart went by. But at the sight of a plague-ridden mother trying to give suck to her dead baby, Extra-Day nearly swooned and Big-as-a-Fist threw up. Sir René decided it was time to rally his brothers together and prepare them for the worst.

"Death —" he began softly, lowering his voice an octave or two.

"No!" cut in Big-as-a-Fist, covering his ears. "Not that, no, no, no! We've hardly lived. We've just started on our adventures. And . . . and I just can't stand it. I'm allergic to death!"

And turning his back on life, he retired to his corner, pouting.

Sir René took up his speech again from the beginning, calling the company together and trying to make the young adventurers understand that they could not always emerge victorious from life's battles, that destiny was destiny no matter how hard they fought against it, that Dulle Griet . . .

"That's enough!" stormed the dwarf, who refused to budge from his obstinacy. "We gave the hangman a good run for his money before. And as you may recall, it wasn't exactly easy. We can't just give in to him now."

He spoke with his finger raised, as if that finger alone had been responsible for sending the hangman down into the netherworld.

Figure-Head sensed that his task was not going to be easy; if it was difficult to prepare a dying man for death, how much more difficult it would be to tell four healthy fellows that their end was near. And four healthier fellows had never walked the earth: how the devil was he to make them understand that no man is immortal?

All of a sudden his attention was drawn to an unusual commotion in the square in front of the church. Several old men, too weak even to call out, were dragging themselves up the church steps and pointing to the bells. The ancestor saw his brothers watching them, their curiosity aroused; they moved towards the steps and raised their heads to look at the bells, which had begun to ring. What was going on?

"I don't know," said the dwarf, who had forgotten his fear, "but it seems very odd. Apparently there's a child locked in the bell tower — Extra-Day saw him up there."

Bit by bit, the news spread throughout the village that a desperate mother, just before dying herself, had chained her child to the clapper of the big tenor bell to arouse the pity of passersby when they heard the bell ringing. The first to feel any pity, however, were John-Bear and Big-as-a-Fist.

"He'll be crushed against the bell," cried the dwarf.

"Either that, or he'll work himself loose and fall off the tower," added Extra-Day.

"Do you think," asked John-Bear, "that the tower is strong enough for me to climb it?"

"It's made of wood," said Big-as-a-Fist, "and a bit worm-eaten. But it's holding up those heavy bells."

Sir René joined his brothers.

"You're too heavy, John-Bear," he said. "Let the dwarf go up."

Big-as-a-Fist stifled a cry. "Going up's no problem," he said. "But how will I get down, carrying a child three times my size on my back?"

If he's referring to his size, thought the ancestor, he must be in quite a state. Figure-Head was about to offer to go himself when he was forestalled by Extra-Day.

"What about me?" he asked. "Just because I'm the youngest, you tend to forget me."

"No, not at all."

"I'm going."

"No, let me climb it."

"It's a dangerous job, and I'm the one to take it on."

"Get back, this is my baby."

The four brothers began jostling each other so much that they ended up shaking the tower — the poor, worm-eaten tower, which already looked as if it would cave in under the weight of the giant, and which now had to stand the combined assault of four eager comrades racing up it three stairs at a time. Before they could think, before they heard the splitting of the rotten wood, before they asked themselves how they were going to get out again, our heroes found themselves in the top chamber of the tower where, by struggling to get free, the child had started every bell in the cathedral ringing.

Fifteen minutes later, when their exploit was over, none of our heroes could say for certain what had happened, except that one of them had released the poor child and passed him into the arms of a second, who had passed him down to a third, and so on down the chain — a chain that ended up with the child standing safe and sound on the ground at the foot of the tower, surrounded by a swelling crowd of onlookers.

And what a triumphal welcome it was!

Then: "Look out!" cried the pigeon to the company. "The tower!"

And the tower collapsed to the ground with a din of bells and clappers; the great tenor bell rolled right to the feet of the four heroes and the rescued child, who had just barely escaped with his life.

They had been saved from the collapsing tower. But there was still the plague. A plague that could be clearly seen in every face now turned towards them, on every arm that reached out to touch the orphan — one of the few children who had somehow escaped the notice of Mad Meg.

Sir René, who alone knew all the tricks the Madwoman had up her sleeve, realized the importance of keeping the child out of her sight, of hiding him somewhere far from this pestilential population and this climate of contagion. They must get him away from the rats, the fleas, the bedbugs; they must bathe him in disinfectant; they must bury his head in the sand.

"He'd die of fright, if not boredom," protested Big-as-a-Fist.

"Not with you around," retorted the ancestor. "Anyway, we have to do our best with what we have."

They did so well with what they had that after eight days they had succeeded not only in saving the child, but also in finding him a wet nurse — Marco Polo had discovered her holed up in a cave on the side of a mountain, along with a dozen other panic-stricken pilgrims who dared not return to their village. Using great quantities of creosote and benzene, they disinfected the houses, burned the cadavers, whitewashed the battlements with quicklime, buried the dead, cared for the sick, and quarantined the survivors.

Without stopping even to catch their breath.

"The bitch has just been here," Big-as-a-Fist would shout. "This way!"

And the other three would run to his aid.

"She's leaving this house — after her!"

And they would dash off, hot on her trail.

"I saw her heading east!"

And they'd head east.

"North!"

They'd swerve north.

"Over here!"

"Over there!"

"Faster, faster!"

"Oof!"

Finally, Sir René stopped and sagged down on the edge of a well, mopped his brow, and sighed:

"Comrades, brothers, let's face it: we're never going to catch up to her. This time, she really is the strongest. I'm afraid the village is done for, alas!"

The other three let their heads droop to their chests and felt like crying: John-Bear for the village; Extra-Day for the village and the child; and Big-as-a-Fist for the village, the child, and himself. Once again the dwarf blurted out the first thought that came into his head — a thought born of despair, revolt, and defiance:

"At least we can sell our lives dearly, brothers. Let's not let Meg win the day without a fight!"

In expressing his idea, Big-as-a-Fist had come to see it more clearly. He even began to find it intriguing.

"What if, instead of attacking the plague, we attacked its source?"

The other three caught their breath. All things considered, it wasn't a bad idea. Get to the root of the problem, go straight for the sower of the evil seed. But how?

"I can hit her," said John-Bear. "She's bigger than me."

"I can talk to her," said Sir René. "She may have a weak side."

"If she has a weak side," put in Big-as-a-Fist, "maybe we can lure her into a trap."

Extra-Day had nothing to add to this, having complete confidence in his older brothers.

And so our heroes armed themselves for their final encounter with the sower of the scourges.

Along with his life, John-Bear had inherited strength, courage, and a sense of honour that was hardly common for his time. He could no more lie to himself than he could deceive others. After a twelve-hour, hand-to-hand struggle, he realized that he would never emerge victorious from this battle; but according to his third maxim, he had to finish the fight once it was started, even if the fight finished him.

And by the evening of that first day, John Strong-as-a-Dozen had already received so many blows that his companions foresaw the blackest of outcomes. He had to withdraw from this unequal contest.

"Come away, John-Bear! Give up!"

Impossible. He was picking on someone bigger than he was; he was coming to the aid of someone weaker than himself; and he was finishing what he'd started.

Hell and damnation! said the dwarf to himself. What have you done now? Why couldn't you count to ten before spouting your brilliant ideas, you little blatherskite? And he pummelled himself savagely while heaping obscenities on the Madwoman.

"I'm going in there," Figure-Head suddenly resolved. He took a deep breath and warned his two younger brothers not to move from their observation posts. "Take care of your brother."

Which they did. They dropped him into a cart which Extra-Day pushed into the shade of an oak tree, and Big-as-a-Fist, who had already bathed himself in benzene, proceeded to swab the swollen tumours as quickly as they appeared on John-Bear's body.

"You're not done for yet, my old friend, my giant. We're going to lance these boils for you. She won't get you that easily."

While the dwarf was busy putting his brother's fears to rest by rocking them in a cradle of loving words, the ancestor was using rather stronger language to deal with the maddened sower of the worst scourge of all time.

"Do you really take pleasure in making the poor and the innocent suffer? Why don't you take those who've earned the wrath of the gods? Instead you do the exact opposite. Everyone knows how you like to spare sinners. You should attack them, you should be ridding the world of evil parasites like yourself. Not tearing the suckling babe from its mother's breast; not weighing down the aged with extra burdens; not adding more misery to those who are already miserable enough. At least have the decency to spare the victims of storms, famines, and wars; aren't you ashamed of always taking those who are weaker than yourself?"

No, she wasn't ashamed. Such a sentiment was unknown to Dulle Griet. In fact, the old crone knew nothing of any sentiment. No shame, no humanity, no compassion. And the laugh she threw out to the distant hills came echoing back and squeezed the lungs and glands of Sir René as if in a vice. But then it was his turn to laugh.

"You won't get me this time, Dark One. You left me to die once, four hundred years ago, and I survived that. Now I'm immune to you; you won't get me a second time."

The Madwoman glared furiously at the ancestor, then turned and went off to shake her mantle over the poorest, most desperate section of the village.

"It's my turn," said the dwarf, speaking softly for the first time in his life. "Nothing ventured, nothing gained."

Then, to give himself courage and to reassure his comrades, he added:

"Anyway, they say that death has no dominion over the Devil and his kind, so I should be pretty safe."

And without looking back, Big-as-a-Fist set out to track down Mad Meg. He was the least brave of the four heroes, and as he made his way he concocted plan after plan in his head, then rejected them one by one. In the end he decided that, when the time came, his instinct would be of more use than his reasoning reason.

"Well, if it isn't my old friend Marco Polo. Where've you been?"

"In a hole in an oak tree; I've been passing the time of day with an old owl."

"An owl? At this hour? And what a time for a chat! Wouldn't you rather help me set a trap for the Madwoman? You know what grave peril the village is in — and all of us, too!"

By way of response, the pigeon made a superb looping dive and passed between the legs of the dwarf, lifting him up into the air on his back. Big-as-a-Fist barely had time to shout, "Giddyup! Hyah, hyah!" and think of his stormy youth before letting himself be carried away by this steed.

"She's right down there," cooed the pigeon. "Walking through the dirtiest, most miserable part of town."

"The shrew! Let's go down and put a flea in her ear."

He meant it figuratively, not realizing that the pigeon was the type to take him at his word. But in fact, Mad Meg's hat had two large slits in the sides to make room for her ears. She had huge ears — all the better to hear the moans and groans she left in her wake. Ears as large as a badger's lair, or a fox's den . . . a fox . . . "I wonder what Cousin Renard would do in these circumstances," he said to himself.

Marco Polo was heading for the gaping opening of the Madwoman's ear. "He'd hide in there," he said. "Let's go!"

And without waiting for a reply he landed on the auricle and shoved the dwarf into the ear canal.

"Whoa!" cried our reluctant hero; then "Woe!" when he realized what a pickle he'd landed himself in. He'd never get out of this one alive. That's what you get for asking a birdbrain for advice, he told himself. He couldn't just stay quietly at home, in the land of his fathers, could he, to propagate the grand old lineage of his ancestors? Oh, no. He had to go out and risk his life on the most dangerous — not to mention the most uncomfortable — roads he could find!

"Talk about uncomfortable! Why . . ."

But he never finished his sentence. Suddenly his retreat was cut off completely: the opening to the tunnel had been covered up.

"Hey! What's going on here? Who's blocking the road?"

Blocking it more and more. It was Meg, of course; feeling a twitch in her eardrums, she had clapped her hands over her ears, imprisoning Big-as-a-Fist right in the plague-sower's head.

Well, as you might imagine, the little maneen started hopping about and hollering for help. He bellowed for his comrades, his brother, even his mother, Goodwife. He shouted, stamped his feet, and generally yelled up the worst storm the Madwoman had ever heard — though she'd scattered enough of them in her day. Never had any stalwart knight penetrated so deeply into her defences. For the first time, the spreader of scourges had encountered a scourge not of her own making — and it was almost driving her crazy. She danced on one foot, then on the other; she yelled, she poked her ears, her entire body shook like a leaf. Big-as-a-Fist had given her her very first headache.

Then she started to cough; something was choking her, caught in her windpipe, sliding down her gullet, tumbling into her belly. Suddenly she wrapped her arms around her stomach and rent the sky with a horrific screech.

Meanwhile, the three other brothers were on their guard, nearly deafened by the Madwoman's cries, and growing more and more concerned for the fate of their comrade. They couldn't imagine how the dwarf could be getting the better of the ogress by himself. And yet they could plainly hear her cries of anguish. Someone was dealing her a deathly blow. By what miracle, what master stroke, was our hero Big-as-a-Fist triumphing over a giantess the size of Dulle Griet?

"He's got a few tricks up his sleeve," mused the ancestor, "but even so . . ."

"He's pretty brave, all the same . . . ," ventured John-Bear, trembling for his brother.

"He's got a wicked kick, our Tom Thumb," added Extra-Day. "If he can just put his boot to her backside."

Extra-Day was right about the kick, but the location wasn't quite what he imagined. Big-as-a-Fist was getting his wicked kicks in, but from the wrong side.

"Shit, shit, shit!" he spat with disgust, splashing about up to his waist in the Madwoman's stomach. "What a cock-up this is! How am I ever going to get out of this stinking hellhole? Damn it! Now I've really done it, sticking my nose in someone else's ear! Look where it's got me: in a bucket of shit up to my neck! Ugh, ugh, yuck!"

All the time he was lamenting his fate, Big-as-a-Fist was floundering about and clutching at the insides of Dulle Griet, who was doubled over with pain. But where he was was dark and silent, and so our explorer of the deep couldn't hear his victim's cries, or even guess at the success of his mission. On this one time when he was on the verge of success, our hero — ordinarily so full of self-confidence — was completely unaware of the enormity of his adventure in the very stomach of Death.

And by the time he was aware of it, he was out. Here's how.

You surely haven't forgotten the third gift he'd claimed as his rightful inheritance from his godmother, Clara-Galante. And you can bet that Big-as-a-Fist hadn't forgotten it either. Except that, ever since his fiasco at the feet of his beloved princess, he'd lost faith in all his gifts and was reluctant to use them — the third gift in particular. After a long debate with himself, however, he decided that he had to get out of his present situation, which was becoming more and more entangled; that he couldn't spend the rest of his life bunged up in this shit-hole. And since one orifice was blocked up he had to find another one, if it meant moving heaven and earth. And that's what he did, right in the bowels of Mad Meg; he used his gifts for all they were worth.

It was the third gift that did it. As soon as he sneezed, the Madwoman let loose a fart that covered the earth with noise and wind, and landed none other than our hero Tom Thumb, also known as Big-as-a-Fist, on his feet.

Well, if he'd been looking for adventure, he'd found it!

Of course, when he related his tale to his brothers he filled it out a bit. As if a voyage through the guts of the Grim Reaper weren't adventure enough, he had to go and embellish it.

"You know," said Sir René, "that little fellow will find a way to make eternity last longer, to keep himself out of the dock on Judgement Day."

While waiting for Judgement Day, however, Big-as-a-Fist and his three brothers were planted pretty firmly on the ground, and were still faced with the sower of scourges; purged of her stomach ailment, she'd come out of the battle nastier than ever.

"We've got to put a stop to her," muttered the dwarf, who'd come so close to doing just that.

"We've got to," echoed the other three, who were as determined as he was.

"But we've tried everything!" bemoaned John-Bear.

"What about me?" said the youngest brother in reproach. "You haven't tried me yet."

It was true. There was still Extra-Day. He was their last hope. A slim hope, to be sure, but a hope nonetheless.

"Did you notice anything unusual about her, Tom Thumb," asked the ancestor, "on your way through her innards?"

Come to think of it, he had; she had no heart, he'd noticed, and her intestines had gone bad.

"Anything else?"

An enormous brain, full of little pigeonholes . . .

"A universal memory," said Figure-Head sadly.

"And oh, yes, there was something else," added Big-as-a-Fist, looking perplexed. "Where her heart should have been, I saw a kind of vase made of two vials joined together. I think it may have been an hourglass."

Extra-Day looked up and smiled.

"An hourglass in place of a heart, eh? If you're willing to lend me a hand, I think the four of us still have a chance to do her in."

The three comrades soon put themselves at the disposal of their youngest member, declaring themselves ready to follow him blindly. Just say the word.

First, he told Big-as-a-Fist to call the pigeon. For this, their final assault on Dulle Griet, the companions would need all their reserves. Then the child born on an extra day began doling out the tasks.

Marco Polo would start by calling the shrew by all her various names. That would make her spread herself all over the place at the same time, shaking her apron at the four corners of the world. Meanwhile, Big-as-a-Fist would play his magic flute, which would make her dance until she was ready to drop. At that point Sir René, who was immune to her and therefore had nothing to fear, would come along and casually engage her in conversation. He'd mention, among other things, that her feet must be getting tired, and suggest that she give them a rest by dancing on her hands for a while. As soon as John-Bear saw her with her backside in the air, he'd grab her by the heels and hold her fast, upside down, until Out-of-Time had time to complete the master stroke of their lives.

"Has everyone got it?"

"Got it!"

"You all know what you have to do?"

"We know!"

"Okay, let's go. And break a leg!"

"Break a leg!" cried the others in unison, while Marco Polo dropped one of his lucky messages on his master's nose.

Everything went according to plan. There was one moment when Sir René thought all was lost: when he heard the tune that Big-as-a-Fist was playing on his flute — a *danse macabre* that almost aroused the Madwoman's suspicions. But the ancestor glared so sternly at the incautious musician that the little joker switched over quickly to a fiendish farandole. As soon as Sir René had persuaded the Madwoman to relax her vigilance and dance on her hands, John-Bear rushed in, hobbled her, and held her dangling upside down until Extra-Day, the grand master of time, arrived on the scene.

"Nobody move," he ordered. "Hold her like that until her hour-glass is completely refilled. She's passing through every hour backwards: it's our only chance to make her run out of time."

The three others — even the pigeon, who had travelled to the far corners of the earth — watched with their mouths gaping and their eyes as big as saucers.

"Well, I'll be . . ."

The rest was child's play. Extra-Day stretched the skin of time until it split open, leaving a hole just big enough to allow the shrewish Mad Meg to slip through — with the help of John-Bear's seven-league boots. With a wail straight out of Hell, she plunged head first into the infinite void.

The sound of an avalanche rose up to fill the four comrades' ears: even the pigeon heard it. Then they realized what it was: tumbling through the far side of time, Dulle Griet had dropped all her scourges, and they were banging into one another like rocks from a mountain struck by a thunderbolt.

"Watch out one of them doesn't hit us," said Big-as-a-Fist.

But for once, the ancestor's face remained calm. He even smiled.

"No," he said to his brothers. "This time — thanks to Extra-Day and all of you — she has gone, and will leave us in peace. For a time. The plague will ravage the earth no more than once every century or so, hardly ever more often than that. It'll take her a least a hundred years to get her foot back out through her arse."

It was the first time the ancestor had spoken so freely.

He must really be pleased and content, Big-as-a-Fist told himself.

Indeed, they were all more than pleased and content to see the last shreds of the plague — the worst of the century — rushing out of the houses and up from the holes in the ground.

"Let's go find the child we saved from the bell tower," suggested Extra-Day.

"Good idea," put in John-Bear. "And keep him with us."

"Now that we've beaten the Grim Reaper . . . ," added Big-as-a-Fist.

But he didn't have time to finish the thought. Sir René raised his right arm for silence, his eyes fixed and his ears perked.

"What is it?"

"Shhh! Listen."

They listened. And heard, barely perceptible in the distance, the rumble of wheels. The three brothers couldn't see how the sound of wheels crushing pebbles on a distant road could be so upsetting to the soul of their ancient comrade.

"It's just a cart, Sir René," Big-as-a-Fist cried happily.

"It is the Coach," murmured the other, drawing out the "oa" in coach like the rumble of an empty coffin.

Then, feigning composure so as not to alarm his friends, he said:

"Let's go! We've still got a good stretch of road to cover. Let's not tarry here."

"What about the child?" asked Extra-Day, his eyes full of tears.

"We'll leave him with his wet nurse. What lies in store for us is much too dangerous for a newborn babe. When he's older, he'll learn that it was we who saved his life, and that we are in some respects his true parents. Perhaps . . ."

He stopped. The others fell silent, too, thinking of a child whom they themselves had almost brought into the world, and who might very well have been their heir.

15

If the earth is round, then where is the end of the world?

First thing next morning, life took up where it had left off.

Big-as-a-Fist noticed, however, that Sir René kept clapping his hands over his ears. Was he sick? Or was he just trying to keep out the unhealthy noises of the world?

"Not exactly unhealthy," said the ancestor, who felt the time was past for playing hide-and-seek with Destiny. "But nerve-racking."

Big-as-a-Fist burst out laughing. For him, the time for playing games was never past. If Destiny had time to play, well then, he'd play with Destiny — and for keeps!

He bit his tongue, that forked tongue of his that never hid anything that was on his mind . . . Maybe it was time for an internal reassessment, he told himself, time to start assigning a more important role to reason. All your life you've trusted your instincts and your intuition. And it's true these gifts have served you fairly well. You're still here, anyway, happy, healthy, lively, astute, ingenious, handsome, young, tall . . . Whoa now, Thomas, let's not get carried away. Better settle for happy and healthy.

At this point our hero was jerked out of his self-contemplation by a shout from the edge of the woods. It was John-Bear, calling him to come quickly and see their oldest brother in a heap.

"A heap of what?"

"Of himself. He just broke down for nothing."

The dwarf went up to Sir René and tried to distract him and cheer him up.

"It's nothing, don't worry. The sun got in my eyes, that's all. There's so much light here. And so little air."

"So little air?" said Extra-Day, astonished. "But we're outdoors."

John-Bear, who wasn't in the habit of questioning the wisdom of his twin brother, started sucking up air into his own lungs and blowing it into the face of his ailing ancestor. All three of them worked to such good effect, in fact, each in his own way and according to his own gifts, that after three days Figure-Head raised himself up on his elbows, opened his eyes, and asked for a drink.

"A drink!" crowed Big-as-a-Fist, so loudly that every tree in the forest felt summoned.

Little by little, and with the help of a few flagons of wine, the ancestor's strength was restored. Soon he was able to reassure his comrades.

"Peace be among ye, my children," he said to them. "Be ye without sorrow, crainte, or doubt. This malady that has afflicted my poor shell shall not be visited upon ye."

Oh-oh, thought Big-as-a-Fist, he's gone back to talking in his ancient language. I don't like the looks of it — it's a bad sign, if you ask me. To the others, he said:

"We've got to purge him. Extra-Day, go into the woods and pick some yarrow and some wintergreen."

As his strength returned, so did his infallible memory and his indisputable wisdom. Once again he took to instructing his comrades on foul and fair weather; the difference between mushrooms and toadstools; the circulation of water; the revolution of the planets; and the history of the world in general. In this way, the dwarf was convinced that the old dotard was fully recovered, and that they could get back on the road.

"If we're ever going to prove that the world is round, we'd better push off."

Once again, the ancestor's brows furrowed:

"You three, perhaps. You're still young, in spite of everything."

Each one protested in his own fashion, one by wringing his feet, another his hands, the dwarf his whole body.

"We're not that young. Anyway, as far as this venture is concerned we're all the same age, because we all started out on it at the same time. Let's change the subject."

And they stopped talking altogether.

Finally, to break the heavy silence, Sir René said, "Very well, then, I'll tell you what it's all about."

"Can't you tell us later?"

"No, it's time now."

"All right, then, let's hear it!"

And so Sir René of the Renaissance, also known as Figure-Head, told his three brothers the story of the Coach of Death. The brothers were intrigued at first, then completely stupefied, When he'd finished, he added in his rough, grave voice:

"And that's why you shouldn't be surprised if, from time to time, you see me cover my ears: I'm trying to shut out the dreadful sound of those wheels."

So that was it!

Now it was difficult to count on the future, faced with this new vision of their enemy. Without a doubt, their adversary had a thick skin. What good did it do to beat the cowled figure of the hangman and to banish Mad Meg to the farthest reaches of time if that deathly Coach was still waiting up ahead to block their route? Ah, me!

"So?" said the dwarf to himself. "So what if the Coach does exist? So what if it's spotted us and decided to take us on board? It still has to catch us: catch John-Bear, with his seven-league boots? Catch Extra-Day, who can run faster than time? Catch Sir René for the second time — when he knows it like the back of his hand? And catch me? Well, I admit I'm the most likely — but I've still got my pigeon, and he'll carry me up into the clouds. But no — this time let's take the offensive, and not let adversity beat us or get us down. We just won't let it catch us off guard, that's all."

And to get off on the right foot from the start, Big-as-a-Fist proposed to his friends that they drown out the squeaking of the Coach's axles in a sea of even louder sound.

"Music! Music, my brothers! We'll throw ourselves into such a hullabaloo of new sounds that the noise of those pebble-crunching wheels will be driven out of our ears forever."

"If it's new sounds you want," cooed the pigeon, "I know some marshes near here that can give you enough to last a lifetime."

"Musical marches?" asked the others, intrigued.

"They're called the Tintamarre Marshes," said the pigeon.

Are they, now!

Well, good enough. And following in the wake of the pigeon, the little troupe headed off in the direction of Tintamarre.

When they got close to the marsh, all they could hear at first were ducks shouting to each other to take cover, as strangers were approaching.

"They mean us," translated Big-as-a-Fist, the only one of the company who could understand animal language.

Then, turning to the pigeon:

"Is this what you call musical marshes? It sounds like a lot of out-of-tune twanging to me."

"Just listen."

So they listened.

"What's that?"

There came a strange assortment of noises from the wild salt grasses: murmurings, whisperings, sudden sharp shouts. And somewhere in the background, rifle fire, then an explosion.

"Did you hear that?"

Now they could hear the clashing of swords, the whistling of bullets, and the rumbling of heavy cannon. They could hear it; they could still see nothing.

"There must have been a big battle on these Tintamarre Marshes."

"Must've."

Suddenly, directly under their feet, the grass began to quiver and quake and let loose a low booming sound, as of thunder or drums. Then came hissing, humming, buzzing, blustering, and grinding, getting louder and louder until the marsh resounded with a clamour that grew ever closer and more shattering. Whatever was washing over the Tintamarre — holus-bolus, bacchanale, or charivari — one thing was for sure: it had fallen into complete cacophony.

"I can't stand it any longer," wailed Sir René, covering his ears, "I'd rather listen to axles grinding."

The other three were appalled, and refused to give in. But Big-as-a-Fist suggested that they catch the rebellious sounds and force them into a harmony . . . Go on, Extra-Day, run after them, grab them in mid-air, straighten them out, snip the tails off the quarter notes . . . No, no, John-Bear, don't swallow them whole — you'll get a bad case of wind.

The Tintamarre Marshes were nothing more than a vast collecting ground for musical notes, tones, and chords, in which our four bold cavaliers did battle with the sounds in order to drown out the noise of the Coach.

"Pass me a groan, would you?"

"How about lending me a rumble, John-Bear?"

"Well, I seem to have three voices too many. How about trading them for a long sigh and two explosions?"

And so, from explosion to groaning sigh, our musicians climbed the scale to create harmonics: they mixed sounds, sprang rhythms, reinvented a few melodies, and ended up by returning to the Tintamarre its primitive symphony, which time, wind, and war had smashed to smithereens.

That evening, our four heroes dropped down onto the wild grass and slept to the sound of the music they had re-created from the dissonant chords of nature and history.

"At least tonight," though Big-as-a-Fist, "neither the old man nor anyone else will have to listen to the grinding of the Coach."

And it stayed night for eight days.

Eight days later, our heroes woke up in fine fettle, aware that they had managed to clip the wings of fate. With such melodies running through their heads, they felt strong enough to get back on the road to adventure, to roll along neck and neck with the Coach itself, if need be, without paying the slightest attention to the sound of its wheels.

"Let's be off, old buddies! It's time we seized the day," exclaimed Big-as-a-Fist, too fired up to stop to ask himself what day he was seizing.

In fact, it was Hallowe'en — which in those parts was called "trick-or-treat" day.

Tricks! Now there was a word our heroes could never hear with cool indifference. Without tricking and treating, and folktales and popular legends, they would probably never have been born in the first place.

"This is my lucky day!" cried Big-as-a-Fist suddenly, for he had just conceived another of his brilliant, audacious ideas, and was eager to share it with the entire company. "What if we play a trick on the Coach, you know, have ourselves a little fun . . ."

Sir René choked and nearly fell over. The very idea of playing with Death was enough to tie a knot in his throat. "Thumbkin, surely you could think of something a little more fun than that."

The dwarf begged the ancestor's pardon; he hadn't meant to alarm him, he was just trying to take the company's mind off its fears and anxieties . . . Anyway, as far as he was concerned the best way to forget about the Coach was to trick it and make fun of it.

Figure-Head was about to launch into the distinction between universal death, which was anonymous and lay in store for everyone, and personal death, which afflicted each of them individually . . . when he stared off towards the horizon with a wild, distracted look, and told his brothers to be quiet.

"Don't look around. I'm the only one it's seen."

But this time his comrades refused to obey. If that old bus was coming their way, it would take all of them or nobody. It was only a wagon, after all. Black, maybe, and drawn by six horses, but, like any other wagon, it had to have a driver.

"It's not even a wagon," corrected Big-as-a-Fist. "It's more like a carriage. You've seen carriages before — they're no worse than taxicabs, sedans, or buggies. If every time we pass a black baby carriage on the road we take it into our heads to . . ."

Give it up, Big-as-a-Fist. It was all very well for the dwarf to run off at the mouth like that, trying to keep his spirits up, but even he was beginning to feel his humour turning sour. For as the Coach passed he caught a glimpse of the driver, and thought he remembered seeing him before somewhere . . . No, Big-as-a-Fist, you're getting senile. Don't go getting your nose all out of joint. You don't know who he is, you've never seen him before, you know nothing about any of that, change the subject and talk about the rain or the sunshine or whatever . . .

But when he opened his mouth to talk about something else, this is what he heard coming out:

"You know that hangman we met back in our younger days? Does anyone remember what he looked like?"

None of the others could recall his face very well; they hadn't seen much of his face. He'd been a big man, and he'd always worn a hood.

"And we killed him," finished John-Bear, trying to settle his brother down.

Time passed.

Then one morning, just when the troupe had cheered up again and was in a good mood, Marco Polo turned back to drop another one of his messages on the heads of his masters — as he did before every spot of danger along the road. This morning he borrowed the five-syllable cry of the blue jays:

"Break camp, lazybones! Break camp, you sluggards!"

Big-as-a-Fist was affronted that a bird should take such liberties, and was about to teach the pigeon a lesson in manners and linguistics when he saw a black shape drawn by six horses barrelling along the road. The four comrades barely had time to leap out of the way into the bushes.

Swissshhh . . . !

Then, nothing.

Two minutes later, they heard the funeral knell tolling from the tower of a neighbouring village.

"Did someone die?" Sir René asked a local fellow who was on his way back from the marketplace.

"Poor man!" exclaimed the passerby. "So young. A chimney fell on his head."

The four heroes took to studying the tips of their shoes, as if their toes would send up the answer to this serious metaphysical problem.

"I'm pretty sure," said Big-as-a-Fist, "that that face wasn't entirely unknown to me."

Bit by bit they began to talk, each of them searching his memory for a forgotten face that could be the one they'd seen on the coachman.

"You remember old Mathias, John-Bear? And Clovis, the blacksmith? And that little guy, what was his name, Syrien, who used to sell bibles door-to-door?"

In such a way they reviewed all the old men they'd known in the country of their youth — who'd all long ago disappeared from the world but were suddenly called up in their common memory — which at least proved that they hadn't dreamed their whole lives up. Suddenly, Big-as-a-Fist slapped his forehead with both hands:

"Marshal!" he cried. "That was the spitting image of old Marshal!"

"But Marshal died," replied John-Bear nervously.

And so he had, died at the age of a hundred. Passed away just like that, without leaving a trace except for the echo of his muffled laugh and his lighthearted greetings. They said he'd died with his finger up his nose, saying "See you later" to everyone instead of "Goodbye." He was a nice old man, was Marshal.

Remembering the good old days put our comrades in such

high spirits that they once again took to the road. Any coach driven by Marshal or Mathias or Clovis couldn't be all that formidable.

"I'd even be tempted to climb up there with him," joked Big-as-a-Fist. "We could talk about a few things that have always bothered me, that lately . . ."

Lately, the dwarf had been dreaming a lot about his mother, and occasionally about his father, and more and more about his godmother, Clara-Galante. And in every dream, one or another of them would come up and tap him on the shoulder to get his attention, and say . . . but what did they say? He always woke up at that point, shouting, "Damn it all! Will I never get to hear it?"

"I'd really be tempted," he repeated quietly to himself. "Just to stop the driver as he went by, maybe have a few words with him."

He needn't have worried: the driver stopped all by himself. To everyone's surprise. And to the terror of Big-as-a-Fist, whose teeth suddenly began to chatter and whose body went all trembly. He tried to tell the coachman to forget it, keep going, we don't need a thing, thanks all the same. But the words banged into one another, and the dots on the "i"s and the crosses on the "t"s were scraped off.

The coachman seemed to feel sorry for them. He stuck his head out the door and, addressing them all at once yet each one in particular, suggested that they might want to climb in to rest their tired old bones in his cab.

It was the words "tired old bones" that saved the troupe. How dare he address four noble adventurers in such a way? "I'll show you how tired my old bones are!" retorted Big-as-a-Fist. And his anger dissipated his curiosity and kept him from doing anything stupid. That day, the Coach went off empty-handed.

But Sir René, who knew a thing or two about a thing or two, judged that it was time to gather his troupe together and fill them in on a few of life's realities, one of which was called death.

There it was. The word was out. And from the ancestor, from

Figure-Head. He shouldn't have done that. There was no need to use that word. It was dangerous, it was . . . irresponsible. Why go around calling such things down on your head?

It's just being smart. You have to look life in the face.

Life, yes. But not . . . that other thing.

It's just the other side of the coin, it rounds it out.

What do you know about it?

He knows a lot about it. He's earned his knowledge.

Big-as-a-Fist fell silent. He had to admit that Sir René knew more than he did, having lived two lives, and that he was even wiser by temperament. But the dwarf had one advantage over the others, one trump card: more than anyone else in the world, he loved life. And the time to prove it was now or never. Taking a deep breath that swelled his chest out like a balloon, he said, in a tone usually reserved for baptisms, confirmations, and first communions:

"Listen to me. I think it's time we took our lives into our own hands, if we don't want someone else to take them in his."

Good start, said the dwarf to himself. Keep it up.

"We've met the Coach, fine, and we've agreed to call it a coach even though it looks more like a taxicab to me, but never mind. Let's say we have seen the Coach. So what? Am I supposed to die from drowning just because I've seen the ocean?"

Figure-Head fidgeted uncomfortably. You'd think the dwarf would have enough consideration to come up with some other example. But Big-as-a-Fist was trying to save the world; he was too busy constructing the basis of his argument to consider the feelings of his listeners. He went on:

"Ever since the world was made, one generation has succeeded another, so I'm told; nature has renewed itself each season, and the grain has ripened and died . . . We're agreed on that: the grain has to ripen and die on the ground. But the grain has no other choice because it doesn't know that it's grain."

John-Bear's face glistened with tears. It was years since he'd heard his brother speak with such eloquence and authority. All those grains dying on the ground, they made *him* feel like dying, out of pity and sympathy with poor innocent nature, which didn't know it had to die every season. The giant was bowled over, he wanted to run out and save all the plants and trees, protect every flower, every caterpillar, every blade of grass, make the twigs stay on the branches and the branches stay on the trunks, restore all of creation to the way it was on the first day.

"The eighth day! We are the children of the eighth day, that's the difference!" exclaimed a transfigured Big-as-a-Fist. "We don't need to renounce that precious heritage, to give in to the inevitable or settle for only those things that are called possible. We must make the impossible possible!"

He said it, cried it, forced it out of his heart and guts like a rotten apple that had been blocking his soul since the dawn of time. And it was gone forever. He had decided in the deepest reaches of himself that he would sell his skin so dearly and so late that it would be as if a new peel had formed under his old one, to let him begin his life over.

"In the meantime," he said, to bring his comrades back to the business at hand, "we can start by nourishing these tired old bones of ours with the fruits of this blighted land. Come on, I'm hungry."

And so they entered the village, in search of the marketplace.

The village had been repainted and touched up but, like a fine old lady, still retained vestiges of its former elegance. And an adventurous old lady she must have been, too, with a seductive history and a destiny unrivalled anywhere. Her past glory still shone through, despite the meagreness of the nearly dried-up stream that trickled through her core from east to west, and the round hills so scoured by the wind that they were little more than sloping fields.

"Time has passed this way," said Figure-Head. "You can see it in the decayed walls and the worm-eaten beams."

"Someone should have stopped Time from doing so much damage," added Extra-Day, knitting his brow.

John-Bear clenched his fists, ready to attack this foe who was bigger and stronger than he was.

The dwarf just smiled nostalgically, thinking about his own native village and the changes Time must have made in it. And lifting his eyes to the church tower to watch the angelus being rung at noon, he was disappointed when no sounds emerged. Time must have taken a heavy toll on this place if they no longer even rang the hours.

"I've got half a mind to climb up there," he mused, "and ring those bells myself."

And without waiting for his comrades' consent, he took off, dashing across the square, up the steps of the church's courtyard, into the church itself — which must have been quite a cathedral in its day — and climbed up into the bell tower.

"Yoo-hoo, here I am," he shouted to the others below.

His brothers, still flummoxed by the dwarf's sudden disappearance, didn't see or hear him. But they guessed he must have gone up into the tower, and knew they'd better join him quickly if they wanted to avoid disaster.

Which is how they happened to be looking down into the square when the Coach pulled in, right under their noses and just as they'd begun ringing the village bells.

"Stop the bells!" cried Sir René. "Muffle that big tenor bell. We don't want to attract the driver's attention to the tower, he'll see us for sure."

"I think he's seen us already," replied Big-as-a-Fist. "Look, he's hauling in the reins to stop the horses. Now he's opening the door and getting down."

"He's looking up here," added John-Bear.

"Do you think he's looking for us?" asked Extra-Day nervously.

"He's saying something to the verger. Poor old man, he's done for."

But Big-as-a-Fist was mistaken. The verger was in no danger. It wasn't his own death knell that the driver wanted him to ring, but that of . . .

"No!"

They had to stop the verger. Instinctively, the four brothers took hold of all the bell cords and wrapped them around their wrists — Big-as-a-Fist wrapped his around his waist. The verger would be ringing no tocsins that day. And to be on the safe side, to send an unequivocal message down to the coachman — who was pacing back and forth in the courtyard, calmly smoking his pipe — the dwarf persuaded his three companions to ring out a whole volley of carillons — for weddings, baptisms, holidays, and joyous carnivals!

"He wants bells? We'll give him bells!" panted Big-as-a-Fist as they rang the changes. Below, the entire village had assembled in the square and was dancing around a black coach that happened to be parked there.

"We've got him!" cried John-Bear, who in a single hour, all by himself, had rung for divine service, the angelus, matins, nones, vespers, and the curfew.

Our four heroes threw themselves into each other's arms.

"Heads up!" called Marco Polo, who had stayed on watch, hidden among the dozens of other pigeons perched on the shoulders of the parish's patron saints.

"He's coming!" cried Big-as-a-Fist. "Every man for himself!"

Then he had a better thought.

"Follow me!" he hollered to the others.

A plan had just popped into his head. If a pigeon could camouflage himself up on the cathedral's parapet, why couldn't four comrades, fearless, peerless knights-in-arms as they were?

"Quickly, my friends. Stand here, open your mouths, stick out your tongues, twist your whole bodies into fantastic shapes, and don't move a muscle. And break a leg!"

"Break a leg!" replied the three others before going rigid with fear, suspended up there on the roof, hanging out over the void, their feet wrapped around the church's rain gutters.

The coachman passed by with hardly a glance at the row of gargoyles that decorated the cathedral's façade, or the odd little fiend that grimaced down from the peak. He scratched his head and wondered where the devil those mortals could have stashed themselves.

And he left.

Is he really gone?

Not yet. His cart's still down there in the square.

Are you sure it's the same one?

There are some shapes and colours and sounds that are unmistakable.

We've got to get him out of here.

I'll go along with that.

Or else get out of the village ourselves without him seeing us.

Too risky. He could easily pick us out of a crowd.

Why the devil is he after us, anyway? Why not one of the villagers?

Because the villagers don't spend all their time provoking him, the way we do.

"All right, all right," said Big-as-a-Fist, "from now on I won't so much as point my little finger at him, I promise."

Not his little finger, thought Sir René; just his whole arm.

The ancestor was too optimistic: the dwarf promptly proceeded to raise his head, his eyes, and *both* arms to the heavens.

"Hey!" he shouted to his pigeon. "What are you doing? Who said you could wear my hat? Who do you think you are?"

"My master," replied Marco Polo. "And so do they," he added, indicating the horses hitched to the Coach. "See, they're pawing the ground and whinnying something fierce."

"My word, so they are! The Coach is moving out. Hurry up, let's take advantage of this case of mistaken identity and get the hell out of here."

And he dragged the three gargoyles out of the church, pushed them down the steps, and led them down the first dark and winding side street they came to, while Marco Polo — shaking his head and tinkling the bells on the dwarf's multicoloured cap — lured the Coach in the opposite direction.

"This way," Big-as-a-Fist called to his brothers. "Turn left! Straight on! Fork in the road! A dead end . . . about face! Over that way! Towards the town gate, we've got to find that gate!"

They found it, but . . .

"It's blocked."

"Oh no! He's put the Coach right across it."

"Is there any other way out?"

"Of course not."

"The rotten bum!"

And the three comrades sat down on the curb of the sidewalk to catch their breath and regain their spirits.

"How long do you think he'll stay there?" Big-as-a-Fist asked after a few minutes.

"He's got all the time in the world, and he knows it," answered the ancestor.

The sadist!

Extra-Day tried to comfort his brothers.

"What's our hurry, anyway? We're well enough off here."

"Oh sure, we're well enough off. We can drink, eat, and sleep; eat, sleep, and drink; sleep, drink, and eat . . . But with that Coach blocking the exit . . . you call that living?"

"Have you got a better idea?"

"We have to think of something. We won't have much appetite — or get much sleep — as long as we see that death-wagon blocking our way. We've got to get around it somehow."

Around it . . . or over it.

The dwarf looked slyly at his brothers, his eyes bright and a smile playing at the corners of his mouth.

"My friends, my comrades, my brothers," he said, his voice climbing the scale: "Would you lend me your ears?"

John-Bear lent his unreservedly; Extra-Day with curiosity and compounded interest; Sir René lent only half an ear because he knew full well that, so far, every proposal from this audacious little article had turned out to be a two-edged sword.

Big-as-a-Fist bristled at that:

"Who got us out of the cathedral just now without a scratch?"

"You did, of course. But who got us in the cathedral in the first place?"

"Hmmph!"

The dwarf was silent for a whole minute, to show that he was sorry, then plunged back into his extravagant plan. He was willing to admit that he'd make a mistake or two in his life, he'd ask forgiveness for past sins and even do penance for them — but he wouldn't think of promising not to do them again. What's the good of learning from experience if you never go back and repeat it? When you get right down to it, life is a series of infinite variations on a single theme.

"My friends, my brothers," he began again, "about that damned cab driver, I think I've found his Achilles' heel."

This time all ears were bent to the breaking-point, and our hero wasted no time letting his brothers in on the boldest, grandest scheme ever concocted this side of the cosmos.

"It's very risky," he warned them. "We could lose everything. But if we win, we win everything."

The other three waited. They couldn't think what he had in mind, but they feared the worst.

The worst!

No, not the worst; if they'd foreseen where this little manikin born in a breadbox was taking them, they'd have imagined something far worse.

"It's quite simple," he told them. "The best way to hide from the coachman is to climb up on top of the Coach. As long as we're on top, we can't be inside."

And he slapped his hands together, certain that this time he'd done it.

He'd done it, all right. But what's done can be undone — or done for. The ancestor wanted to know what they'd do once they were up on the Coach . . .

But this was no time to split hairs, Sir René, or to give too much thought to the morrow. In the fix they were in, they'd best take it one step at a time, and hope they could seize the day.

The first day passed fairly pleasantly, for the most part. From their perch our heroes watched the horses become frisky, and the driver turn the Coach around. The Coach itself seemed to sense an odd wind sweeping through the square and the courtyard and along the narrow alleys, and to become aware of an absence in the village. Its axles squawked, its doors banged in the breeze.

Have those cocky little devils escaped? How did they manage it? What hole did they find? What kind of stuff are these mortals made of?

And without bothering to put out his pipe or push his hat down tighter on his head, the driver cracked his whip and with a loud "Giddyup!" loosed the reins on his six horses. In a trice the horses were off, leaving the village at full gallop.

"Hyah! Hyah!" shouted Big-as-a-Fist, who was sitting on John-Bear's feather. The giant was standing up on the wagon's rear footboard; the two others, squatting on the roof, watched the countryside flying by on either side.

The devil's cavalcade!

"It sniffed us out, and it's after us like a donkey chasing a carrot on a stick," laughed the dwarf.

"At this speed, we'll soon be at the end of the earth," put in the giant, who was being blinded by the dust.

"I've always wanted to know what that was like."

"What what was like?"

"The end of the earth. When we left our parents' home that fine morning, weren't we in search of the earth and all her planets?"

"But once we got there . . . where would we go after that?"

"After that? . . . After that, you big dunderhead, there'll still be lots left to explore. You know the world never ends."

No, John-Bear didn't know that at all. He had complete confidence in his brother, though, because his brother always knew exactly where he was going, knew how to solve everything, and could get his comrades out of any stew or close call.

Listening to his big lughead of a twin brother prattle on with his praise, Big-as-a-Fist began to feel nervous. The world was rolling by on both sides of the Coach at a speed that was accelerating like a geometrical progression, and all of a sudden he covered his eyes with both hands and wanted to cry out. But he couldn't.

The Coach was taking them away, whether it meant to or not — and whether *they* wanted it to or not! It didn't know it had picked up four hitchhikers, but it was carrying them off all the same. What dead end had he plunged them into this time? His own and his brothers'! And without further thought — convinced once again that he could rely on nothing but his own instinct — he cried:

"Jump!"

What? Jump?

"How can we jump from a coach careering at full tilt along a bumpy, winding road?" protested Sir René, who was having his own misgivings about the depth of the chasm closing in on them from all sides.

"We have to jump!" repeated the dwarf, who had regained his spirits and, with them, his sense of responsibility towards the company. "Don't discuss it, for crying out loud! Jump!"

His tone brooked no reply. The first to obey Big-as-a-Fist's imperial command was his most faithful, most loyal brother, the one who had obeyed him from the very first day when, in their father's workshop, the dwarf had ordered him to be born.

After John-Bear, it was Extra-Day who jumped — or rather, took a soaring leap that looked more like a launch into flight and landed him on the roadside several leagues along from the giant.

Big-as-a-Fist calculated that if he was ever going to meet up with his brothers again he'd better not delay his own jump, and he steeled himself for the effort . . . now . . . now . . .

"Go on, little brother, hurry up!" shouted the ancestor, who was sitting comfortably on his haunches, and had decided not to budge.

The dwarf looked up at him and met his eyes, and saw in them a fond but firm farewell.

"No! Not that! Age before beauty!"

"I'm staying. I'm too old for this; I'd break every bone in my body."

"So what's a few broken bones? They'll heal. We'll make you a splint!"

"Go, little brother. You're wasting time. Jump and don't look back."

"Nooo!"

And with a sudden rush of adrenalin that charged through his muscles and strengthened his bones, the dwarf shoved the old man off the top of the cab at the very instant that Marco Polo plucked his master up by the collar and lifted him into the air.

The Coach must have felt suddenly lighter, and must have figured out what load had just been unloaded, for it stopped dead in its track and turned around.

And now it was coming back.

It advanced slowly along the road, looking behind each blade of grass and every pebble along the way. Every now and then the driver would poke his head out of his window and scrutinize the shrubs and undergrowth.

"Marco Polo, my old friend, help me," whispered Big-as-a-Fist into the bird's ear. He was too frightened to look down.

He didn't need to look down, because he knew what was taking place as surely as if it were happening inside his own brain. The Coach now filled the entire width of the road where his brothers had fallen, one after the other. It would surely find them; they lay right in its path.

My pigeon, my brother . . .

But for the first time the pigeon was stalled in mid-air, hovering right above the Coach — which also seemed to have stopped moving.

"Good lord, it's the ancestor. They're picking up our Figure-Head."

And Big-as-a-Fist covered his eyes with both hands.

Then the pigeon took off, carrying his master higher. Nearly overcome with grief, Big-as-a-Fist watched as his youngest brother, Extra-Day, was lifted into the Coach.

Big-as-a-Fist would have thrown himself from his safe refuge, but the pigeon lifted him still higher in the air.

"Stop, Marco Polo!"

But Marco Polo had set his wings and was gliding into the open sky, carried by a light breeze that was ruffling his feathers.

Big-as-a-Fist's voice had left his throat, and his blood had left his veins. His strength, senses, and reason were gone. Nothing remained but his memory — but oh, what a memory it was! His whole body bubbled with it, his whole life passed before his eyes, again and again, invading him, turning him on his heels . . . I'm nothing but a pot of soup, he told himself, with every word and gesture of my life floating in me like peas . . .

Thinking about pea soup took him back to the follies of his youth, that time of great expeditions, of bold and perilous endeavours. He'd been so sure of himself in those days. He had simply set off, armed with only a sack and a stick, in quest and conquest of the world. A world that was either flat or round, no one was sure, but was eternally at the mercy of the stars that twinkled in the firmament like so many peas in a pot of soup . . .

"Marco Polo," Big-as-a-Fist suddenly said, stroking the bird's wings. The blood in his veins had started circulating again, and his brain had yawned and stretched and woken up. "Marco Polo, do you think you could fly in reverse?"

For the first time in his life, the pigeon lost his rhythm and got one of the wings tangled up in the other: Had he heard right? Fly backwards? What sort of ship of fools had he boarded when he let himself be consigned and conscripted into the world of men?

But after a heroic effort, the pigeon succeeded in flapping his wings backwards and counter-clockwise, and became the first pigeon in history, in the whole universe, to fly in reverse.

"Brrravo!" exclaimed Big-as-a-Fist, who felt he was being transported to seventh heaven. "Now, back up to that black coach that's crunching along on the gravel road down there. I've got a word or two to say to the driver."

"But master . . . I don't think . . ."

"Do as I say, pigeon! It's our last chance. We've got to catch up to it by going backwards."

The bird dove down tail first. Big-as-a-Fist covered his eyes — John-Bear had escaped from the Coach and was trying to get away in his seven-league boots. The dwarf squeezed his eyes shut, but let the pigeon carry him down to the black hearse.

The bird landed on the shaft that connected the team of horses to the Coach, and waited for his master to make the next move.

The horses had already caught up with the giant; now the driver was politely inviting him to climb in and rejoin his comrades. Big-as-a-Fist did nothing; he was biding his time. For now he knew exactly what he had to do. John-Bear's boot was on the footboard, the heel dangling over the bottom step in plain view.

Heel! Achilles heel, thought Big-as-a-Fist, rolling the four syllables between his tongue and his palate like sugar cubes. Achilles, the demigod, the nearly immortal, vulnerable in only one place — his heel . . . Without that one little fault, that single, solitary fault, Achilles would have lived for all eternity.

Big-as-a-Fist continued to stare at his brother's heel . . . Achilles heel . . . the flaw in his invulnerability!

"Come and get me!" he shouted in a sudden access of inspiration: "Come and get me, coachman!"

He felt the syllables hopping about on his tongue, felt the words regrouping themselves, creating new images, forming new ideas.

The immortals could be made mortal by a single tiny flaw — a heel, a knee, a wound no bigger than a lime leaf between their shoulder blades . . . The gods were vulnerable in one spot, a tiny pinhole, yet a hole big enough to let their destiny through . . . What if the opposite was true for mortals? What if mortals were also vulnerable in one tiny spot — the size of a heel, say — and by means of that could become immortal?

"Marco Polo!" he called out. "Wait for me outside the Coach. I'll be back."

"Don't do it, master . . ."

"Don't worry, my precious pigeon, I'll return."

"No one returns from there."

"They do if they're invulnerable in the heel."

And without looking back, he emptied his lungs of their last breath of bad air, placed his left foot on the Coach's running board, and, bracing his whole body, went inside.

Big-as-a-Fist didn't waste time greeting or grieving over his brothers, who were lying prostate on the bottom of the Coach. He went straight to the front of the cab, where the coachman welcomed him warmly, two fingers touching his temple and his pipe still stuck in his mouth.

"Good day," said the dwarf, stressing the two syllables carefully. "I'm not interrupting you, am I? You probably weren't expecting me so soon."

"I've been expecting you," replied the other. "Early or late, it's all the same to me."

"I guess it doesn't happen often that people come early."

"Not often, no. But *when* you come doesn't matter much: it's *how* that counts."

"I see," said the dwarf, nodding his head. "You mean the style. You're right. Everyone should have the decency and the dignity to leave the world as he entered it, to remain faithful to himself and his fate right to the end."

The driver raised one eyebrow, smiled, and took his pipe from his mouth. The musings of his new friend seemed to please him. It was the first time one of the Coach's passengers had taken the time to chat with him. And it didn't hurt; in fact, it was the best way to keep your mind off the bumps in the road.

So the conversation continued. They talked about the weather, Halley's Comet, whether the earth was round or not, how the universe, seen from above, looked like a huge bowl of lentil and split-pea soup with all the bits bumping into each other.

"You get quite a nice view from up here," said Big-as-a-Fist, casually sticking his head out the window.

"Watch it! Don't try to get too close to that hole."

"I don't suppose it would do me much good."

"No . . . none at all."

After that they fell silent, though they continued to look at each other from time to time and smile. Suddenly, Big-as-a-Fist leapt to his feet, pulled his cap down firmly on his head, and looked the coachman straight in the eye:

"I won't try to bargain with you," he said. "I know it'd be a waste of time."

"A complete waste," said the other, putting his pipe back in the corner of the mouth.

"And there isn't much time left . . ."

"Damned little . . ."

"But there's something else I want to ask you."

The driver raised an eyebrow.

"I'd like to take you up on what you said about style . . . method."

"Ask away."

The dwarf leaned his weight on his left leg, then switched to his right, then said:

"Give us the chance to die more . . . appropriately."

"How do you mean?"

"Well, take Extra-Day for example: He should die in full sunlight, at noon; he should lose his head on a block in the public square. That would be fitting and have style."

"Sure, why not?"

"As for the ancestor, Sir René, he should drown in the frigid waters of the Arctic. That would be very grand."

"I suppose so."

"And the giant, John-Bear, he should be hanged from the highest oak in the forest."

"Good enough."

"And finally . . . as for the last one . . ."

". . . ?"

"Suppose I agree to be thrown into a cage with wild beasts?"

This time the coachman raised his eyebrows; he could hardly believe his ears.

"There's no need of that, my friend. I've known bigger men than you who couldn't face that."

"Bah! What have I got to lose, eh?"

"All the same . . ."

"No, I insist. We only pass this way once, let's do it with panache!"

"Well, well."

The driver was almost moved to take pity on the little fellow, but he had too much to do that day, and threw himself into his preparations. He placed a block in the middle of the village square and arranged for the executioner; he found an old ship languishing in dry dock; he selected an enormous oak in the middle of a clearing in the woods, and hung a rope from it with a slip-knot at one end; and into a cage with very close-set bars he shoved half a dozen wild animals, whose growling and roaring awakened echoes in the mountains such as had seldom been heard before.

"They'll make short work of him," the driver said to himself. "He won't feel a thing." Then, aloud:

"Time, gentlemen! Let's get it over with. Ready?"

"Ready or not, here I come!" cried Big-as-a-Fist, with a wink of his eye to that distant country that had once sheltered his childhood games, his dreams, his first steps towards adventure.

And without more ado, he himself helped the Coach deliver his brothers to the block, the oak, and the frozen Arctic waters. Then he stepped resolutely into the cage of ferocious beasts and banged the door shut behind him — to the utmost astonishment of the coachman.

An astonishment that lasted several seconds, during which the coachman's attention was distracted, diverted. It took less time than that to find his Achilles heel. If life can have a chink in its armour, so can death.

While conducting his long conversation in the Coach, Big-as-a-Fist had had plenty of time to discover the heel's opposite in each of his brothers. And that's how he'd come upon the ultimate way to play trick-or-treat with Death.

Let's recap.

On the driver's word, and with encouragement from Big-as-a-Fist, Extra-Day allowed himself to be led to the block in the public square. He said not a word, but he was filled with a sadness that was not without its own beauty and nobility. He placed his head on the block, when the time came, and awaited the sound of the first stroke of noon.

The first stroke rang.

The last stroke rang.

But between the two, nothing. Time had stood still for a brief second, but long enough for Extra-Day, born Out-of-Time, to return whence he'd come. He disappeared, leaving not a wrack behind but a mompus of curiosity seekers asking one another where he'd gone.

Big-as-a-Fist had just enough time to wave goodbye and to shout after him:

"Break a leg! See you again some day, old friend!"

And to catch the wink tossed back to him by his lifelong companion.

The coachman ran up to the block, tore the hat off his head, and bombarded the dwarf with questions: What had happened? Where was the kid?

Big-as-a-Fist shrugged his shoulders and twisted his mouth into an upside-down croissant.

Well, there're still three left, the driver said to himself. His day wasn't shot yet. And he herded Sir René into the old boat, then shoved it out to sea with all his might.

The sea grew rough and thick, and finally hardened in the cold air. The ancestor, standing stiffly at the bow, felt himself grow sleepy as he studied the stars and the tail of Halley's Comet, seeking to read his destiny in them. Then he became a figurehead once more, and for another half a millennium.

"Break a leg!" Big-as-a-Fist called after him, and caught the old man's final look of amusement. "Now you'll have a whole new century to tell your descendants about."

But the dwarf's teardrops froze in two lines down his cheeks.

"Blast!" stormed the coachman, pulling his Coach right up to the edge of the water. "Another one got away! Well, it won't happen with the next one. I'm going to hang him myself, high and quick, and this time we'll see who has the last word."

Big-as-a-Fist signalled to John-Bear to let himself be led away without resistance, not to be afraid, that his little brother had everything under control, that he had found the giant's weak spot, his Achilles heel through which his immortality would pass.

And so John-Bear was strung up from the top of the most venerable oak in the forest, which turned out to be the giant's great-grandfather. The ancient tree recognized his descendant, and let him fall gently to the soft moss at his feet, even placing a branch in his hand by way of inheritance. The giant emerged from his descent with nothing more than a bruise on his bum, and immediately looked around for his brother, to tell him about the most extraordinary adventure of his life.

But his brother had disappeared. John-Bear beat the bushes and searched through the underbrush, to no avail.

"Big-as-a-Fist! Here I am, I'm back! Where are you, little brother?"

The driver turned to Big-as-a-Fist and hurled a blood-curdling laugh . . . Three down, eh? Well, no matter. He still had the fourth, and he was worth all the other three put together. And this little devil wouldn't slip through his fingers. And he shoved him into the cage where six starving mouths were waiting for him, six of the most ferocious beasts of creation. Creatures of the sixth day.

John-Bear found the growling and roaring of the animals more unnerving than the grinding of the Coach's axles . . . No! He wouldn't let it happen! He'd break into the cage, destroy the beasts, save his brother!

But when the giant entered the cage, ready to take on the six giant-sized beasts single-handed, he beheld a scene that took his breath away and left him feeling foolish and ashamed of his own fury.

"What's going on, Big-as-a-First?" he finally managed to stammer, shuffling his feet.

Big-as-a-Fist called his brother over to him, saying he had some friends he'd like him to meet.

"Don't be afraid, John-Bear. Come here; I've been telling them our adventures. These beasts aren't wild at all if you get to know them, and speak their language. Come and join us."

And the two heroes sat there in the middle of the pit and conversed at great length with the animals, speaking of many things that were close to their hearts.

Suddenly they heard a devil of a noise at the gate: the coachman had come to take out the full measure of his anger on his two remaining victims.

"Do you know that fellow?" asked the dwarf innocently, turning to a magnificent she-bear who looked half starved.

"I do indeed! He's dragged us all over hell's half acre!"

Big-as-a-Fist winked at John-Bear out of the corner of his eye.

"Well," he said, "he's all yours."

And opening the cage, he released all the beasts. Like flashes of greased lightning, they stormed after the Coach. The driver barely had time to leap up onto the footboard and wrap the reins around his fists.

"This is one day he won't have time to stop and collect anybody," hooted Big-as-a-Fist, and the two heroes collapsed at the side of the road and laughed to their heart's content.

Then the giant turned serious.

"Will we ever see them again?" he said sadly to Big-as-a-Fist.

The dwarf wiped his nose and tried to swallow, then said in his gravest voice — which registered somewhere between tee and doh:

"They've gone back where they belong, John-Bear. Back into

folklore and legend, into the folds of history and time. Where they came from."

"But will they come back to us?" pressed the giant.

"They're with us all the time, they'll always be nearby. Each time you stop to savour a fleeting moment of time, you'll know Extra-Day is smiling at you, hidden on the other side of it. And when you want to go back in time to trace your family history, to find out where you came from, you'll hear Sir René delivering his interminable lessons, swamping you with his antique wisdom and his flawless remembrance of things past."

And to cheer himself up and pull his brother out of the doldrums, he added:

"He'll swamp you with so many stories, you'll be doing your damnedest to get rid of him."

The very first thing next morning, our two heroes took to the road, heading for the rising sun. The ancestor had told them not to give up, that if the world truly was round . . .

"Look, John-Bear. Wouldn't you say that was Clara-Galante's place, down there in the hollow beside the stream?"

"But the stream looks pretty small. Not much more than a trickle of water under the moss."

Big-as-a-Fist grabbed his brother's pant leg. "Stop!" he said. "Shhh! Listen. Do you hear it?"

The giant opened his ears as wide as he could — which was wide enough to catch the ticking of a clock ten miles away, but too wide to pick up the peeping of a chick at this feet. He stood stock still and listened with all his might, but he had to give up and ask his brother what he was supposed to hear.

"John-Bear, my brother, my faithful friend, my boon companion . . . I think we've made it home."

John-Bear opened his eyes, his nostrils, his mouth.

"You think so, Tom Thumb?"

"I'm positive!"

And without another word the dwarf climbed up the giant's boots, up his legs, along his side, over his chest, up his neck, and, using his nose for a foothold, hopped up onto the ostrich feather waving from his hat. Shielding his eyes with his hand, he could just make out the village on the horizon; but what was this bird doing blocking his view?

"Marco Polo!" he cried, holding out his arms. "But what's happened to you? You're all white!"

Marco Polo made three or four loops, turned a few figure eights, and landed softly on the giant's shoulder.

"I flew to close to the Coach," he cooed. "It turned me into a dove."

And for the first time, Big-as-a-Fist thought he heard the bird chuckling.

Suddenly, and as if what he was saying hadn't the slightest importance, he stage-whispered into his brother's ear:

"What do you say, John-Bear? Do you think a white dove would deign to stay with us if we went back to our own country?"

The pigeon shook his feathers, fluttered his wings, clicked his beak, and shook his left leg vigorously under his master Big-as-a-Fist's nose. The dwarf's eyes widened and sparkled. Slowly, timidly, he stretched out his hand.

"Are you going to tell me who your message is for? And . . . what it says?"

Marco Polo winked at the two heroes and took off, flying straight for the yard of Goodman and Goodwife.

"He's going to our place!" shouted both brothers at the same time.

"Catch him, John-Bear. We should all get there together. Giddyup, hyah, hyah!"

Running as fast as he could, John-Bear said to his brother:

"You know what, Big-as-a-Fist? I saw a brownish spot on Marco Polo's left leg. Do you think it could be a birthmark?"

Big-as-a-Fist didn't answer, but he thought about it for a few minutes. Then he smiled to himself.

"Hurry up, John-Bear, shake a leg. And comb your moustache. We should spruce up before we go home."

Outside the yard, Big-as-a-Fist stood in front of his brother and, spreading his legs and sticking out his chest, said:

"How do I look, eh?"

"Pretty tiny."

"Oh yeah? Well, you look a bit overweight."

The two brothers joined hands and went through the garden gate. One stepped over a hay wagon, the other jumped over a rake. They both picked an apple from the apple tree as they passed it; then they went up onto the porch and opened the back door of the house. Inside, Goodman and Goodwife were talking to a pigeon, asking him if he had any news of their children.

Epilogue

And so our two heroes lived with their mother and father ever after, and had many children.

The old servant's dry voice fell silent.

I left the dilapidated old cabin, blinking in the harsh sunlight and laughing softly to myself. The squirrels were still shaking from head to tail; the rabbits were hopping, the crows crowing, the leaves rustling in the trees. When the blue jays saw me coming, they again took up their twelve-toned warning.

Stepping over Dr. Landry's stream, I left the forest. As I went down the little sand-cliff, I heard the yap of a fox that had poked its nose out of its den. Well, well, I said to myself. Then I continued my descent to the village nestled peacefully between the sea, the hills, and the woods.

Peacefully, did I say? . . . It seemed to me a whole beehive of people were swarming in the courtyard in front of the church, and around Robichaud Brothers' general store: many more generations than had been there in my father's day, when I'd curled up into a ball under the family desk and listened to the story of my ancestors . . . a story with roots going all the way back to Paradise, and with ancestors descended in a direct line from Adam and Eve.

I'd been a bit cramped under that desk, but I'd felt wonderful. Like being in a cocoon, or a shell, or a womb. Words drifted to my ears, bits of phrases, sometimes whole sentences. I caught as many of them as I could, tried to put them together, to weave them in a way that would turn mere speech into story.

There was the story of the Cormier family, my mother's family on her father's side. Oh my, what a bunch! Little devils they were, I can tell you. Built low to the ground and all hairy, like little monkeys they were, and real tricksters, too, though most of them were a brick or two shy of a load. Braggarts and swaggerers, they'd just as soon tell you a lie as look at you. And brave as all get out, as long as someone else was doing the fighting. But they could be gentle as a loaf of warm bread, and wonderful company. They never gave in to a thing except temptation. And they'd simply refuse to suffer or pine away or die. All things considered, they were the best ancestors in the world to have.

On my mother's mother's side there were the Goguens. We used to say at home that the Goguens were put on this earth to keep the Cormiers in line, to stop them from getting up to no good every morning as if they wanted to start the whole world fresh. Most of my mother's side of the family were big and strong, headstrong, too, chips off the old block. Old Grandmother Célina, you'd never catch her at a loss for words, or failing to finish something once she'd started it. She was a tough old bird, was Célina, an enormous woman. She didn't just dream about setting things right in the world — she went out and changed them, day after day, without stopping to think where it would lead. She did it because she believed it was her right, her duty, her act of loyalty to the life that had put her here on earth in the first place.

From my father's side, my father's father's father, comes my family name, and that's a whole other story. They were a wise people, the Maillets, and they go way, way back — we've had the family tree traced back as far as the sixteenth century without missing a leaf, so we think we can say without exaggeration that our roots lie somewhere in the time of the builders of the great cathedrals: Notre-Dame and Saint-Julien-le-Pauvre. There's a story in the family — a legend, really — that the Maillets turned up for the first time in the year 1603, in Paris, three brothers who were master masons, guild-masters. The mallet was their main tool for building cathedrals, and that's how my father's ancestors got the name I bore in my cradle: "Maillet," which means "mallet." It's a proud line, the Maillets, with strong traditions and a rich heritage that's been handed down from generation to generation from the very earliest times.

My father's mother died in childbirth, and no one in our family knew her; she disappeared without trace, without leaving even the recollection of a face in the memories of her descendants. She came and went, catching up a bit of breeze-borne pollen from the flowers as she passed. The years have not tarnished her beauty. Age has not touched her. Our paternal grandmother, whose maiden name was Allain, has remained forever outside of time.

These are the stories I gathered under the family desk, as I lay there contemplating the birthmark on my left thigh, which I took to be the stain of Original Sin.

Little by little, I learned that the mark was for a sin I hadn't even committed — although I'd committed plenty of others! — but had inherited from my first parents, who'd done my sinning for me, four thousand or four million years before I was even born. And I decided right there and then, at that precise moment, that one day I'd go up to those people and demand an explanation, and at the same time exact from the author of Genesis a promise to give the world a second chance, through me.

This Creation of yours is too small, I'd say to him, or so I told myself; too short, too thin, too — unfinished. Which is hardly surprising, given the fact that He took only seven days to do it including the whole day of rest. In a case like that, you'd think He could have asked someone for help, and been able to pay more attention to the people He'd left hungry, or unclothed, or living under the rule of idle and foolish kings. He could have asked the world's dreamers to dream; asked the inventors to invent something; or asked me to add to his seven days an eighth day.

I crossed the village, my head empty but my heart and body buzzing with electrifying dreams. I crossed the marsh and the dunes, went into my lighthouse counting the steps to the top of the tower. I didn't know why I was hurrying . . . unless it was because I had decided not to leave Paradise. I gathered my papers together, my pencils, my pen. I was sure of only one thing: after the eighth day — the ninth day!

The possibilities were limitless.

— *Montreal, April 30, 1986, at noon!*

Photo: Manon Elder

"The great role of the artist," Antonine Maillet has said, "is to add an eighth day to creation, to render the impossible possible."

Antonine Maillet, a native of Bouctouche, New Brunswick, has spent her life conjuring the impossible into being. She is the author of wry and wildly inventive adult fiction, children's books, radio and television scripts, and more than a dozen plays.

Maillet's sparkling imagination, her versatility, and her commitment to giving Acadian culture a voice have been recognized at home and abroad. She was the first non-citizen of France to win the prestigious Prix Goncourt, which she received for her hilarious homeric novel *Pélagie-la-Charette*. Her now classic monologue *La Sagouine* won the Chalmers Canadian Play Award; *Don l'Orignal* won the Governor General's Award for Fiction; and *On the Eighth Day*, Wayne Grady's rollicking translation of *Le Huitième Jour*, won the Governor General's Award for Translation.